Praise for
New York Times and USA Today Bestselling Author

Diane Capri

"Full of thrills and tension, but smart and human, too."
*Lee Child, #1 New York Times Bestselling Author of Jack
Reacher Thrillers*

"[A] welcome surprise....[W]orks from the first page to 'The
End'."
Larry King

"Swift pacing and ongoing suspense are always
present...[L]ikable protagonist who uses her political
connections for a good cause...Readers should eagerly anticipate
the next [book]."
Top Pick, Romantic Times

"...offers tense legal drama with courtroom overtones, twisty
plot, and loads of Florida atmosphere. Recommended."
Library Journal

"[A] fast-paced legal thriller...energetic prose...an appealing
heroine...clever and capable supporting cast...[that will] keep
readers waiting for the next [book]."
Publishers Weekly

"Expertise shines on every page."
*Margaret Maron, Edgar, Anthony, Agatha and Macavity Award
Winning MWA Past President*

FATAL DAWN

by DIANE CAPRI

Published by: AugustBooks
http://www.AugustBooks.com
ISBN-13: 978-1-942633-10-5
ISBN-10: 1-942633-10-6

Original Cover Design: Cory Clubb
Digital Formatting: Author E.M.S.

Published in the United States of America.

Visit the author website:
http://www.DianeCapri.com

ALSO BY DIANE CAPRI

The Hunt for Jack Reacher Series
(in publication order with Lee Child source books in parentheses)
Don't Know Jack (The Killing Floor)
Jack in a Box (*novella*)
Jack and Kill (*novella*)
Get Back Jack (Bad Luck & Trouble)
Jack in the Green (*novella*)
Jack and Joe (The Enemy)
Deep Cover Jack (Persuader)
Jack the Reaper (The Hard Way)
Black Jack (Running Blind/The Visitor)
Ten Two Jack (The Midnight Line)

The Jess Kimball Thrillers Series
Fatal Enemy (*novella*)
Fatal Distraction
Fatal Demand
Fatal Error
Fatal Fall
Fatal Edge
Fatal Game
Fatal Bond
Fatal Past (*novella*)
Fatal Dawn

The Hunt for Justice Series
Due Justice
Twisted Justice

The Hunt for Justice Series
Due Justice
Twisted Justice
Secret Justice
Wasted Justice
Raw Justice
Mistaken Justice (*novella*)
Cold Justice (*novella*)
False Justice (*novella*)
Fair Justice (*novella*)
True Justice (*novella*)

The Heir Hunter Series
Blood Trails
Trace Evidence

CAST OF PRIMARY CHARACTERS

Jessica Kimball
Henry Morris
Emilio Fernandez
Carter Pierce
Mandy Donovan
Lynette Tierney
Ross Tierney
Earle Gotting
Shane Hallman
Henrik Metcalfe
Zander Norell
Tanya Norell
Ammerson Belk
and
Peter Kimball

FATAL DAWN

CHAPTER ONE

Monday, May 29
6:30 a.m.
Humboldt Prison, Kansas

SHANE HALLMAN WATCHED EARLE Gotting's spindly body shuffle down the wireframe steps from the upper cell block. His orange prison jumpsuit hung off his shoulders and rolled up sleeves exposed stick-like arms. In his hands were a few threadbare clothes and a couple of pictures. His worldly possessions. All of them.

At the bottom of the steps lay the recreation area. A dozen steel tables all bolted to the concrete floor. Each table had a bench on either side, also bolted to the concrete. A strict code determined who could sit at which table and Gotting wasn't welcome at any of them. He turned straight for the wall and moved along the side of the recreation area.

Hallman crossed the room and put his foot on one of the benches, blocking Gotting's path.

Gotting moved to go around.

Hallman blocked his progress. "You're getting out."

Gotting's face remained impassive. "Done my time."

Hallman snorted derisively. "So did I. Year ago I was up for parole. They denied me. Because of you."

"Not my problem."

"Really?"

"Really."

"You've been inside for some chicken shit stuff. Drug running. Unlicensed guns. You'd have been here for life if they knew what you'd done." Hallman glowered. "Six more months and I'm done here. Then I'll make all of this your problem. Count on it."

"You've hung out with the wrong crowd in here, repeating the mistake you made out there with that thug Metcalfe." Gotting tilted his head toward the exit and shrugged as if the threats were water off his back. "Got to pick your friends more careful."

Hallman leaned forward. He saw the strain around Gotting's eyes as he enunciated each syllable separately. "I. Wasn't. There."

"And I'm going to remember that after your gang beat me senseless," Gotting said, chin jutting forward. He patted his right leg. The one they'd mangled.

Hallman shrugged. "You should have told them what they wanted to know."

"You mean what you wanted to know," Gotting said.

"I wasn't there!" Hallman growled. "You should have told them. You'd be walking straight."

Gotting snarled back. "You've been drinking the Kool-Aid and listening to the wrong stories. Think if I had some secret stash somewhere, I'd be limping out of here?"

Hallman leaned closer and cracked his knuckles. "I think

you're so stupid it'll take a lot more than a damaged leg to get that secret out of you."

A guard stepped up behind Hallman and spoke over his shoulder. "You leaving or hanging around, Gotting?"

Hallman stepped aside, and gestured to the exit door, painted with the words "Way Out," like any inmate was likely to mistake the exit for something else.

It was the warden's idea of a joke. A lame insider's joke meant to convey that no inmate could find his way out. In the battle of the guards against the inmates, inmates made better jokes. Crude and vulgar. Cutting and remorseless. But the warden and his guards always got the last laugh. Walking out free was the only thing most of the inmates wanted.

"Yeah, big day," Gotting said to the officer.

"We should meet up when I get out. Catch up on old times." Hallman punched Gotting on the shoulder. "I insist."

Gotting tucked his bundle of possessions under his arm and rapped on the door with his knuckles. He glanced back at Hallman one last time before he walked out and closed the door from the other side.

Hallman stood for a while watching the door. He should have been the one walking out. And he would. Soon. Only six more months. *Make the best of it, Gotting. I'm coming for you. This will be the last six months you'll draw breath. Trust me.*

CHAPTER TWO

Six months later
Monday, November 27
8:00 a.m.
Denver, Colorado

JESS THREADED HER POWERFUL Dodge Charger through the Monday morning Denver traffic on her way to work. She rarely spent enough time in Denver to battle rush hour traffic. She definitely remembered why she hated it.

The weekend's dusting of snow lingered in doorways and corners. She tuned into a radio report on the decline of the bee population. A specialist was encouraging conservation efforts before large-scale agriculture production was affected, he said.

She turned off onto a quiet street well behind a white Lexus sedan. The traffic light turned red a moment before the Lexus reached the intersection. A Toyota cut across the lane into the cushion she'd left herself.

Jess braked hard.

The Toyota rear-ended the Lexus. Both cars rocked on their suspension.

She stopped barely two feet from the Toyota's rear bumper. She checked her rearview mirror. The car behind her was too close. She couldn't back up.

An elderly driver stepped out of the Lexus. He sorrowfully looked at the broken bumper on his car.

A passenger stepped from the rear of the Toyota. He was too thin. Long blond hair straggled from his baseball cap. On the back of his neck was a tattoo she couldn't make out from this distance.

Jess leaned forward.

The older man pointed at his car and said something.

The skinny guy covered the distance between them in two strides and swung a punch. He had another tattoo on his hand.

The Lexus driver toppled backward onto the sidewalk.

Jess grabbed her phone and dialed 911.

She stretched forward to see. The Toyota couldn't move because it was trapped between her and the Lexus.

The operator answered. "911, what's your emergency?"

The Toyota passenger rifled through the old guy's clothes, taking his cell phone and wallet.

"Police. Robbery. Junction of Fletcher and Bonnell."

The thin man jumped into the Lexus and screamed off in a cloud of smoke. The Toyota did the same right behind the Lexus.

"Make that a carjacking. White Lexus sedan. Suspect also in a white Toyota." Jess stabbed a button to transfer the call to her car's speakers.

"Are you safe?" the operator said.

"It's not my car. There's an elderly man injured."

The old guy struggled to his feet.

"Do you have the plate number?"

Jess moved up to where the old guy was standing. "Get in."

"Do you have the Lexus's plate?" the operator repeated.

From the passenger seat, the old guy said, "I'm the owner. Ronald Walsh," and reported his license plate. "They've got my wife."

The Toyota and Lexus were almost two blocks away already.

Jess pulled away hard. She told the operator, "We're pursuing the Lexus."

"Please don't put yourself in any danger. I have alerted police," the operator replied.

Walsh fiddled to fasten his seat belt.

"Two patrol cars are on the way. ETA two minutes," the operator said.

Jess stopped at the next light. Cross traffic was sparse, but running the red light was a risk she wouldn't take. "They'll be too late."

The Lexus and Toyota took different directions at the block ahead. When her light changed, Jess went after the Lexus.

Walsh finally secured his seatbelt. "He had a gun. My wife has a weak heart."

"We'll follow him until the police arrive. Then we'll leave it to the professionals."

"She has asthma, too."

The road opened into two lanes. The Lexus raced away. Jess took the outside lane, struggling to keep up with the more powerful car.

"Lexus is now heading east on Wilson," she said to the 911 operator.

"Please ma'am, the police are on their way."

"Tell them to hurry or these guys will be long gone."

The Lexus braked hard and whipped left through a gap in the traffic. Angry horns blared.

Jess slowed. There was no gap in the traffic for her.

Walsh strained forward to see the Lexus. "I can't find them."

Jess accelerated for a space in the traffic.

Walsh struggled to hold onto the grab handle and dashboard when she turned sharply at the next left.

The street was one-way with two lanes. Jess used the left lane, racing between gaps in the traffic, slowing to search for signs of the Lexus. Four blocks down, she took another left.

She whipped her head left to right. No sign of the attacker.

The road ended at a T-junction with a street that ran along a steep grass embankment.

She turned left again.

Walsh pointed down the embankment. "There she is."

The Lexus was on a parallel road at the bottom of the embankment.

Jess accelerated to chase them.

The Lexus's wheels locked up in a cloud of smoke. The car fishtailed. Traffic behind it screeched to a halt.

The Lexus did a one-eighty.

The passenger door opened. A gray-haired woman was thrown from the vehicle. She rolled on the pavement like a rag doll.

The Lexus raced away.

Jess braked hard. "The attackers have released Mrs. Walsh. Lexus now heading west on Simpson."

"Responders are thirty seconds out."

Jess stopped directly up the embankment from Mrs. Walsh.

Mr. Walsh unbuckled and rushed out of the car.

"Get in. We have a half mile to cover to get over there," Jess called.

Leaning over the guardrail, Walsh stared at his wife who struggled to her knees, clutching her chest.

Jess jumped out of the car and grabbed his arm. "We have to get your wife."

Mrs. Walsh rolled over on her side and lay on the road.

Her husband held out a small gray tube. "I have her inhaler."

Mrs. Walsh was curled in the fetal position.

Jess grabbed the inhaler and zipped up her coat. The railing along the top of the embankment had posted warning signs. It was too steep. She couldn't walk down.

Mrs. Walsh thumped her chest. She was suffocating.

Jess rolled over the guardrail and shuffled a few steps before she lost her footing. She turned sideways as she hit the ground. She held her arms and legs out to try to control her descent, but the forces of gravity were too great. She wrapped her hands around her face to protect herself as she tumbled over and over.

Grass and rocks tore at her coat. She dodged a stick of a tree laid bare by winter.

Her hands were stung by cuts and scrapes. Her back pounded into the concrete retaining wall at the bottom of the slope, forcing the air from her lungs in a hard whoosh.

She climbed over the concrete above a ten-foot drop to the sidewalk. She lowered herself as far as her arms would allow and let go. Her left foot imprinted her impact on the damp ground.

Mrs. Walsh was gasping and choking. Jess ran to her, jammed the inhaler in her mouth, and pumped the trigger twice.

The woman strained to breathe.

Jess pumped two more shots.

Her breathing slowed. Still long and labored, but not wheezing.

Mrs. Walsh put her hand on Jess, keeping the inhaler in her mouth. Her gasps turned to normal breathing. She took the inhaler in her hand.

Jess laid her tattered coat over Mrs. Walsh. She heard the ambulance siren in the distance.

"Hang on. Help is on the way," she said.

Jess looked up the embankment. Mr. Walsh was leaning over the rail. She gave him a thumbs-up. He nodded before putting his head in his hands, in tears, Jess figured.

Mrs. Walsh gripped Jess's arm. "You're an angel."

Jess shook her head. "Shhhh. Save your breath."

CHAPTER THREE

Monday, November 27
10:00 a.m.
Denver, Colorado

BY THE TIME JESS made it to work, her body was already complaining about her tumble down the embankment. As she approached the elevator, Thelma Baxter slipped her bony hand along the edge to hold open the doors.

Thelma was the special assistant to the owner of *Taboo Magazine*, and Jess loved her to pieces. Many a time over the years Thelma's warm heart had buoyed Jess's spirits when it seemed like the entire world was against her.

Thelma's infallible memory for every story that had ever run in the magazine's pages came in handy often, too. She knew more about what was going on at the magazine than the owner himself. Jess secretly wondered if Thelma actually ran the operation using Carter Pierce as the figurehead.

When she entered the elevator, Thelma raised her eyebrows. "What happened to you?"

"Carjacking," Jess replied without thinking.

Thelma gripped Jess's wrist. "Are you all right?"

Instantly mortified because she'd alarmed Thelma, Jess patted her hand and nodded. "Perfectly. I'm sorry. It wasn't my car. I just tried to help out."

Thelma whistled. "And it looks like it. What happened to your coat?"

The elevator doors opened. Jess followed Thelma out.

Jess's assistant, Mandy Donovan, was busy at her computer as Jess approached. Mandy did a double take, too. "What the hell happened to you?"

"Carjacking," Thelma said, with a wink.

"Someone else, not me," Jess added quickly before Mandy could go into full-on alarm mode.

"You okay?" Mandy asked.

Jess nodded. "A little sore, maybe a couple of bruises. I fell down. I'll tell you about it later."

Mandy stood and held her hand out. "Give me your coat. I'll get it cleaned."

"Don't bother. The coat's not worth the price of cleaning now." Jess shrugged the coat off her shoulders and handed it over. "Just toss it in the trash. But could you—"

Mandy laughed. "Coffee coming up." She poured a mug from a pot on her desk and handed it to Jess.

Jess smiled. "You're a star, you know that? Let's ask Carter to pay you more money."

Mandy laughed again. "Hey, works for me."

Thelma frowned and muttered on her way to her office, "Based on what I hear, there won't be any raises around here for a while."

Mandy and Jess exchanged knowing looks.

Jess went to her office and settled in at her desk. Her computer monitor was covered with several sticky notes that served as today's to-do list. She was more than a little behind schedule, and the carjacking stole a couple of hours. But for now, the spirit of the past Thanksgiving weekend reminded her to be grateful that she hadn't been seriously injured and both Mr. and Mrs. Walsh would be okay, too.

Thinking about the long weekend carried her to memories of Peter again. She'd only spent two Thanksgivings with him before he was abducted. He was twenty-three months old then. He would be fifteen years old now.

Feelings of guilt, sadness, and loss invariably overtook her during the holidays, which was one reason she seldom accepted the invitations she received from friends and co-workers to join their family celebrations.

She pulled up a spreadsheet with a long list of names and dates. She scrolled right. Addresses with street names and apartment numbers were listed in the area where she and Peter had lived.

She'd run down to the basement, started her laundry, and run back up to her apartment. Not more than five minutes. Probably less. Peter was sleeping when she left. He was gone when she returned.

Although he'd never climbed out of his crib even once, she'd wasted precious minutes looking everywhere inside the small apartment, growing more frantic by the moment. But of course, Peter wasn't there. Some part of her had known that from the start but refused to accept reality.

She'd chased around her apartment building in ever-widening circles until she'd ended up waking all the residents. She'd knocked on doors and stopped pedestrians on the street.

Neighbors had joined her. They spread out around the streets and alleyways.

No one could believe Peter had simply disappeared. When she'd finally faced the truth, she'd called the police. A cruiser arrived quickly, and the officers organized a more efficient search.

Peter was gone without a trace. *How could that be?*

There was only one answer. Peter couldn't have run away. Some bastard had taken him.

The night was cold, but more than the temperature chilled her heart. She was nineteen back then. A teenage mom. Her life was a precarious balancing act between caring for Peter, classes, and a part-time job. Peter had been everything to her and still was. From the moment he was conceived, her entire life had revolved around him and always would.

Jess's phone rang. She saw the caller ID. Her boss. "Hi, Carter."

"I'm in New York, but I just heard about your heroics this morning. Nice job."

"Carter—"

"You're about to tell me it was nothing?"

"It didn't end very well. Mrs. Walsh was terrified, and so was her husband. The carjackers got away."

She heard the pleasure in his voice as he said, "CCTV is a wonderful thing. The thieves are in custody right now."

"That's something, at least."

"Mrs. Walsh wouldn't have made it until the ambulance arrived if you hadn't helped her, Jess."

"So the medics said."

Carter paused.

Jess knew why he'd called. Just as he knew she only

FATAL DAWN | 25

tolerated the personal spotlight as a means to an end. When the glare of media attention helped her search for Peter.

He said, "Denver Broadcasting called. You know the owner's a friend."

Jess sighed. "Uh huh."

"He said you'd turned down a spot on *Denver PM*. I know what you're like and I know the last thing you'd want is hero worship, but—"

"Carter—"

"Just listen to me, Jess. We need it. The magazine. Our star reporter is caught on camera saving a life, and…well. We need all the positive publicity we can get." He paused to let his begging soak in, and when she didn't relent, he said, "It's not for me, Jess. I'll be fine if *Taboo Magazine* goes under. My ego will be bruised. I don't like failure. But we employ a lot of people. Your friends and colleagues. This kind of publicity could really help. Can't you do it for them?"

Jess sighed. Everything he said was true. The magazine was failing. Online competition was strong. Demand for print magazines had fallen dramatically, but the production costs remained the same. Carter was wealthy. The complete collapse of the business wouldn't cause him much hardship. But the employees? Mandy and Thelma? All of them would be looking for new jobs, which were not easy to find these days. And her search for Peter would be a lot harder without Carter's support, too.

"I really wish you'd reconsider, Jess. They promised to do a short segment. They have surveillance camera footage from a hotel nearby, and they'll ask a few questions. Personal questions are off limits unless you want to talk about Peter. That's up to you."

Carter was right. She could help *Taboo*. After everything Carter and *Taboo* had done for her. Not to mention Thelma and Mandy. *Taboo* had been her only real family, helping her when she needed it. She shouldn't even hesitate.

"Don't make me beg, Jess. Please." His tone was downright pitiful.

She laughed, as he'd meant her to do. "I'm sorry, Carter. I was just preoccupied. I'm glad to do anything I can to help. I hope you already know that."

"Thanks, Jess. I owe you one."

"That's crazy talk. You owe me nothing. I should have volunteered in the first place." She frowned. "But is the magazine in seriously bad shape? Should I be looking for a new job?"

"Let's just say we need to keep our foot on the gas. I'll make the call," he said before he disconnected.

A few minutes later, an assistant producer from *Denver PM* called and rattled off a list of instructions for her evening appearance.

CHAPTER FOUR

Monday, November 27
11:00 a.m.
Humboldt, Kansas

SHANE HALLMAN STEPPED OUT of Humboldt prison dressed in the same clothes he'd worn when he entered. It had been summer then. The late November cold seeped through his jeans and T-shirt in moments.

He resisted the temptation to rub warmth into his bare arms. The guards were watching, he knew. They'd be laughing at him as he tasted his first freedom in five years.

"Here's your stuff, Hallman," the guard said, tossing the paper bag. Gleefully, he said, "The next bus into Kansas City's in two hours. Miss it, and you'll sleep outside on that bench 'til tomorrow. Forecast tonight is near freezing."

The wait meant nothing to him, though. He'd breathe free air. That's all he cared about.

The last guard unlocked the inner gate and taunted, "See you again soon."

Inmates spent years thinking about how they would respond to that last jibe. He refused to give them the satisfaction. He simply turned his back before the guard finished speaking.

Hallman walked away from the looming bulk of the prison, down the long road to the outer perimeter fence. He glimpsed a surveillance camera turn to follow his progress, but he kept his attention on the road.

The outer perimeter guard house was expecting him. They took his thumbprint and made him wait outside in the cold while they compared it to a stored version to verify him as the right inmate to be released. The heat inside wafted out as the door opened and closed.

Comparing prints was a quick process. They were flashed up, side-by-side. The computer returned a score on how well the prints matched in milliseconds.

But the guards made him wait because they could. *Sick bastards.*

He relaxed. Shoulders down, arms dangling by his sides. He gazed around the prison grounds, ignoring the building behind him.

The cold turned from unpleasant to bitter. The joints in his fingers stiffened. He whistled aimlessly, making up random tunes and rhythms, to show they hadn't broken his spirit. A guard eventually pointed him to the gates through the two layers of barbed wire that ringed the prison.

It was an airlock system. The inner gate opened and closed before the outer gate opened. He waited as electric motors whirred and finally, finally strolled out to freedom.

The prison was miles from the nearest town, yet the velvety blacktop ran arrow straight in both directions. Along one side of the road was a sidewalk, equally smooth and equally black. It dead-ended at the bus stop, open to the air, topped by a small canopy to keep the rain off the benches.

He reached the canopy as raindrops began to fall. The air was cold and the icy rain even colder. The pelting rain bit through his jeans and shirt as he squeezed himself into the corner of the bus stop for as much shelter as he could get.

A black BMW SUV with dark windows approached and stopped. Hallman stepped forward, hoping for a ride.

The window lowered. The driver didn't lean out. Instead, he spoke from inside the SUV's warm, dry cocoon. A deep voice said, "Well, well. If it isn't Shane Hallman."

He recognized the driver. Henrik "Snap" Metcalfe.

Snap earned his nickname playing football in high school because of what he did to the bones of his opponents. Later, his brute strength won him a lucrative job as an enforcer using the same methods. Later still, he took over the business after the owner mysteriously disappeared. Metcalfe bragged about killing his former boss whenever his clients seemed unwilling to pay.

Hallman knew Metcalfe would show up once he got out of prison. He hadn't expected Metcalfe to materialize out of thin air the moment he was released, though.

He nodded, ignoring the icy rain. "Metcalfe."

"Figured you'd be out of there two years ago," Metcalfe said.

"Me, too." Hallman shrugged. "Guy picked a fight before my parole hearing."

"Bad news for you," Metcalfe grunted. "Because of your debt."

Hallman eased back an inch. "Yeah. Twelve grand."

"And five long years interest." Metcalfe laughed derisively. "We'll just call it fifty. That's a nice round number. Easy to remember."

Fifty. Hallman's heart skipped a beat. He didn't have fifty pennies, let alone fifty thousand dollars. Arguing would no doubt be absolutely fruitless and result in a few snapped bones, at the very least.

Metcalfe had to know there was little chance of getting that kind of money from Shane Hallman. He wanted leverage. To keep the debt running and growing.

But Hallman had a plan. All he needed was a little time. And to keep Metcalfe off his back until he finished.

He swallowed hard. "I… I don't have that much."

"You've had five years to think about it. You've come up with a payment plan in all that time, I'll bet." Metcalfe raised his eyebrows. "You've got friends. Family. They'll help you out. When you explain the consequences."

"They don't have—"

Metcalfe beckoned him closer with a crooked finger. "I don't want to hear it. I don't care about you or your pathetic excuses. I want my money. Fifty. Tonight. And you can keep your limbs intact." Metcalfe pointed to Hallman's arms and legs, one at a time like he was defining the order. "All four of them."

The BMW rolled forward and the window began to close.

Hallman held out his hand. "Wait." He took a deep breath. "A month. Give me a month. Two months is better."

The SUV stopped, the window half open. Metcalfe looked at his watch. "You've got one week. Monday morning. Ten a.m. Fifty grand."

Hallman finally drew a breath.

"Not a minute late. Otherwise, I'll let you choose the first bone I break." Metcalfe pulled a baseball bat from under his seat and brandished it before the BMW drove off.

Hallman glanced around. The prison was still. The guards

were inside their security hut. No one was standing on the sidewalk or in the bus shelter. The road was devoid of traffic.

He breathed a sigh of relief. No one could have possibly overheard. More important, he'd bought himself some time. Metcalfe wouldn't leave him alone for a week. But with luck, he'd have a few days, which could be enough if he handled things right.

He pressed himself back into the corner of the cold shelter. By the time the bus arrived, he was shivering uncontrollably. He handed the driver a standard issue prison travel ticket good for the ride into Kansas City and huddled in the rear of the bus for warmth.

The journey took two hours. He spent every minute working on his plan. The secret he'd learned in prison had been burning a hole in his belly. He couldn't use the secret while he was locked up.

But now he was out.

It was time for action.

CHAPTER FIVE

Monday, November 27
1:30 p.m.
Kansas City, Kansas

HALLMAN RODE THE BUS all the way to the terminal in
downtown Kansas City.

The bus had picked up growing numbers of passengers as
they traveled through the outskirts. They wore coats in somber
shades. Some wore hats. He waited until they had all stepped off
before sweeping down the aisle, his eyes scanning the empty
seats in the hope a hat or gloves had been left behind. He didn't
find anything he could use.

Buses were lined up at an angle, front sections nestled under
a canopy that did little to stop the cold wind and rain from
stealing his body heat.

He hustled into the bus station.

It was an oddly shaped area with a concession stand and a
line of ticket windows. Posters on the walls showed artificially

glamorous images of the destinations serviced by the city's transportation system.

Rows of metal seats were filled with people looking off into the middle distance, all desperate not to make eye contact with fellow travelers.

He consulted a giant Greyhound timetable with tiny print. He'd missed the bus to Dallas.

In a corner were two payphone booths. One was empty, the phone made obsolete long ago by the irresistible force of technology. The other had a phone covered in stickers and graffiti. The handset dangled by its metal coated cord.

He picked up the handset and cycled it on and off the cradle a couple of times until he heard a dial tone.

Satisfied the phone would work, he headed for the concession area, and toured around the small tables, searching for paper and a pen. The smell of grease excited his stomach, but he shoved the thought to the back of his mind. He had no money for burgers or fries.

A teenager in a yellow shirt and hat watched his every move. Hallman smiled at him and left. They didn't have what he needed.

The ticket windows sealed the staff away from customers. Even if someone back there had a pen, they were unlikely to lend it to him.

An automated lottery ticket machine stood in one corner. An empty chain next to the blank tickets showed someone else before him had also needed a pen. He searched the floor around the machine and found a small pencil in the dust behind it.

He took a lottery ticket form and returned to the payphone. He found enough change to make a call and dialed his brother's cellphone.

"Shane?" Thomas Hallman's nasal voice was unmistakable because of the slight lisp he'd developed as a kid.

"Yeah."

"You out?"

"Just made it into the city. Bus station, like you said. You found me a place?"

"Yeah. A *Dollars & Cents* store. The reference number's 888 4798. Go north to Independence, turn right. It's about a mile."

Hallman jotted down the reference number on his blank lottery ticket. "You couldn't find anywhere closer?"

"You haven't been allowed to walk a mile in a straight line for the past five years, and you're complaining?"

Hallman sighed. "It's cold."

"There's a few shops nearby. I sent two hundred."

"Two hundred?"

"Should get you a coat and a Greyhound ticket to Dallas."

Hallman shifted his weight. "You couldn't make it a little more?"

"Two hundred will get you a ticket and a hot meal. You're getting out of Kansas, remember? It's what we agreed."

Hallman breathed in and out. "I… I just need to do one or two things."

His brother's voice hardened. "Not just no, but hell no. Everything bad that's happened in your life has happened because of the people you mixed with in Kansas."

Hallman grinned to himself. If only Thomas knew the whole story. But he was useful right now, so Hallman let him think he was a Good Samaritan. Hallman intended to play the poor sap for all he could get.

"'Kay brother, but the Dallas bus has already gone. I've got to stay over one night at least."

"Two hundred," Thomas said firmly.

"Three would make it easier. I haven't slept in a decent bed for five years."

His brother gave a big sigh.

Hallman waited. One thing a guy learns in prison is how to wait.

Eventually, Thomas spoke. "Okay. Three hundred. A coat, a hot meal, a hotel, and the first bus to Dallas in the morning. No messing around. No booze, no drugs, no nothing."

Hallman smiled. "You're a good one, brother. What would I do without you?"

"Once you get to Dallas, I'm not going to give you the chance to find out. You'll do everything I say, and I'm never letting you out of my sight again."

"You got it, brother. See you tomorrow."

Hallman hung up. Three hundred wasn't much. Not for his plan. But he'd manage. He always did.

CHAPTER SIX

Monday, November 27
3:00 p.m.
Denver, Colorado

JESS RECEIVED A CALL from Denver PD after lunch. As Carter suggested, they had apprehended a suspect in the carjacking and wanted her help with a lineup. They didn't have to ask twice. She arrived at the low, modern building on Forty-Ninth Street early.

The receptionist made a call to Detective Leon Treseder. Jess relaxed slightly because she knew him. Thirteen years earlier he had been a beat cop in a squad car when Peter was abducted. He'd been kind to her then when she needed it most. Occasionally since then, their paths crossed. He never failed to ask how she was and how the search for her son was going.

A minute later he arrived.

Treseder was a hulking figure, a six-foot linebacker with a buzz cut in a close-fitting suit. She braced herself for his handshake, and then recalled that he had a light-but-firm touch. "Nice to see you, Miss Kimball."

"We've known each other way too long for that, Leon. Call me Jess, please."

He grinned. "You got yourself in the headlines this time, Jess."

"Seems that way."

"I'm sure Mr. and Mrs. Walsh are grateful."

She shrugged to brush off the compliment.

He paused a beat. "Any news?"

She offered a flat smile. "You mean about Peter? No."

"Stephenson still on the case for you?"

She nodded. "I'm glad to say he is."

Brentwood Stephenson was the private investigator Jess had hired to lead the search for Peter eight years ago.

They'd connected well from their very first meeting. He was a genuine southern gentleman, educated, refined, and courteous. He managed to pull off this feat without sounding patronizing or like he was mired in the past.

That wasn't why Jess had hired him, though she did appreciate his manners. With thirty years in the Dallas PD, there wasn't much he hadn't seen, and he knew how to pace himself on long cases. His phone calls were always measured affairs. Even when he had a tantalizing possibility to report, he was careful to frame it against the background of the search for Peter that had lasted well more than a decade.

"He's a good man," Treseder said. "You heard he found the guy they called the camping killer from his bank records?"

Jess nodded. "After twenty years. Pretty impressive."

"Good detective. Nobody better for your situation, in my view."

Stephenson was a good investigator. Every few months he reviewed every person who had any connection to the case. He watched for disappearances, unexplained wealth, and of course, criminal convictions. He chased down every lead, even though they'd all gone nowhere.

One day all that work would pay off. She hoped.

Treseder got back to the lineup. "Ready?"

"Let's go."

He led her through to a dimly lit viewing room. Dark drapes covered the window into the identification room.

"I'm guessing you know the drill, but I need to give you the full instructions." He pointed to a tape recorder. "Everything you say is recorded. It may be used in a trial." After that, he ran through a list of dos and don'ts.

When Jess confirmed she understood, he left the room to organize the parade of potential suspects.

Treseder's comment about her being in the headlines was a useful reminder to let Stephenson know what had happened today. She was in the headlines, which always brought attention to her search for Peter. A moment after she sent him a summary of events, he sent back a note thanking her for the update and to say she should be cautious about the possibility of hoaxes and scams, as usual.

Detective Treseder returned. "This is a double-blind test, meaning I don't know the identity of the suspect. So it's all up to you."

She nodded, and he opened the drapes.

Jess peered through the glass. The identification room was brightly lit, the contrast in lighting between the rooms made her invisible to the seven men seated in the lineup on the other side.

Jess frowned. "Are they going to stand?"

Treseder shook his head. "Seated reduces differences in

height. Sorry. Standard practice here. But if there is one you feel particular about, we can ask him to stand."

Jess passed her gaze across the figures. All seven had blond hair that covered their ears and, in some cases, reached their shoulders. One man's hair draped down his back. Jess ruled him out, the man she had seen had long hair, but not that long.

One man had a large nose that she felt she would have noticed, so she ruled him out, too.

The remaining five had different facial features, but in the few moments she had glimpsed Mr. Walsh's attacker, she had barely seen the man's face.

Five possibilities. She wouldn't guess. Lawyers had told her there would be no negative evidentiary impact if she failed to make a choice. But if she misidentified an innocent person, that could be used effectively in the suspect's defense.

She cast her mind back to the intersection where the man got out of the Toyota. She saw the blond hair first, and all five of these men had blond hair. He was thin, and they were all thin.

"Could I see them walk?" she said.

Treseder pursed his lips. "It's not standard. We'd have to lead them out and let them walk one at a time. Do you have one you're considering?"

Jess looked at the seven men and shook her head. She glimpsed a tattoo and inched closer to the glass. "Can I see the backs of their necks?"

Treseder keyed a switch and spoke into a microphone. The men turned around. Three of them had tattoos.

Three.

"Ask them to show me their hands, please."

He asked. The same three guys also had tattoos on their hands.

She studied each man, imagined him climbing out of a car, swinging a punch. She did it again and again. Each of the three, again and again.

"Anything?" Treseder asked.

She shook her head as she looked through the glass one last time. "I can't say for sure. The man had tattoos. One on his neck. More on his hands. But between the three with tattoos… I can't say."

She turned her gaze to Treseder. His face was impassive, as it should have been, but it pained her that she couldn't identify the suspect.

She breathed a long sigh. "Maybe something will come to me later."

CHAPTER SEVEN

Monday, November 27
4:00 p.m.
Kansas City, Kansas

HALLMAN ARRIVED AT THE *Dollars & Cents* store
shivering and soaked. Despite the cold, he walked the block
either side twice before going in. The area wasn't the best, but he
didn't see anyone hanging around on corners or in doorways.
There was no point in picking up his money only to get mugged
as he returned to the street.

The temperature inside the store was little better than
outside. There were a few uncomfortable plastic chairs and a
counter at the back. The counter was shielded by thick glass and
wire mesh. A small hatch allowed money to be passed back and
forth. A microphone and speaker hung over the gap at the top.

Behind the glass, a man in a red coat watched him idly. A
name tag stitched into his coat identified him as Frank, which
could have been his first name or his last.

"I've come to collect some money," Hallman said.

Frank sneered. "Wow. There's a surprise."

After five years in prison, the sarcasm rolled off Hallman's back. "I have the number."

Frank grunted and pushed a clipboard through the hatch. A pen and a small form were clipped to the board. "Fill it in."

"Wow. There's a surprise." Hallman mocked as he picked up the pen.

Frank said nothing.

The form was simple. Boxes for sender's name, recipient's name, and the reference number. Hallman had memorized the reference number. He pushed the completed form through the hatch after a few moments.

Frank typed on a computer keyboard and stamped the form. He laid out ten twenties on the counter. "Count them."

"Should be three hundred."

Frank glanced at his computer screen. "Nope. Two hundred."

"I talked to my brother. He changed it to three hundred."

Frank worked the keyboard a moment and shook his head. "Two hundred."

Damn Thomas. Never could do anything right the first time.

He printed out a receipt and pushed it through the hatch. "The computer doesn't lie."

Hallman inspected the receipt. His brother had apparently transferred two hundred earlier in the day.

"He only agreed to change it an hour ago."

Frank shook his head. "He hasn't changed it."

"He told me—"

"Don't matter what he said. He didn't change it."

Hallman scowled. "Maybe the change hasn't come through your system yet."

"Maybe."

"So how will I know when it has?"

"When you come back and ask." Frank gestured to the short stack of twenties lined up behind the glass. "Count them."

"Ten."

"Bingo." Frank assembled the bills into a pile, placed them in an envelope, and sealed it. He pushed it through the hatch. "Don't spend it all at once."

Hallman wanted to punch the guy in the face, but the barrier between them made that impossible. So he stuffed the envelope in his jeans pocket and left.

Two blocks south he found a thrift shop. He combed the rails for the cheapest coat that looked water resistant. He found a black one with a hood. He skipped the gloves. He could keep his hands in his pockets for warmth. But he grabbed a dark blue fleece hat that he could extend below his nose. He'd make two holes, and he'd have a mask.

The coat and hat were twenty-three dollars including tax. He took the change in coins and left.

Hallman continued walking south in the cold rain. He kept off the main roads and zigzagged between blocks and streets. He remembered the area pretty well after five years away. He only doubled back once. But he didn't like being out in the open where he might be noticed and recognized or remembered. He knew too many people in this city. He wanted his whereabouts untraceable.

But he needed to see Max Spinney.

Max could talk to anyone. He had a natural way of bonding with people that led him to a life of conning. People trusted him. He'd abused that trust for profit. Until he got caught.

He'd served his time. Four years, with time off for good behavior. After he was released from prison, he took up permanent residence on one end of the bar at the Blue Roof Tavern.

Hallman saw the sloppy drunk as soon as he stepped through the front door. Max smiled. Hallman waved and grinned back.

Max had gained a few pounds. His thin nylon jacket stretched around his middle over a T-shirt with a faded picture of a beach on the front. His clothes hadn't been washed in a while. Neither had Max.

"Shane Hallman, as I live and breathe." Max gestured to the stool beside him. "Take a seat."

Hallman sat down. "Buy you a drink?"

Max hefted an empty glass. "You need to ask?"

The barman sauntered over. Max ordered a vodka over ice, Hallman requested tonic water.

The barman left without comment.

"You on the wagon or something?" Max said.

Hallman laughed. "No choice. Five years at Humboldt."

"Right. They let you out finally."

"I did my time. All of it."

Max nodded. "That's good. No parole. None of that halfway house crap."

"I'd have coped with any crap to get out earlier."

"You say that now." Max arched his eyebrows knowingly.

The bartender returned with the drinks. Hallman peeled a twenty from the cash his brother sent, and carefully counted his change.

He waited until the barman left. "I need to find a guy."

Max chugged a half inch of his vodka. "Who?"

"Earle Gotting."

Max frowned. "Why?"

"We were inside together."

"Together?"

"Same wing at Humboldt."

Max nodded. "Yeah. Right. He got out a year ago."

"Six months."

Max downed another inch of his drink. "Really? Hard to keep track of time."

Hallman understood Max was testing him. Max wouldn't hook him up unless he was sure there'd be no blowback. Max had always been deeply suspicious of ulterior motives. Given his own talents as a con artist, suspicion was probably a defense mechanism.

Max shrugged. "Haven't seen Gotting in a while. I'll put the word out. See if I can find him."

"Losing your touch, Max? You used to know everyone."

Max finished his vodka.

Hallman gestured to the empty glass on the bar. "Another?"

Max nodded. "Double would be good."

The bartender stared at him expectantly. Hallman nodded. The bartender poured another vodka. A larger glass this time. He placed it in front of Max and left.

Max spoke without looking at Hallman. "Gotting drinks at Ged's Place. A sorry little bar in a strip mall on Compton, down in Burlington."

Hallman didn't know Ged's Place, but he knew Burlington. A rough area in the south-east corner of the city. He'd watched a man get beaten to death there once.

"Does he drink much?"

Max laughed and leaned forward, peering into Hallman's eyes. "Did you really know him at all at Humboldt?"

CHAPTER EIGHT

Monday, November 27
5:15 p.m.
Denver, Colorado

JESS ARRIVED AT DENVER Broadcasting's offices a few minutes early. A receptionist called an assistant who led her to the *Denver PM* studio. The host's name, Mia Luna, was written in splashy script across the walls.

She was familiar with the show. *Denver PM* aired daily at 5:30 p.m. Content was local light news to carry into the local hard news show that ran immediately before the network news. After that, the nightly game shows kicked off prime time. Because of its feel-good content, *Denver PM* was more popular than anything newsy the local station offered.

This close to airtime, the set was abuzz with people. Camera operators set up for their shots while rolling cameras across the area in front of the elevated staging on set. A woman rushed back and forth, checking cables until a monitor behind the stage jumped to life. On the left of the stage, a young woman stood in front of a giant blue wall, waving her arms and gesturing to imaginary places that would soon be advised about the weather forecast.

Other staff members scurried around the stage preparing to air.

The assistant led Jess toward the set, reeling off instructions as she went. "You'll enter from the left, cross in front of the armchairs and take the one on the left. Mia will greet you. Say something like 'Pleasure to be here,' just to get the ball rolling. Aim for a conversation with Mia, try not to look at the camera." The assistant checked a clipboard. "You'll be second. After the segment on the new China trade deal."

"We're making a change to the lineup," a woman said.

Jess turned to see Mia striding across the room, somehow managing to clear each of the cables snaking across the floor without so much as glancing in their direction.

She'd met Mia earlier in the year at a charity event race. Jess ran hard and came in fourth. Mia was waiting for her at the finish, barely breathing hard. Mia was all muscle. Not the bulging sort like a bodybuilder, but the long, lean kind that produced endurance.

Mia stepped onto the stage just as a man with a handful of papers walked over. The executive producer, Jess guessed.

Mia said, "We need to start with positive human interest. All the political topics will get covered later. There's no local impact to the trade deal story yet, anyway."

She turned to Jess and held her hand out. "Good to see you again, Jess."

"We have the introduction and all the graphics laid out already, Mia," the executive producer said.

Mia looked at her watch. "Seven minutes. The team can change it easily."

He stuffed his papers under his arm and walked away grumbling.

"You don't have to change things for me," Jess said. "I can wait."

Mia smiled. "Don't worry. He complains, but he's the best. Besides, he knows I'm right. He'll have it done in half the time. Your story is something people will feel good about. That's what we do here."

Jess shrugged.

A young woman attached Jess's microphone to her lapel.

"We've been working with the police," Mia said as the woman threaded a cable through the back of Jess's clothes. "Sharing what CCTV footage we could collect on your car chase." She grinned, "You'd make a good street racer."

"I haven't seen any of the footage."

"We even have your roll down the slope and the inhaler. We got lucky with that one. A taxi driver had a dash cam pointed in your direction." Mia paused and frowned. "I'm thinking the last time we met you were still searching for your son."

Jess offered a flat smile, surprised Mia had remembered.

"Any news?" Mia asked.

Jess shook her head.

"One minute," the executive producer called out.

The crew left the set, shrinking into the shadows around the studio.

Mia pointed Jess to the armchairs.

"Thirty seconds," the executive producer said.

Mia looked at Jess and arched her eyebrows. "Our audience numbers are in the millions. Peter, right?"

Jess frowned. "My son? Yes."

"We'll mention him. Maybe someone knows something."

Jess never missed a chance to ask for help from the public to find Peter. "That would be great. Thank you."

"Thirty seconds." Mia winked at Jess, "I can shave that off politics any day. Do you have a photo?"

Jess fished out her phone, found the age-progressed photo of Peter and offered it to Mia who handed it to the executive producer. "Get this ready to show at the end of our interview."

"Okay. Live in ten," he replied.

A large timer above a camera counted down.

Mia straightened her back and assumed a calm, wide-eyed smile.

The counter reached zero, and Mia's smile broadened. "Good evening, and welcome to *Denver PM*. With us tonight is Jessica Kimball, *Taboo Magazine's* star reporter. Jess interrupted a carjacking this morning, almost certainly saving the life of the hostage."

Jess handled Mia's questions, modestly accepting her praise, and discussing the good work done every day by her coworkers at *Taboo*. She even had a chance to put in a plug for Carter Pierce.

In the last thirty seconds, Mia pivoted to Peter, explaining that he was missing and showing the photo of a blond-haired, brown-eyed fifteen-year-old. She gave Jess the chance to announce her website and her toll-free number for tips. The website and the tip line were added to the crawl across the bottom of the screen.

Finally, Mia implored anyone with information about Peter to come forward and reunite Peter with his mother for Christmas. Then she moved to politics.

Jess remained in her armchair until the commercial break, listening to the next segment. Mia was right. The trade deal was political mumbo-jumbo that no one would want to dwell on very long. Maybe Mia's audience would be more interested in finding Peter. She hoped.

CHAPTER NINE

Monday, November 27
5:30 p.m.
Kansas City, Kansas

HALLMAN WALKED SOUTH THROUGH the city. Fine drizzle came and went while the sky remained resolutely gray. He zipped his jacket up hard against his neck and buried his hands in his pockets.

The streets changed as he worked south. More empty industrial units here. Doorways gathered trash. Colorful shop windows farther north were replaced by seedy bars.

He passed a sign that vandals had broken in two pieces. The remaining section announced he was entering "Burli."

At a gas station, he asked a girl behind a wire mesh for directions to Ged's Place, but she just shrugged.

He walked toward a cluster of bars and strip joints he'd visited before he went to prison. The places were still there, but he saw no Ged's, and no Compton Street.

A truck delivering beer to one of the bars was parked near the exit. One man stayed with the truck while two others hefted metal barrels onto a dolly and wheeled them inside.

Hallman removed his hands from his pockets and smiled as he approached the guy at the truck to ask for directions.

The driver kept the window up, probably to trap the heat inside. But he knew Ged's and gave directions through the glass. Hallman guessed he probably wanted to get rid of the stranger, which was fine by him.

He reached Ged's Place shortly afterward. It was located in a strip mall with only one other occupied store, a charity consignment shop.

Inside, Ged's Place was dark but warm enough. Hallman's boots stuck to the carpet as he crossed from the door to the bar. Two men sat at one of the tables, and a woman was perched at the end of the counter. He didn't see Gotting anywhere.

The bartender ambled in his direction and theatrically flipped a coaster on the bar. "What're you having?"

Hallman shook his head. "I'm looking for Earle Gotting?"

The bartender sneered. "We serve beer and liquor. We aren't the yellow pages."

Hallman checked to be sure he wasn't attracting attention. "Earle and I were at Humboldt together. I just got out."

The bartender shrugged. "Still don't know him."

"How much is it worth?" the woman at the end of the counter asked.

Hallman shook his head. "I just got out. No money. I can come back later. I know he drinks here."

The bartender grunted and walked off.

The woman pulled an unhappy face before she spoke. "Palm Tree Court. Apartment 225." She frowned. "Or 227. Definitely on the upstairs floor. At the back. Got a hole kicked in the door."

Hallman didn't ask how she knew, but he figured her for a junkie, like Gotting. He thanked her and left.

CHAPTER TEN

Monday, November 27
6:10 p.m.
Kansas City, Kansas

HALLMAN HAD SEEN THE Palm Tree Court apartments
earlier while he looked for Ged's Place. It took him less than two
minutes to find them again. The parking lot boasted few vehicles
with lower than triple-digit mileage on the odometer. Several
cars were propped up on blocks.

Three-story concrete block buildings that had seen better
days housed dull brown apartments. The weathered wooden
steps leading to the upper floors had long ago lost all trace of
color. The handrail flexed as his weight landed on the treads.

A large square of plywood was screwed over the lower
portion of the door to apartment 227, behind which was the hole
the woman had mentioned, he figured.

He looked for a doorbell. Finding none, he knocked and
waited.

Five seconds later, he knocked again and placed his ear to the door. He heard the murmur of a radio or television. He hammered on the door with the flat of his fist.

The door opened.

Earle Gotting's haggard face stared at him. He leaned slightly to the left. Maybe because of his bad leg or because he was drunk or high or all three.

"What do you want?" Gotting said.

"Talk to you."

"Not interested." Gotting pushed the door toward the frame.

Hallman stuck his foot in the way and shoved the door open again.

Gotting shifted his weight. "Do I know you?"

Hallman stepped forward. He used his forearm to push Gotting backward into the room.

Gotting shoved Hallman's forearm away. "Get off me."

Hallman stepped sideways and closed the door. "We were at Humboldt together."

"Yeah? What of it? Lotta guys at Humboldt." Gotting scowled.

In the dimly lit room, Gotting looked even worse. Smelled worse, too. Gotting might not have showered within the past six months, he smelled that bad. His home wasn't much better. The odor of trash and dirty dishes and stale marijuana smoke hung in the air. And something else that smelled of decaying flesh. Hallman glanced around for dead rodents, but only saw a couple of live mice scurry away from a half-eaten hamburger bun.

"You remember me," Hallman said. "You got out six months ago. I got out today."

Gotting shook his head. "I ain't taking you in if that's what you're thinking."

"I'm not looking to crash. And if I was, I wouldn't stay in this pigsty. I want to talk to you. About what you told me. When we were at Humboldt."

Gotting leaned on the door handle. "I ain't told you nothing. Get out."

"It's important. What you said."

Gotting frowned. "What'd I say?"

Hallman cocked his head and took a closer look at Gotting. He was struggling to pay attention and getting confused. Did he have brain damage? Definitely possible, given the various substances he seemed to be ingesting.

"Let's talk about it." Hallman steered Gotting toward a chair in the filthy living room. He instead limped fluidly around a coffee table that had a lamp on it and poured himself onto the sofa. Hallman sat on a chair across from Gotting.

The apartment was a studio with the kitchen behind a counter. An open door led to the bedroom and bathroom. Gotting was far from a neat freak. Like the living room, every inch of the kitchen was covered in dirty dishes, fast food wrappers, empty bottles, and overflowing ashtrays. The mixture was revolting.

Hallman ignored it all and concentrated on Gotting. "You told me about a baby you took."

Gotting laughed and shook his head. "Nah. No, no. I didn't take no baby."

"You told me."

"Nah."

"The mom's a celebrity now."

Gotting inched backward, drawing his bad leg with him.

Hallman nodded toward Gotting's leg. "I didn't do that to you."

"You gotta go."

Hallman didn't move. "I want to know about the baby. Tell me, and I'll go."

Gotting shook his head.

Hallman pushed Gotting back into the sofa.

Gotting breathed out. His shoulders relaxed.

Hallman leaped forward, grabbing the lamp from the coffee table and whipping the electrical cord over Gotting's head.

Gotting reacted too late. The cord was already around his neck.

Hallman snugged up his garrote. "I don't want to hurt you, but I need to know."

Gotting's eyes widened along with his big, black pupils. The effects of whatever drug he had taken diminished by the flood of adrenaline building in his bloodstream.

"Whose baby was it?"

Gotting gagged.

Hallman tightened the cord. "Whose baby?"

Gotting's eyes bulged.

"Whose?"

Gotting pulled back, lying flat on the couch.

Hallman put his knee on Gotting's scrawny chest. "Tell me."

Gotting's face turned bright red. Hallman relaxed the tension on the cord. "Tell me."

"Jess… Jess Kimball," Gotting said between snatched breaths. "But she ain't no big celebrity, Just a reporter. I made out like she was big. Back inside. Boasting. That's all. She ain't rich."

Jess Kimball. He had a name. How much more could he squeeze out of this miserable cretin? Hallman forced his smile into a frown. He growled, "Good enough."

Gotting gasped. "Why are you doing this?"

"Money." Hallman relaxed the cord further.

Gotting stared. "How you going to get money out of her? She has a reward. She ain't rich."

Hallman shook his head. This guy was a waste of good air. It would be easy enough to strangle him and be done with it.

Gotting stared. "You're going to turn me over to the cops."

Hallman snorted. "No, I ain't. Not unless you give me a reason to."

Gotting clawed at the cord. "Then you should cut me in. I took the kid. By rights—"

"Tell me how you did it. How did you take the kid?"

Gotting took a deep breath. "A baby. She left him. Went to get laundry in the basement of her apartment building."

"You were watching her."

"Well, duh." Gotting pried the cord another half inch from his tender flesh. "Watched her for a couple of weeks. Single mom. No help. Just her and him. It was an easy take."

"What was she wearing?"

Gotting scowled. "What are you—"

Hallman jerked the cord tighter.

Gotting choked. "Jeans. T-shirt. I don't—"

"What sort of T-shirt?"

"It… I don't…" He frowned. "Like the big lips with the tongue thing."

"What tongue thing?"

Gotting pulled on the cord. "The…the…"

"Rolling Stones?"

"Yeah, yeah. That's it."

He was too stupid to lie. Which meant Hallman had learned another usable piece of information. "You're sure?"

"Yeah. She wore it all the time. Like it was the only one she owned or something."

Gotting was too weak to fight back, but was he telling the truth? Hallman narrowed his eyes. Gotting's face was screwed up. The lack of oxygen and the compression on his throat was getting to him. The drugs and alcohol swimming in his system were a good thing. He was too far from reality to make up convincing lies.

Hallman needed just one more thing, and he'd be good to go. "Where is the kid now?"

Gotting screwed up his face in disbelief. "How the hell would I know?"

Hallman tightened the cord. "I need to find him."

"It's been years—" Gotting choked again.

"Blackmail won't work without the kid." Hallman leaned more weight on his knee, pushing the oxygen from Gotting's lungs. "Where is he?"

Hallman waited, watching Gotting's eyes bulge. A cold chill ran through his blood. There was one giant, obvious, plan-destroying answer to his question. He tightened the cord. "Did you kill the baby?"

Gotting found some strength somewhere. He shoved against Hallman's weight. "You think I'm stupid? I'm no baby killer. I gave him to a guy."

"Sold him, you mean."

Gotting dug his fingers into his neck and strained against the cord. "A fence. I gave him to a fence."

A fence? Whoever heard of fencing babies? "Who'd you sell him to?"

Gotting gagged. His eyes bulged. He shook his head.

Hallman tightened the cord another notch.

Gotting thrashed his legs. He squirmed and bucked.

Hallman kept his weight on Gotting's chest, not enough to

crush his fragile ribs, but forcing him down into the sofa's sagging cushions. "Who!"

"N… Norell. Zander Norell."

"You're lying."

Gotting's legs kept moving. He gagged as he shook his head. He gasped, "No. No. Not lying. Norell. Fenced the kids I took."

Hallman raised his eyebrows, feeling like he'd actually won the lotto all of a sudden. More than one kid meant more than one potential blackmail opportunity, didn't it?

He snarled and loosened the cord to let Gotting catch his breath. "How many kids did you take?"

"I don't know. I didn't keep count." Gotting sucked in as much air as he could get. "Norell spooked when I went inside. Won't do no more."

"But you weren't sent in for kidnapping." The guy was a blabbermouth now with very little persuasion. Hallman didn't believe Gotting had kept his secrets from the police.

"Where do I find Norell?" Hallman demanded, giving the cord one more solid yank.

Gotting had lost his fight. He seemed exhausted all of a sudden. His eyelids closed. "North Elm. 1734."

"You kidnapped any babies since you got out?"

"No point without a fence. Not like I can sell the damn kids myself, can I?"

"You're pathetic, you know that?" Hallman shook his head, released the tension on the cord, and moved away from Gotting.

Nobody in his right mind would buy a child from a train wreck like Gotting, no matter how desperate they were. A broker of some kind was the only reasonable way it could have been done.

He'd never heard of Zander Norell. Gotting could have lied, but he was too stupid to come up with a moniker like that.

Gotting remained still. His eyes were closed. He barely moved.

Hallman slapped Gotting's face. He grunted and opened one eye.

Kidnapping, blackmail, and ransom were all a giant leap from Hallman's specialty, which was burglary. He'd spent enough time in prison. He didn't want to add the murder of this worthless piece of crap to the list. Simply put, Gotting wasn't worth the price.

He loosened the cord from around the bony neck. Gotting's head lolled sideways before jerking back.

"I want to rest," Gotting said, glassy-eyed. He lay motionless on the sofa.

Hallman looked at the coffee table. Among the junk, he found a bottle of pills and a couple of syringes with a bag of white powder. He didn't touch any of the drugs or paraphernalia. Gotting must have been in the process of using these when Hallman arrived.

He'd intended to use a combination of bribery and threats to persuade Gotting to hold his tongue. Now, he was flat out on the dirty sofa. Hallman figured it unlikely that Gotting would even remember his visit.

Which was probably a good thing. Eventually, the police were likely to become involved. They'd dig into everything, including the spaced-out waste of breath lying on the couch.

The blinds on the windows were already closed. Gotting was a serious addict. With the pills and powder he had on the table, he probably wouldn't emerge from here for days. He might even die here. Hallman tried to feel sorry about that, but truth was, the world would be a better place without Gotting in it. Lucky for Hallman that Gotting didn't die before now.

Hallman found a rag in the kitchen sink and did his best to wipe away his fingerprints. He spent more time on the lamp and its cord. He put the rag in his pocket. He'd toss it when he was far enough away.

On the coffee table was an old cell phone. The battery was half full. He turned the phone off and dropped it in his pocket.

Before he exited the apartment, He used the spy hole in the door to check the corridor. Quiet out there. Excellent. He wiped the door handle with his sleeve as he left.

At the bottom of the steps, he noticed the exit at the rear of the parking lot. He put on his hat, pulled up the collar of his coat, and walked fast. His steps were buoyed by success and optimism now. Things were falling into place.

He didn't stop walking until he was well past the broken Burlington sign.

CHAPTER ELEVEN

Monday, November 27
6:35 p.m.
Kansas City, Kansas

FARTHER SOUTH WAS A big box electronics store with a parking lot the size of an aircraft carrier. The store was warm. He could feel the heat flowing into him and drying his jeans.

In the middle of the store, dozens of PCs and laptops were on display. He headed for the most expensive. Two salespeople converged on him. He fended them off and brought up the web browser.

The internet connection was slow, but he was safer using it in the store than he had been in the prison where everything was monitored. The last thing he wanted was some overzealous screw finding anything in his search history.

He searched for Jess Kimball.

There were several pages of hits. Her full name was Jessica. She was an average height blonde. Her hair had a natural curl to it. She stood confidently, her shoulders square, her back straight, and her brown eyes piercing the camera's lens. He scrolled through more photographs. Her clothes had a no-nonsense edge, but they weren't sophisticated or obviously expensive.

He found a set of pictures from a magazine awards ceremony. She was accompanied by a very well-groomed older man.

His name was Carter Pierce. Hallman looked him up. Pierce had inherited a fortune and made it a bigger one. If the yearly lists of the richest people in America could be believed, he had doubled his inheritance every decade. He was an only child. Even though he had been romantically connected with several women, he had never married.

Hallman grunted. Either he had impossible standards, or he was impossible to get along with. Whatever, Carter Pierce was as alone in the world as it was possible to get.

Pierce owned *Taboo Magazine*, a high-end glossy, noted for its in-depth reporting and photography. Pierce also ran *Taboo*. He was credited with articles about the rich and famous, and he'd gone to court to protect his journalists. He splashed money at all sorts of worthy causes. Charities, his staff's medical bills, and crime victims, whether they appeared in his magazine or not.

Which brought Hallman back to Jessica Kimball.

Looking over the front pages of the last twelve editions of *Taboo Magazine*, her reporting appeared on the cover nine times. She was the magazine's star reporter. That's why Carter Pierce stood by her side at the awards ceremony.

He said many times that he considered Kimball like family. Family.

People did a lot for family.

Hallman scrolled through the images until he found what he was looking for.

Jess Kimball's son, Peter.

Hallman clicked on a link. An article about Peter Kimball opened. Peter had been abducted before his second birthday. His mother, Jess, had spent her life searching for him. Hallman scanned the story quickly, absorbing the few specific details that might prove useful.

There was an age-adjusted picture of Peter's face at fifteen, but it looked to Hallman like a generic image that probably matched thousands of teenagers. On the same page were a toll-free number for tips and a notice that Jess Kimball would pay up to fifty grand for information that led to her son's safe return.

Fifty grand would pay off Snap Metcalfe, but fifty was way less than what Hallman had in mind.

He scrolled through another page listing Kimball's work tracking down criminals and helping the victims. He laughed. What sort of crime-fighting hero can't even locate her own kid?

Hallman found the *Taboo Magazine* website. Her biography didn't list a phone number, but there was a general one for the magazine. He wrote it down on the back of his lottery ticket form.

He left the store and walked another mile to a gas station with a rare outdoor phone booth. Even better, the booth was on the edge of the parking lot, out of CCTV range. The once shiny metal structure was rusting, but the phone looked functional.

Behind the gas station were rows of low-income houses. He guessed they didn't have fancy security video cameras. He could call from here without being recorded.

He used some of his change from the charity shop to place the call.

A woman answered. She had a warm and inviting voice. He summoned his most casual tone to ask for Jessica Kimball. The woman put him through without question.

"This is Jess Kimball."

Her voice was exactly what he expected. Businesslike. Straight to the point. A busy professional.

He kept his tone the same. "Have you found your kid?"

"Who is this?"

"Have you?"

There was a long pause. "Who is this?"

He snorted. "You don't have to drag out the call so it can be traced. Question is, have you found your kid?"

"Do you have information or not?"

"You need to get some money together."

"I have a reward for anyone with information that leads to his discovery." She was calm and controlled. Not easily rattled, this one.

He scoffed. "Fifty grand? You call that a reward? That ain't worth getting out of bed for."

"If you know where he is, the reward is higher."

"Here's what I know." He clucked his tongue against his teeth. "I know you need to get serious about my money."

"Do you know where he is or not?" She was getting a little testy.

He smiled. "One million. Chump change. Your sugar daddy Pierce spends more than that on lunch."

"What do you—"

"Get it. Fast. Before anything happens to your little boy."

Hallman hung up. He glanced around the gas station. A woman was filling up an old Chevy, and a man was loading a propane bottle into the back of a pickup. Neither paid Hallman any attention.

He needed to get moving. Kimball might contact the police immediately. She might even have sent a message while they were on the phone. It could take her a few minutes to get the message through to the right people at Kansas City PD, but he wasn't taking any chances.

He left through the back of the lot and weaved his way past the small houses. There was no sidewalk, so he walked along the curb. Several people eyed him, but no one spoke to him.

He kept his head down and kept moving. After ten minutes, he hadn't heard a police siren or seen a cruiser, which boosted his confidence.

They would trace the call eventually. Nothing happened on the US phone system these days without being recorded on a hundred computers. Finding the phone wouldn't get them very far. He hadn't threatened her, but he was pretty sure he had captured her interest. He grinned.

Leave her stewing for a while, and the next time he called she'd be desperate.

CHAPTER TWELVE

Monday, November 27
7:10 p.m.
Denver, Colorado

THE EXTORTION CALL HAD come into the *Taboo* offices after hours, and the answering service had forwarded the call to her cell phone. She'd picked it up from her car as she left the *Denver PM* studio.

All calls to *Taboo's* offices were recorded, which was stated automatically when calls were received before a human came on the line.

Jess had listened to his demand for money in exchange for information about Peter. She'd heard similar demands over the past fifteen years. Every time, her stomach somersaulted and every nerve in her body hummed until she chased down the caller and dealt with him herself.

These calls had always been hoaxes before. This one felt different, but she couldn't say precisely why.

When he hung up, she punched a code that allowed her to replay the conversation.

His voice came back at her, solid and strong. No hesitation. No doubt that his position was superior to hers. He didn't threaten. He taunted. And he wanted her to believe he had facts to back him up.

She listened to the recording twice more. His vocabulary was plain. No real accent to his voice, but he'd sounded confident. Too confident to be bluffing? Maybe.

He'd called to prepare her for future threats. He wanted to plant anxiety in her mind. She nodded and wrote "anxiety" on her notepad.

By the fourth repetition, she managed to detach from her feelings and consider the call objectively. From hard experience, she knew emotional reactions could only have a negative impact. She'd have time to figure out her feelings later. Right now, she needed a professional to deal with the caller.

She dialed Henry.

FBI Special Agent Henry Morris was the closest Jess had come to a personal relationship since Peter's father deserted her. They'd met while chasing a pair of Italian criminals, and kept in touch after the case closed. Later, Henry had transferred from Dallas to the Denver office to close the physical distance between them.

The relationship was progressing, albeit slowly. The lagging pace was more her doing than his. Peter held her total emotional focus. She couldn't make room in her life for anyone else until she found her son. Henry said he understood. She hoped he did.

Henry was a straight arrow, tight-lipped about his work, and only talked with her about his cases after information was publicly announced. Jess respected his professionalism because he also respected hers.

Despite his heavy workload, Henry always found time to help Jess when he could. In matters related to Peter, the FBI had jurisdiction if Peter had been moved across state lines. Both Jess and Henry believed he had, although neither had any proof.

Henry answered her call after the fourth ring before his phone switched to voicemail. "Jess?"

She didn't waste his time or hers on pleasantries. "I just got a blackmail call about Peter."

"How threatening?" Henry asked.

"Nothing specific. Implied he knew Peter's whereabouts and demanded money. He'll call again with details."

"Hoax?"

"Maybe." She shrugged reflexively. "Most of what he said was generic. A couple of minutes of internet research, probably. Anyone could have made the call."

"How well can you remember his exact words?"

"It was an incoming call to *Taboo*. I'll get you a recording."

"Do that. I'll give it to the audio guys. Caller ID?"

"No. So probably a pay phone. There aren't many of those left in the world."

"I'll get records from telecoms." He paused a beat. "You've had calls like this before. What do you think?"

"Yeah, plenty. Comes with the reward and the tip line and my high profile." She breathed slowly, considering his question. "But this guy seemed different. He had unusual confidence, or maybe determination. I'm not sure how to describe it. But he sounded believable."

"Did he have any unique information?"

"No, but he just…"

"Gave you goosebumps?"

She swiped splayed fingers through her curls and sighed. "Yeah. Something like that."

"Okay if we monitor your calls?"

"You'll get no complaints from me."

"I'll set it up. And send me the recording. I'm headed to the DA in a few minutes, but the audio guys can still work on it asap."

She closed her eyes and forced air into her lungs. "Thanks, Henry."

"No thanks needed. The kidnapping of a child with transportation across state lines. FBI territory. Front and center."

"Even after thirteen years?"

"Absolutely. The case is open until it's closed. No question." He paused. "I'm sorry. I'm running way behind. We can talk later. Send the recording, and I'll get my team going on this. I'll get back to you as soon as I can."

CHAPTER THIRTEEN

Monday, November 27
7:15 p.m.
Kansas City, Kansas

METCALFE SAW MAX SPINNEY'S name appear on the phone's display while he sat in his BMW waiting to collect another debt.

Spinney wasn't good for anything besides sitting on a bar stool, but he had the best ears in the whole of Kansas City. A smarter guy might have turned that skill to greater profit. As it was, Spinney was always looking for his next drink. When Spinney called, it usually meant someone was getting in the way of Metcalfe's business.

He pressed the button to answer. "Yes?"

"I just had a visitor. Came to find me specifically."

"Hmmm. Who was it?"

"Shane Hallman."

"And?" Hallman popping up twice in one day rang alarm bells. Metcalfe leaned back in his seat and paid closer attention.

"He owes you a bundle, right? I remember from when he went inside. He got out today."

"That so," Metcalfe said, not wanting to reveal he already knew.

"Thought you might be interested."

"What did he want?"

"He was looking for a guy," Spinney said shakily. "Don't know if you know him."

"Try me." After Spinney failed to reply, Metcalfe sighed. "If it's good, I'll pay your bar tab for the day."

"Right. Okay. Thanks… Hallman's looking for Gotting."

Metcalfe frowned. "Gotting?"

"Earle Gotting. Two-bit low-life from ages back."

Metcalfe permitted himself a small smile. Max Spinney calling someone else a two-bit low-life was remarkable irony. "Why does Hallman want Gotting?"

"Said they were inside together. Same wing out at Humboldt."

"Possible, I guess."

"You questioning me?" Spinney demanded.

"Don't get your boxers in a wad, Max," Metcalfe said. Spinney's tab for the day was always substantial. If Metcalfe didn't want to pay for his information, someone else would. There were plenty of others Spinney could sell good info to. Hallman owed money all over Kansas City.

Spinney harrumphed and pouted a little before he replied. "Gotting was released six months ago. Now Hallman gets out, and the first thing he does is come looking for him."

"So they're having a reunion?"

"Not likely. He didn't even know that Gotting's one of those people that drinks like a fish."

Metcalfe ignored Spinney's second bit of irony. "Maybe."

"Word is, Gotting's into drugs. Sells and uses."

Metcalfe raised his eyebrows. News like that was always worth having in his pocket. "Hallman a user?"

"Hard to say. But he wasn't looking for a fix today. There's something going on, I tell you. Cooked up some scheme together while they were inside, maybe?"

Metcalfe nodded. Made sense. "Hallman wasn't thinking of skipping town though, right?"

Spinney hesitated. "Dunno. Just looking after your interests, like you asked me to."

Metcalfe grunted. Spinney barely looked after himself, but the information might prove useful. "So, where's Gotting?"

"Ged's Place. Burlington."

Metcalfe thought for a moment. "On Compton?"

"That's it."

"This stays between us and no one else. Got it?"

"On my word."

"Tell the bartender I'll be by later to pay your bill."

"Thanks, Henrik."

Metcalfe hung up. He realized Spinney had embellished a bit because he'd been looking to convert what he offered into payment for booze. But it was a worrying message anyway.

First order of business for an ex-con like Hallman was a roof over his head. So either he planned to crash with Gotting, or they were leaving Kansas City. Neither possibility was comforting, given the fifty grand Hallman owed. Metcalfe didn't feel like chasing a deadbeat all over hell's half-acre, either.

Metcalfe started the BMW. He'd waited a long time to get his money back from that loser. The last thing he'd do now was let Hallman walk away.

CHAPTER FOURTEEN

Monday, November 27
8:00 p.m.
Denver, Colorado

JESS CLEARED THE PAPERS from her dining table, organized and stashed them in a desk drawer in the spare bedroom.

Her apartment was small, sparsely furnished, and barely used. Not because she disliked the place or avoided memories. Like romantic relationships, she had no time for decorating or hobbies or entertaining. One event had overwhelmed all others. Peter. Until she found him, he was her primary reason for being.

Henry Morris was due at eight o'clock. He arrived precisely on time, to the minute, as always. His reliability was one of his most endearing qualities to Jess. She'd had very little in her life she could count on before Henry.

She opened the door.

He held out a shopping bag from the local organic produce store. "I come bearing gifts."

She peered inside. "Does one of your gifts have a cork?"

He grinned as he pulled out a Cabernet. "Ah, yes. The main ingredient of the best salads."

She arranged the vegetables on two plates while Henry found salad dressing in her fridge.

He sat facing her at the circular dining table and poured two glasses of wine. They clinked glasses before they began eating. Jess noticed again how pleasant he was to have around. She'd been eating alone for too many years.

"They traced that call you asked me to track down to a payphone at a gas station in Kansas City, south of the city center," Morris said after the small talk.

She nodded. "Kansas, not Missouri?"

"Right. But either way, not in the state of Colorado," Morris replied. "Which is enough to suspect interstate child kidnapping. If so, that's FBI jurisdiction. Which means I can help you with this, using bureau resources."

She nodded slowly but said nothing. She'd received calls from out of state before. None of them had panned out. "Any usable prints on the phone?"

He shook his head. "It's a public phone, and it was raining. They took the coins. We'll get what prints we can. DNA, too, if there is any. We could get lucky. But we don't expect much."

"Did he make any other calls from that phone?" She twirled her fork around the lettuce on her plate.

"Not likely. It's not a popular phone. Not used much. I have a list of calls over the past two weeks. Nothing lights up our computers so far."

An exasperated sigh escaped her lips.

He refilled her glass. "The call could be nothing, Jess. A hoax. Some scam artist looking to make a quick buck from the reward.

Like all the ones you've received before."

"Maybe. But the others didn't have the… I don't know what to call it. Passion, maybe? This guy had passion in spades."

"I've listened to the recording several times," Morris nodded. "He sounds like he's hyped up, but that's not uncommon for someone in the middle of…"

"A shakedown?" she arched her eyebrows and frowned.

He nodded again. "If he calls again, try to get some facts from him. We'll continue to monitor your numbers for a few days. A week, maybe."

"I've got my work calls redirected straight to my cell now."

"I know." He held up his phone, "You get a call, and I get a computer-generated notification immediately."

"On the first round, he was only trying to soften me up. Make me anxious, so I'll give him the money."

"Right."

"I've got news for him."

Henry laughed. "Didn't work, huh?"

"Damn right." She picked up her wine. "Who does he think he's dealing with?"

CHAPTER FIFTEEN

Monday, November 27
8:25 p.m.
Kansas City, Kansas

HENRIK METCALFE SWUNG HIS big BMW across the road and cursed. The rush hour traffic was gone and almost no one was walking around in the cold night. It should have been easy to find a lone walker. Despite doubling back and covering the same ground repeatedly, he'd seen no sign of Hallman.

Spinney's tip had taken him to Ged's Place where the barman confirmed that a man, presumably Hallman, had been looking for Gotting. The barman didn't know where Gotting lived but said some woman had given Hallman an address. The barman hadn't overheard the address, and the woman was nowhere to be found.

Which reduced Metcalfe to unsuccessfully cruising the neighborhood. He'd approached one or two groups clustered in nearby parking lots, but they claimed not to have seen Gotting or Hallman.

He'd continued the search, but the darkness impeded positive identification. He slowed to illuminate each walker with the BMW's powerful fog lights. Inevitably, they covered their eyes against the glare, which obscured their faces, too.

He pulled into a drugstore parking lot. He made a few calls seeking Gotting's address but struck out. The answer from all quarters was that Gotting was a washed-up, drug- and alcohol-addled wreck not worth talking to.

Metcalfe slammed the BMW into gear. He'd do one more circuit of the Burlington area. He rolled out of the parking lot's exit.

Straight across the street was a rundown liquor store. Metcalfe recalled the store was a drug hangout and only a block from Ged's Place. Gotting was likely to stick close by to feed his habits. Maybe someone inside would know where Gotting lived.

Metcalfe crossed the near-empty street and parked directly in front of the liquor store's armored door. There was no glass across the front of the building, just advertising posters stuck to thick plywood boards. The suggestion was that the place had been burglarized in the past, but Metcalfe suspected the point was to prevent cops and junkies from looking through the windows.

He locked his BMW and went inside. The man behind the counter eyed him suspiciously. Metcalfe walked straight to the counter, his empty hands held straight out. He was well known in certain circles. His appearance might ring alarm bells in an area of town where extortion and intimidation were commonplace.

"I'm looking for a guy," he said.

The cashier put his hand on a telephone. Metcalfe assumed he'd paid the local gang for protection, and one call would bring a couple of heavies.

"I'm not here to cause trouble. Earle Gotting. Thought he might buy from you sometimes."

He kept his hand on the phone. "Earle ain't been in today."

A couple of customers were loading up a cart with beer. They stopped to watch the activity at the counter.

"Does he come in here every day?" Metcalfe asked.

The guy shook his head.

"You got an address?"

He pursed his lips.

Metcalfe put a fifty-dollar bill on the counter and kept his hand on it. "It's important."

The guy glanced at the men loading a cart before pulling a book from under the counter. "Two-two-seven," he said pointing west. "Palm Tree Court. Few blocks down the street."

Metcalfe took his hand off the bill. "Thanks."

The cashier nodded and swept up the money.

Metcalfe found the apartment complex. Palm Tree Court was curiously named, since there wasn't a single palm tree growing anywhere in Kansas City, as far as he knew. Empty flower beds surrounded dilapidated siding, and trash collected under wooden steps as though the stairs were designed for the purpose.

He checked his gun and took an aluminum baseball bat from under the rear seat. It slotted neatly into an enlarged pocket inside his long coat. The handle protruded enough for a quick grab.

He stepped out of his BMW and checked the area over before locking the vehicle and walking up the steps to Gotting's place, number 227.

CHAPTER SIXTEEN

Monday, November 27
8:45 p.m.
Kansas City, Kansas

EARLE GOTTING STARED AS if he was unable to comprehend that Henrik Metcalfe stood in his apartment living room.

Metcalfe cracked his knuckles. "I don't believe you."

Gotting swallowed. "Really. I don't know."

Metcalfe had entered his apartment ten minutes earlier.

Metcalfe slammed his fist into Gotting's stomach.

Gotting doubled over. His stomach churned.

Metcalfe demanded to know why Hallman was looking for him. The answer was simple, but not credible, not when Hallman had said it, and not now when he tried to convince Metcalfe.

He wrenched Gotting upright. The weak muscles in his stomach made him cry out.

"I want to know who, how, and why," Metcalfe snarled.

Gotting groaned again, rolling his head to one side.

Metcalfe's big hand gripped him by the neck of his shirt and shook him. "Don't make me use the bat."

Metcalfe pulled the bat from under his coat with his free hand and smacked it menacingly against Gotting's weak leg.

The pain speared through Gotting's nerves. He squealed before he could get his lungs under control.

Metcalfe lifted the bat above Gotting's head.

Gotting choked. "I… I… I think I'm going—"

With one hand, Metcalfe threw him backward.

Gotting smacked into the wall. He grunted and slapped his hands over his mouth, gagging.

Metcalfe stepped back.

Gotting stumbled into the bathroom and collapsed over the sink. Metcalfe stood behind him while he wretched.

"His first day out of the slammer and that slimy creep is here, paying you a social call. I don't buy it," Metcalfe said.

Gotting splashed his face with water. "I told you. He was looking for a kid."

"Because you used to kidnap kids and sell them for money to feed your habits?"

Gotting nodded, reluctantly.

"Which kid was he looking for?"

Gotting rinsed his mouth.

If he refused to give the kid's name, Metcalfe would beat the life out of him. But if he did give Metcalfe the kid's name, Gotting would make himself a liability, and Metcalfe would get rid of him swiftly.

Gotting wiped the back of his hand across his lips. "Just some kid that I took. Thought he was going to make a fortune blackmailing the parents."

Metcalfe laid the business end of the baseball bat on the sink, in front of Gotting's face. "And will he?"

Gotting pushed himself upright, leaned against the counter and slipped a small deodorant aerosol can into the palm of his hand. "How? I picked kids from single moms and poor families because they had no money to come after me. I'm not stupid."

Metcalfe tapped the counter with the bat. "So you say."

Gotting stared. "He has no hope of getting money out of the trash I stole babies from. Really."

Metcalfe smashed the bat down on the counter.

The plastic surface splintered into chunks. The shock wave through the plastic of the fixture stung Gotting's hands. He cringed, cowering away from the bat. The only way to live through Metcalfe's interrogation was to fight back.

"How many kids did you sell?" Metcalfe demanded.

Gotting shrugged. "I didn't count."

Metcalfe slammed the bat down onto the broken counter, splintering off more chunks of plastic. "Tell me!"

"I… I don't remember. It was years ago. Like…a bunch. Twenty, thirty maybe?" Gotting forced his head down low, close to his shoulders for protection. "I just got paid. Norell handled it."

"Norell? That slime?" Metcalfe's scowl morphed into a frown. "One of those kids must be special."

Gotting shook his head. "I don't think so."

"It's a miracle you can think at all." He dragged the tip of the bat off the counter, sweeping broken plastic onto the floor.

"Yeah," Gotting nodded.

Metcalfe rolled his shoulders. "Tell me how it worked."

Gotting nodded and stepped away from Metcalfe. With his finger on the button, he rotated the deodorant in his hand, searching for the front of the aerosol sprayer.

Metcalfe grabbed Gotting's shirt. He moved the bat behind him for a good solid swing at Gotting's body. "Tell me."

Gotting swept the deodorant can up, pressing his finger hard on the plunger. The aerosol jetted out, a solid spray with clouds of microscopic swirling droplets.

The spray hit Metcalfe in the face. He closed his eyes, twisting his face away, and screamed as he lunged with the bat. His swing hit the wall in the tiny room. The impact stole the baseball bat's momentum.

Gotting gripped the bat and kept the spray going onto Metcalfe's face.

Metcalfe lunged forward, his eyes still closed and his scream now more of a growl.

Gotting sidestepped into the bathtub, using his hold on the bat to lever Metcalfe face-first into the far wall. Gotting wrenched the bat free, leaped out of the bathroom and slammed the door.

He grabbed his wallet, car keys, and a plastic bag of drugs, and fled his apartment, descending the steps in three bounds. His Audi started on the first try. He raced out of the parking lot.

CHAPTER SEVENTEEN

Monday, November 27
9:00 p.m.
Kansas City, Kansas

HALLMAN SLOWED HIS PACE. From down the street, headlights glared at him. They had a familiar look. The kind of rings on high-end BMWs.

He put his hand up to shield his eyes. Expensive Beemers weren't common around Burlington.

His heart rate picked up. He walked slowly and turned right into the kind of seedy alley where a guy could get mugged. Or worse.

Sheltered from the streetlights, he watched the BMW pass by. The driver didn't look into the alley, but his profile was already seared into Hallman's visceral memory. Henrik Metcalfe.

Was Metcalfe following him? He should have been more careful. He kicked the ground with his boot. *Damn Damn Damn!*

He eased to the edge of the alleyway. Every muscle in his body tensed to the quivering point. Metcalfe's BMW slowed but didn't stop. At the end of the next block, Metcalfe turned right.

Hallman realized he hadn't breathed in a while and exhaled to quell the growing fire burning in his limbs.

Metcalfe was searching, scanning the streets. Looking for someone.

Metcalfe wasn't likely to have clients in this area. No one had any money here. He must have come here for a purpose. To find someone in particular. The safest assumption was that Metcalfe was here for him.

Maybe Max Spinney had talked. Even just a casual mention. A few words to the wrong person. But what had he said? Had Spinney said Hallman was looking for Earle Gotting? Safer to assume he had.

Fire burned in Hallman's tense muscles again. What if Gotting already knew Metcalfe? What if they'd worked together? What if Metcalfe was involved with Gotting's kidnapping scheme?

Blackmailing Kimball had been the only thing on Hallman's mind for the past six months since he first heard about the chance. He'd put his plan in motion as soon as he left prison. Metcalfe couldn't stop him. But the risks were growing.

He put his hand in his pocket. The cash his brother had sent was still safe. He could get on a bus, just as his brother had intended. Get out of Kansas City.

But Metcalfe knew about Thomas. He'd find Hallman in Dallas.

And what would he do in Dallas, anyway? He had no marketable skills and even less desire to acquire any. Spend his life under Thomas's thumb? *No, thanks.*

He had a plan, and it was a good one. All he needed to do was follow through.

He'd always known he'd need to escape Metcalfe's claws. But if Snap Metcalfe had partnered with Gotting to kidnap Peter Kimball, the plan had to change.

Hallman had no choice. Moving forward was the only option. But he'd also need to disappear after he got his money. Thoroughly and completely.

Which meant two things.

He needed more money from Kimball than a measly million bucks.

And he needed it fast.

CHAPTER EIGHTEEN

Monday, November 27
9:30 p.m.
Kansas City, Kansas

EARLE GOTTING HAD SOBERED up at a truck stop gas station, grabbed a shower, and located clean clothes. He'd tried to remember Hallman from prison, but the memory wasn't there. Didn't matter. The snail slime was here now, and he'd be damned if he'd let Hallman steal what was rightfully his.

Twenty minutes later, his Audi looked right at home on the tree-lined roads in the Mission Hills district.

Manicured lawns bordered homes that were glossy magazine perfect. Street lights gave the neighborhood a magical quality against the night sky.

Gotting approached Ammerson Belk's home. Belk was a partner at the Somersall-McCree law firm downtown. A mid-size firm with a long history. Solid. Dependable. Plodding.

They'd had a good run. Gotting found the babies, and Belk turned them into cash. Private adoption, he called it.

Gotting didn't care. All he wanted was the money.

He'd been there a few months earlier. Shortly after he was released from prison. Told them he figured his silence had earned him something. He had plenty of dirt on Belk and the law firm, and he'd kept it to himself. He'd protected Belk and Norell, too. Both of those bums had been walking around while he was inside. He'd figured with the right persuasion they'd be grateful, and he'd been right. Within a week they'd handed him the keys to his new Audi.

Belk's house was located on Wisteria Drive. A single story with a detached garage set toward the back of the lot ringed with a low, white picket fence.

The house was brick construction painted a light color unidentifiable in the night. Dark green decorative shutters adorned the windows, and a large portico covered the porch and the front door. Just the kind of house their profitable private adoption business would have bought. And it probably had.

Gotting parked by the garage, away from the glare of the streetlights. He rummaged in the glove box and found his revolver, a Rohm RG-14.

He'd picked it up in a bar a few months ago for thirty bucks. It was the same type of gun that had been used to shoot Ronald Reagan. He wasn't sure if that was a good thing or a bad one, but the seller had made it sound interesting. The gun was small and easily concealed. He'd fired it once at a range where he again confirmed he was no marksman.

He didn't intend to shoot the gun. He didn't expect he'd have to. Belk wasn't that brave. If he had been, he'd have stolen the babies himself. He wouldn't have needed Gotting at all. As a persuasive tool, though, there was none better than a loaded gun.

A single light hung over a side door with a frosted glass

pane. He put his ear to the door and pushed the doorbell. A muffled tune rang inside the house.

He stepped back and waited.

A distorted shadow of the portly Belk appeared behind the frosted glass and stopped.

Gotting knew he was checking a small monitor that showed views from a half-dozen cameras dotted around the outside of the house. Gotting looked up and smiled at one of the cameras mounted on the overhang.

Belk unlocked the door and opened it the width allowed by the chain that held it in place.

Gotting smiled. "Hello, Ammerson."

Belk's fleshy face peered through the gap between the door and the frame. "What do you want?"

"Can I come inside?"

"No."

"I need some help."

"I paid you all I owed you. And more."

Gotting nodded. "I know. The car is nice. But it's not about the car."

"Then what?"

Gotting looked behind him. The low fence did nothing to shield him from the neighbor's view.

"You really want to talk about it out here?"

Belk scowled a moment. He slid back the chain. "Very well."

Gotting stepped into a laundry room and closed the door.

"You know you're on camera," Belk had already begun to sweat.

"I'm not here to hurt you. And after I'm gone, you better delete it."

"Get on with it." He dabbed his forehead with his sleeve.

Gotting cleared his throat. "Thirteen or fourteen years ago, I brought you a kid. Peter Kimball."

"What are you talking about?"

"I need to know where he is."

Belk breathed in and out with a loud hiss.

"I *need* to know. Now."

Belk shook his head. "First of all, you never brought me any kid—"

"Don't try to go all legal on me here." Gotting shrugged. "Same as always, Zander Norell did. After I brought the kid to him. No difference."

Belk snorted. "And secondly, I never knew the names."

Gotting sneered. "Yeah, right."

Belk pressed his lips into a thin line before he spoke. "What's this about? You know you can't blackmail me."

"I don't want to blackmail you. I want to blackmail Kimball."

"The kid?"

"Don't be stupid," Gotting snapped. "The mother."

"Are you crazy?" Belk stared. "Why are you doing this now? After thirteen years?"

In truth, the question still nagged him. But Kimball was his. He'd taken the kid. He'd found her and scoped her out. He'd hooked a credit card behind the latch to break into her apartment. He'd traveled from Denver to Kansas City with a crying baby wedged on the floor in the rear of his car.

He was the one who took all the risks.

Him.

Not Hallman or Metcalfe. Not Norell, and certainly not some dumb-ass big city lawyer.

If there was any money to be made from Kimball, it was his money. Simple as that.

"That's none of your concern," he finally pointed out.

"Well, it doesn't matter," Belk said. "I didn't have the names, so I don't—"

"It was thirteen years ago, not thirty. You can find it. You don't need the name."

"You don't understand—"

Gotting pulled out his revolver. "It's you who doesn't understand."

Belk held pudgy hands with thick fingers up in front of him and stepped back. "Now you don't have to—"

"Just find out where he is. Peter Kimball. Thirteen years ago. Tell me, and I'm gone."

Belk breathed out, the air hissing between his teeth.

Gotting brandished the revolver. "From this distance, I can't possibly miss."

"All right." Belk turned around. "I'll find out."

Gotting lowered his revolver and followed Belk through the kitchen into a study.

Belk pulled an aging laptop from the bottom drawer of his desk and worked the keyboard. A minute later he scribbled an address on a sheet of paper and pushed it across the desk.

Gotting picked it up. The city was nearby. "Higgins?" he said.

Belk nodded. "Now will you leave?"

Gotting stared at the address and the old laptop. "Is this where he lives now? Or where the parents lived when you sold the baby?"

"I didn't sell him, I arranged for his private adoption. There's a difference."

Gotting pointed the revolver at Belk again. It wasn't an empty threat. At this point, Gotting would have gladly shot his kneecap off.

Belk sighed. "It was their address at the time. I don't keep up with these people. No reason to."

"But you work for some fancy legal outfit. You can find him. I know."

"Maybe. Tomorrow. When I get to the office."

"You set him up with a Social Security number and everything. You can find him now." He shook the gun. "Now."

Belk sighed and turned back to the laptop. He typed quickly for a few moments and waited for the ancient machine to do its work.

What felt like an hour but was probably no more than a minute or so later, the computer dinged. Belk wrote a Colorado Springs address on the sheet of paper. "That's where the family lives now."

Gotting verified the written address matched the computer screen, folded the paper and placed it in his pocket. He put the revolver away, unplugged the laptop, and tucked it under his arm. "If this works out, we'll never meet again."

"I sincerely hope so," Belk sputtered as Gotting walked out of the house with his laptop.

CHAPTER NINETEEN

Monday, November 27
11:00 p.m.
Denver, Colorado

MORRIS HAD CLEARED THE table as Jess stacked the plates in the dishwasher after dinner. They watched a movie together before he left.

Her apartment seemed unnaturally empty without him. She'd noticed that emptiness several times lately, and she wasn't sure how she felt about it. For the moment, she moved the worry aside.

She was tiring fast, but one thing she still had to do was contact Brentwood Stephenson.

Jess had come to rely on him in a way that she'd never expected to. But she needed his thorough approach now. If the extortion phone call had originated in Kansas City as Morris said, there were two possible states within easy reach. After thirteen years, the people who'd had any connection with Jess's life when Peter was taken had dispersed all over the country and abroad. It was not farfetched to assume that some would be living in Kansas or Missouri.

She composed an email outlining the conversation and the circumstances surrounding the phone call and requesting names and addresses of anyone relevant who might be living in those states.

When she had finished, the computer's clock said 11:55 p.m. In Baton Rouge, that meant after midnight for Stephenson. No way he would reply tonight, which was fine. She'd had a long day, too.

She turned off her computer and went to bed, wondering how far the guy would go with his scam. She fell asleep quickly, but not for long. Her ringing phone awakened her at two in the morning.

Jess pried open one eye at the sound. Her room was dark and the bedclothes warm, and she hoped the blasted phone would stop ringing. It did not.

She cleared her throat, propped herself up on her elbow, and croaked, "Kimball."

"The price has gone up."

The same voice she'd heard before removed the sleep from her mind in an instant. "Who is this?"

"Three million."

"Who are you?"

"Used bills. Not marked. You've got forty-eight hours."

Jess pressed her lips together. Holding back the torrent of questions and anger building inside her. She needed him to talk. She had to learn what kind of person she was dealing with, what he knew, and whether he really had Peter.

The silence stretched on. She breathed through her nose, keeping her adrenaline as level as possible under the circumstances.

"Why should I believe you? Convince me that I'm talking to the right guy," she said.

"You've been watching too much television." But after he sighed, he said, "You were wearing a Stones T-shirt."

Her skin tingled. No caller had ever said that before. She kept her voice level. "Lots of people have Stones T-shirts."

"When I took him."

"Took who?"

There was a long silence before the man spoke. "You know damn well who. Get the money if you want him back."

"I'm going to need more than that before I believe you."

"You're going to need three million more. Get it."

She felt wired, every muscle taut. "No one just gets three million. I'm a reporter, not a billionaire."

"Lean on your glitzy magazine boss. He's got the cash. No sweat. He'll come through if he wants to keep Peter alive."

Her breath caught. "You have Peter?"

"You tell Carter Pierce what I said. If he wants your boy to live, he'll pay."

"So, you do have him? I need to be certain."

"This will happen quick. Get prepared. Get my money."

"I want to hear his voice." What she heard in her own trembling voice was fear.

"Why? You think you'd recognize a teenage boy? Not a chance. You lost him as a baby before he began to speak. Just get the money. You've got forty-eight hours."

"Listen. Even if I can get three million, I need to make travel arrangements. Where are you?"

He laughed. "What? The police can't trace a phone call anymore? You get the money, or you'll never see him again. No one will."

"I want to talk to Peter."

He hung up.

Jess leaned back against the headboard, the phone trembling in her shaky hand.

CHAPTER TWENTY

Tuesday, November 28
2:15 a.m.
Denver, Colorado

JESS GATHERED HER COMPOSURE and dialed Henry. She spoke as soon as he picked up.

"I just got another call."

"I know." Morris sounded wide awake and focused. "We got lucky. It's a landline phone located in Kansas City. The police are on their way. Two squad cars, a couple of minutes out."

"He'll be on the move."

"They're doing their best."

"He knows the calls are being traced."

"Everybody who ever watched TV knows calls are traced."

"He wants three million in cash in forty-eight hours."

"I heard," Morris replied. "Price has gone up. There has to be a reason."

"Maybe I could find out if I was in Kansas City."

"Three million is a lot. No offense, but it's not like you've got that kind of money. Is Pierce likely to find the three million for you?"

"Maybe." Jess paused. "*Taboo's* struggling, but Carter is worth hundreds of millions. He's offered before."

"Even millionaires don't generally have three million in cash lying around the house, though."

"Well, he mentioned ransom and millions, but he didn't get specific about how many."

Morris thought about that for a full second. "Possible this guy knows about Pierce's offer to help you?"

Jess frowned. "Is he someone who works at the magazine, you mean?"

"Seems plausible. Someone who knows you or knows about you. Doesn't have to be a close associate."

"But it does have to be someone who's currently in Kansas City if you're sure the call wasn't electronically rerouted somehow. I can get a list of employees who've been out of the office over the past few days."

Morris said, "Something's changed to push the price up. He's more desperate now, too. Or he's trying to move things fast before we find out he's scamming you."

"Henry." Her voice cracked. She cleared her throat. The adrenaline running through her veins had her strung as tight as the blackmail. "I-I don't think this one's a hoax. He knew what T-shirt I was wearing when he took Peter."

"That's a detail that's been withheld?"

"I've never put that out anywhere. As far as I know, it was never released."

"But other people must have seen what you were wearing at the time. Neighbors. The police."

She shook her head while she thought things through. "Not

likely. I grabbed my coat as soon as I realized Peter was missing. It was raining, and my phone was in the pocket, so I didn't take my coat off."

Morris whistled. "So, this could be the actual guy."

"Or he knows the actual guy," Jess spoke through gritted teeth. "But I don't think he has Peter. He wouldn't let me talk to him."

"You think he's just using his knowledge to blackmail you?" There was a buzzing on the line. Morris said, "Hang on. I'm getting a call from Kansas."

The phone went silent. Jess pressed the speaker button to keep her hands free while she waited. She wheeled her roll-aboard from her closet. She began tossing clothes and toiletries into the bag. She was half-packed by the time she heard his voice again.

Morris came back on the phone. "Kansas City police found the phone at a twenty-four- hour convenience store called *Convenient 4U*. The caller wasn't there. They're combing the area and reviewing CCTV, but they don't sound hopeful."

She said, "I'm going to Kansas City," as she continued packing.

"I figured. First flight is five a.m. Arrives before eight. I just looked it up. I'll go with you."

Jess threw an extra pair of jeans into her roll-aboard. "What about your work?"

"We delivered our big case to the DA today. The team can pick up the rest for a while. See you at the airport at four?"

She paused. "I'm bringing my gun. Don't try to talk me out of it."

Morris was silent a beat. "I'll expedite the paperwork. Lock it in a case and be at the airport at three."

She looked at her alarm clock. Two-fifteen. Forty-five minutes. She could just make it. "Thanks, Henry."

She hung up, dressed, zipped her suitcase, and was on the road in ten.

CHAPTER TWENTY-ONE

Tuesday, November 28
2:30 a.m.
Kansas City, Kansas

HALLMAN WALKED AWAY FROM *Convenient 4U* at a measured pace, but as soon as he turned the corner, he broke into a jog. He stayed on the grid-like arrangement of side streets, which made his navigation easier.

The first priority was to put as much distance between him and the phone. The police had undoubtedly traced the call. He heard no approaching sirens, but they might make a silent approach on a non-violent crime response in a residential neighborhood at this hour.

Running was a magnet for police attention. He turned another corner. A sedan rolled by, headlights spearing the darkness. He shuffled back against the wall.

The car moved toward the store but didn't stop. He moved away at a fast clip.

A minute later, light glowed over the top of the buildings in front of him. Music and the sound of cars drifted through the air. He entered an alley walking toward the noise and stepped into a bright neon kaleidoscope of bars, cars, and people.

He wanted to get lost in the crowd, but he saw too many police, both on foot and watching from squad cars.

The bars were closing. Foot traffic was heavy. Students mingled with older couples and groups. He followed along behind one of the groups moving north, head down and walking unsteadily as if he'd been drinking all night.

He slowed his pace behind the group as they left the busy area. A couple of minutes later, they entered an apartment building, never seeming to have noticed him.

Hallman glanced around to be sure he was well out of the area the police would likely be searching for him. He walked at a relaxed pace. Three miles past the river crossing, veering toward the darker sides of the streets.

The houses became modern suburban structures, one- and two-story dwellings with what salespeople liked to call architectural features.

He stopped beside a tree and pulled a street map of Kansas City from his pocket. It was a tattered book that he'd stolen from *Convenient 4U.*

Using the index, he found Norell's address, eight blocks away.

Fifteen minutes later, he stepped onto Norell's street. Trees lined either side of the road. Most of the cars were parked in the residents' garages or driveways.

A black BMW SUV was parked a few houses down and on the opposite side of the street. The streetlights illuminated an outline of the driver.

He couldn't see the driver's face, but he recognized the vehicle. Metcalfe.

Hallman knelt on his haunches behind a tree. He was forced to admit that his plan was seriously at risk.

Metcalfe had been hanging around Gotting's, and now he had Norell's place staked out. Spinney was the most likely snitch.

If Metcalfe had directed a few threats at Gotting, he'd have crumbled in a heartbeat. Which meant Metcalfe must know about Kimball.

But why was Metcalfe waiting outside? Why not inside, working Norell over with his baseball bat?

Or had he already been inside?

No. That made no sense. If Norell had told Metcalfe where to find the boy, Metcalfe would be gone already. No reason to delay and the last place Metcalfe would wait was outside a dead man's house if he'd already killed Norell.

Which meant something else was going on here.

A car drove by. Hallman shuffled down lower. The headlights illuminated Metcalfe's SUV and the driver still waiting.

The only option that made sense was that Metcalfe was waiting for him.

His business with Norell could wait. Hallman started down the street, walking slowly and using the line of trees to hide from Metcalfe. He turned left at the end of the street, risking a glance back. The SUV was still in the same spot. Waiting.

He walked two miles back into town, re-tracing his earlier path until he came upon a dilapidated industrial building. A side door gave easily when he pushed it with his boot, and a few minutes later he was huddled in a moth-eaten office chair, snoring.

CHAPTER TWENTY-TWO

Tuesday, November 28
2:45 a.m.
Near Colorado Springs, Colorado

THE HOTEL ROOM WAS cold, damp, and dark. Gotting sat on the bed. The air stank. It was a familiar smell. Beer and earth. Stale and decaying. Decades of filth, but probably nothing life-threatening was growing in the carpet.

He'd never counted the number of babies he'd placed on the floor overnight. They'd all survived. At least long enough for him to get paid. And who cared after that?

The room suited his purposes then and suited him now. Then he'd been traveling to Kansas City, now he was leaving. Then he'd had a drugged-up baby in tow. Now, he was the drugged-up baby. He grinned.

His muscles ached from tension. He'd driven for six straight hours until he reached a rundown motel ten miles off I-70. He was tired, but uppers had kept him going through the night.

He grunted. No, the uppers hadn't kept him going. The kid

had kept him going. The kid was his. Whatever and however there was money to be made, it was his money. He'd always done the dirty work while everyone else got rich. But not this time.

He looked up Jessica Kimball on his burner phone. She was still looking for her kid, which was good. He scoffed at the fifty grand she was offering for information. A puny number like that didn't hold his attention any more than it did for Hallman or Metcalfe.

Gotting put Carter Pierce's name into a search engine. There were thousands of hits, among them was a list of Pierce's good deeds. Money to charities. Coverage in his magazine for worthy causes. On the board of a few nonprofits.

Gotting scrolled down the page and sneered. Hell, the man was an all-round do-gooder. One cause after another. Even his secretary. She'd gushed to a tabloid about how he'd helped with outsized medical bills that would have bankrupted her.

But what about Kimball? She was the top reporter for his magazine, sure. Would Pierce help her to the tune of a few million? That was a big leap from paying his secretary's medical bills. Gotting scrolled back to the charitable donations. A few of them were in the millions.

The alarm clock said 4:30 a.m. He had another couple of hours' drive to reach Colorado Springs. He could grab the kid. If he got there before Metcalfe and Hallman, he could sort out the blackmail later. He knew somewhere he could keep the kid. A boy would be no problem. He had a bag of drugs in his car sufficient to sedate a horse for weeks.

He turned his phone off. It was hard to predict people. You couldn't know what they would do just by asking them stupid questions. People said all kinds of things. Most of it was bullshit.

No, you had to face them with the problem. Stick the issue right in front of their noses.

First things first. Grab the kid.

Then Pierce and Kimball had to decide.

Was Peter Kimball's life worth a few million dollars or not?

CHAPTER TWENTY-THREE

Tuesday, November 28
3:05 a.m.
Denver, Colorado

JESS MET MORRIS AT the airport. He took her gun case and
went off to complete the paperwork necessary to transport it to
their destination.

She checked them in for the flight, but their last-minute
plans meant there were no seats together. He made it to the gate
during the final boarding call.

She handed him his boarding pass, and they hurried to their
seats. She was in row twelve and he was in the very back at
twenty-nine. They were both stuck in the middle seat. The
confined space wasn't a problem for her, but Morris was folded
up like origami paper.

There wasn't enough room to lay her laptop on the tray
table, but if she tilted it at forty-five degrees she could use the
keyboard and still see the screen.

In an email, she gave Stephenson the details of the second phone call and told him she would contact him after she landed.

An hour into the flight, Morris came by and beckoned her to the galley at the back of the plane. He showed his badge to the flight attendant and requested a few moments of privacy. The attendants gathered up snacks and drinks onto a cart and left.

"Got a message from KCPD. They reviewed the CCTV from the convenience store. It's poor quality, and the suspect kept his face away from the camera. He stood outside the door for a few moments before entering. They think he was scoping out the camera location."

"Nothing useful at all?"

"He's wearing a coat and hat. No surprise given the cold. You can see for yourself." Morris held out his phone.

Jess watched a grainy video. The camera was high up in the corner of the store. No sound.

Three employees were all seated when the front door swung open and the suspect stepped inside.

The workers turned as one to watch the customer. He waved his hand and went straight for the pay phone, turned his back and made the call. The camera was fixed, and the phone was on the edge of its field of view.

Jess timed him. From her recollection, the length of time he'd spent on the phone seemed to match the call she'd received.

The suspect seemed to be looking around the store. One of the workers at the counter appeared to speak to him.

Keeping his back to the camera, he marched up and down the aisles, stopping twice before leaving.

Jess frowned. "Why didn't he just run. Why take your time like that?"

"Wanted to avoid looking suspicious?" Morris said.

"Maybe, but…" Jess rewound the video and watched the man leave the store again. "What was he going to buy?"

"I've been wondering that myself," Morris said. He scrubbed the video back and forth examining the store's fixed posts near him when the man stood still.

Jess leaned closer to the screen. The man was at an angle to the camera, facing the opposite direction. "His coat moved," she said, pointing.

Morris peered at the images and nodded. "He could be stealing something."

Jess advanced the video until the man left the store. The shelves where he had been standing were in view, but the camera's resolution wasn't good enough to identify anything he might have stolen.

Morris typed a message on his phone. "I'll have KCPD find out what was on those shelves. Whatever it was had to be pretty important for him to stand around, knowing squad cars would be racing toward him."

"He's very sure of himself."

"Cool and calculating."

Jess grimaced. "Or ruthless and heavily armed."

CHAPTER TWENTY-FOUR

Tuesday, November 28
8:05 a.m.
Kansas City, Kansas

THE FLIGHT LANDED IN Kansas City on time. Jess carried her bag off the aircraft and waited for Morris.

Her phone connected to the cell service and played a chorus of chimes as it received a long string of messages. She spotted Stephenson's name immediately.

She dialed his number and he picked up on the first ring.

"You've received two calls from him, Jess?"

"Right. The FBI has traced both. Two different public phones. Both in Kansas City."

"Any reason to believe he's not some crank? Or a guy looking to make a quick buck?"

"He mentioned my T-shirt."

Stephenson whistled. "First time we've heard that from a tipster. You brought the FBI in?"

"They've been monitoring my calls."

"Good. I've emailed you a list of possibles identified back at the time of the original kidnapping who now live in Kansas and Missouri. Not all suspects at the time. Some were witnesses with opportunity that the locals talked to at the time. A total of eight. Three of those eight live in Kansas City. All three have criminal records and have served prison time since Peter was taken."

"All three?" Jess gulped. "That's, I don't know, disturbing I guess is the only way I can think of to put it."

"It is. Maybe worse than disturbing." Stephenson seemed to be reading from a list. "One convicted of arson, one for drugs, and one for drugs followed by possession of a firearm."

Jess didn't reply.

"The last guy got five years, which was the maximum for an unlicensed gun."

"Seems excessive, doesn't it?"

"It does. Which means there's more to that story."

"All males?" she asked.

"Yep."

"Any of these three guys still in prison now?"

"You're not that lucky," Stephenson grunted. "The last one released was the guy with the gun. Name's Earle Gotting. Cut loose six months ago."

"We can't narrow the list further?"

"Not long distance like this. But I can be there in a few hours."

"I might take you up on that. For now, I have Morris with me."

"Glad to hear it. I'll keep digging from here. If I find anything, I'll call you. Stay safe, Jess," Stephenson said before he rang off.

Jess tapped the phone against her lips thoughtfully as she watched Morris exit the jet-bridge and emerge into the terminal.

"Guess what," Morris said as he approached. "The guy stole a Kansas City street map. The *Convenient 4U* store owner thinks it was an old one. Been on the shelves for ages, he said."

"So, he's not local to Kansas City."

"Or he doesn't have a phone to search internet maps." Morris grinned. They walked toward ground transportation. "And before you ask me, I have no idea why he didn't just buy a burner except he might be low on cash. Burners have to be activated at the time of purchase with cash or a credit card. Stolen ones don't work."

"Regardless of why he stole it, he wanted a local map. Which must mean he's trying to find a specific place or places around here." She frowned and held up her own phone. "I have a list of specific places he might be going."

She filled him in on Stephenson's email on the way to the rental car counter. The list of possibles included last known addresses. Minutes later, they pulled out of the airport parking lot in a dark green Ford Edge heading for the first person on Stephenson's list who might have remembered her Rolling Stones T-shirt.

CHAPTER TWENTY-FIVE

Tuesday, November 28
8:15 a.m.
Colorado Springs, Colorado

GOTTING LOOKED AT HIMSELF in the Audi's rearview mirror, smoothed his hair, and stepped out of the car. His right leg was numb from sitting, and the car's heated seats hadn't improved his backache.

He'd reached Peter Kimball's home an hour earlier. He watched until the mother took the boy to school. Curiously, she dropped him a few blocks away and he walked the last distance. She was well dressed, probably the sort of person who worked in an office, maybe a professional of some sort.

Gotting parked quickly to follow on foot.

The boy didn't talk to anyone. He wore a dark blue coat and carried a backpack and worked his way through the streets, passing a couple of buildings then crossing a park to the rear entrance to Westfield High School.

Gotting watched as the boy met a couple of friends at the gate and walked inside.

Earle walked back to his car.

The park was wide open, a single path across a grassy area dotted with trees. There was a monument in the middle, but it provided no cover.

The buildings had people inside, but they were industrial structures with lots of walls and very few windows. The parking areas were filled with cars, but the people were already at work.

Wind blew the warmth away from his body. His jacket had been heavy enough in Kansas City, but it was insufficient protection in Colorado's early winter-like weather. He'd passed a ski and snowboard shop a few miles back where he could buy a parka, but the less contact he had with people, the better. He shoved his hands in his pockets and hunched into the coat already on his back.

He reached his car and looked back at the buildings. The parking lots were still devoid of human life. Mornings were not good times for kidnapping, but there were fewer witnesses to worry about. People didn't hang around in the cold and stuck to their routines. Especially school kids.

He put his car in gear. He'd come back tomorrow morning after he set up the rest of his plan.

For the second time, he planned to abduct Peter Kimball.

But this time, the money would be all his.

CHAPTER TWENTY-SIX

Tuesday, November 28
9:30 a.m.
Kansas City, Kansas

JESS CROSSED OFF THE first two suspects on Stephenson's list. Morris used an FBI database to trace the first one to Florida, the other was whereabouts unknown, Morris said.

Fine rain streaked the windshield and lights glistened off the wet streets as Jess drove to the third address. Earle Gotting's apartment.

The apartment complex was a series of old brown three-story buildings, all of which had seen better days. Cars were propped up on bricks in the parking lots except for an occasional Cadillac or BMW that probably belonged to the local drug dealers.

She parked facing Gotting's place, apartment 227. Faint light showed around the edges of closed drapes. The wooden steps to the second floor creaked as she followed Morris upstairs.

The door to apartment 227 had also seen better days. The bottom half had been repaired with unpainted plywood.

This place was a dump. Already Jess could easily believe Gotting was the one extorting money from her. If she lived here, she might be desperate enough to resort to blackmail, too.

Morris checked around the side of the apartment. "There's a fire escape. A second exit. I'll keep watch."

She rang the doorbell. There was no sound from the bell, so she knocked.

A minute later, Morris returned and knocked harder.

She went to the edge of the landing and looked over the parking lot. She saw nothing moving. It was still early. Maybe everyone was asleep.

Morris knocked one more time with no result. "I don't have a warrant. We can't go inside."

"There was a leasing office sign on a door near the front," Jess said. Morris nodded and followed her down the stairs.

The leasing office was a converted apartment on the ground floor with a sign over the door. The sign said the office didn't open for another hour, but the lights were on. Jess knocked.

A middle-aged woman peered from behind the blinds. Morris held out his badge. The woman studied it for a few moments before opening the door.

The office was in the apartment's living area, the kitchen off to the right, a pot of coffee on the counter.

The woman stood in front of a desk with a sign that said: "Ask Pam."

Jess raised her eyebrows. "Pam?"

The woman held her hand out. "McGinty. Leasing Executive."

Jess and Morris shook her hand and identified themselves.

"We're looking for Earle Gotting," Jess said.

McGinty leaned forward. "Is he in trouble?"

"We just want to talk to him."

She clicked her tongue against the roof of her mouth. "That's how it always starts."

"We tried his apartment. He didn't answer the door."

"Probably sleeping. He lost his job a few weeks ago."

Alarm bells went off in Jess's head. Serious money problems often pushed people to do things they would not normally do. Blackmail, for example. "Does he still make the rent?"

She said, "Seems to."

Jess nodded.

Morris held out his badge. "I wonder if you could just check. We really need to talk to him."

"I'm…" She screwed up one eye and stared at Morris. "Aren't you supposed to have a search warrant or something?"

"We don't want to search his apartment. We don't even have to step inside."

The woman considered Morris's claim for a moment. "Okay. Guess it can't hurt."

She located the key in a kitchen cabinet and led the way back to Gotting's apartment.

She didn't bother with the doorbell and knocked on the door. "Mr. Gotting. It's Pam from the office."

Jess watched the door for any sign of movement but saw none.

Pam pounded on the door. "Mr. Gotting. The FBI is here. They'd like to talk to you."

In the parking lot, a vehicle started.

The door to the apartment next door opened. Pam waved to an older man. "Just looking for Mr. Gotting."

"He's got a visitor," the man said. "Came a few minutes ago."

"Is he still there?" Jess said.

The old man nodded. "Far as I know."

Jess had no doubt the man knew everything about the people who came and went on the floor.

"Unless they used the fire escape," she said quietly to Morris.

He darted for the edge of the landing to look over the fire escape. "Wait," he shouted. "Stop!"

Jess bounded down the stairs. A man was running across the grass to a black BMW SUV. She held a hand up. "Stop!"

He jumped into the BMW. The engine was already running, and the SUV screamed out of the parking lot.

Jess ran for her rental and backed out of the parking space fast.

Morris came running down the steps and dove into the passenger seat.

Jess floored the accelerator.

CHAPTER TWENTY-SEVEN

Tuesday, November 28
10:00 a.m.
Kansas City, Kansas

THE FORD PULLED HARD, but the BMW was faster. It
moved in a way that didn't seem possible, darting between the
lanes into spaces barely larger than the vehicle itself. Her rental
pitched and rolled, forcing Jess to wait for larger gaps in the
traffic.

Morris called the local FBI for backup.

The BMW screeched across the median, bouncing hard on
its suspension as its wheels hammered into the curb.

Traffic honked and swerved between lanes to avoid the SUV.

Jess waited for a clear space in the traffic.

Morris strained forward, keeping watch on the BMW. "He
turned right."

Jess floored the accelerator, taking the inside lane. The
rental's tires squealed as she turned a hard corner to follow the
disappearing BMW.

The street was a four-lane, two lanes in each direction with no median.

The BMW turned a quick left through a narrow gap in the oncoming traffic. The oncoming traffic braked hard, tires squealing as drivers fought to keep vehicles from spilling into the neighboring lanes and colliding with other vehicles.

The BMW accelerated away down a narrow side street.

Jess followed, weaving through a pair of stationary vehicles, the drivers honking and waving their fists.

Cars lined one side of the narrow road and pedestrians filed in and out of stores.

Jess kept her speed down even though the BMW had disappeared.

A police siren sounded, close and loud. Her Ford was bathed in red and blue flashing lights. She glanced in the rearview mirror. A police car was right on her tail. She sighed and pulled into a gap in the parked cars.

The police car stopped behind her.

Jess lowered her window.

A second police car slid by and parked across the front of the Ford, blocking her in.

An officer with the name Powell on his name tag approached the driver's door. He didn't waste time with niceties. "License and insurance," he said.

Morris leaned over and held out his ID. "We were in pursuit."

Powell leaned in closer and examined the ID, his gaze flitting from Morris's face to his picture. "I'm just going to have to run this."

He held his hand out toward Jess. "ID, ma'am."

Jess handed over her driver's license.

Powell grunted. "FBI?"

Jess shook her head. "A reporter."

Powell's lip curled up at one end. "Wait here."

Two more officers stood watch around the Ford like they thought she might be a flight risk.

Powell ran the details on the computer in his car and returned a few moments later.

He handed Jess her ID. "Sorry to have messed with your pursuit. We get too many fake IDs. You should have registered your plates."

Morris nodded. "Sorry about that. Been a busy morning."

"Who were you chasing?"

"We don't know. We went looking for a man named Earle Gotting, and the suspect ran from the rear of the building."

Powell cocked his head. "Don't know the name."

"He was a person of interest. We wanted to ask a few questions." Morris shrugged. "But now? Seems like more."

"You working with the local office?"

Morris replied, "We flew in this morning."

Powell patted the roof of the car. "Well, better straighten things out with them. Drive carefully."

Powell returned to his cruiser, and the police cars left.

CHAPTER TWENTY-EIGHT

Tuesday, November 28
10:45 a.m.
Kansas City, Kansas

JESS DROVE BACK TO the Palm Tree Court apartments, keeping to the speed limit and obeying every single traffic sign to the letter.

Morris spent the time on his phone, alternating between explaining and persuading a colleague in the local FBI field office to look for the BMW.

Jess only heard Morris's side of the conversation but deduced they would send a police officer to look for CCTV video from neighboring businesses.

As she parked, the blinds in the leasing office opened, and Pam McGinty beckoned.

Morris finished his phone call and they walked into the office.

"Did you call the police?" Jess asked.

Pam laughed derisively. "They said they'll be here when they can. Apparently, after the person of interest has fled the scene, we're no longer a priority."

"Did you see the guy?" Jess said.

Pam shook her head. "Only from the back."

"Was it Earle Gotting?"

"He seemed bigger." She patted her shoulders. "Wider, you know."

Jess glanced at Morris and said, "He was running from Gotting's apartment. So, a crime was probably being committed inside."

Morris grimaced. "Not exactly imminent danger, if you're looking for a reason to enter the apartment."

McGinty stood up. "You can't enter the building without a warrant. Management drums that into us, given where we are. But…follow me."

She led them out of the office and around the back of the building to a steel door with a hefty padlock.

She clicked open the lock with a small key, stepped inside, and disabled an alarm.

Morris followed Jess inside. The room was filled with tools, cans, pipes, and all the paraphernalia Jess figured was required to maintain an apartment complex.

Pam handed Morris a large tank with a hose and spray attachment. "We can enter to spray for bugs. It's in the lease documents. I'd carry the tank myself, but it's heavy."

She walked them around to Gotting's apartment without waiting for a reply.

Morris knocked hard on the door.

The old man from the next apartment poked his head out of his door. Morris waved him back inside.

Pam pulled a bundle of keys from her pocket, sorted her way through them, and finally inserted one in the lock.

The door swung open revealing a studio with an open plan kitchen and living room. Pam grimaced in understandable disapproval.

The place was a mess. The sofa cushions were on the floor. The sofa itself was overturned and the bottom had been cut out of it, exposing the springs and thin wood frame. The coffee table lay on its side, wedged against the far wall.

In the kitchen, the cabinet doors were wide open, and junk was piled up on the floor. Bottles, cans, and dirty glasses littered every surface. The sink was full of mugs and dirty plates. The fridge door had been folded back on its hinges, and the contents were spread over the floor.

Jess put her arm across the doorway before Pam walked inside. "Earle Gotting wasn't the guy in the BMW. This place is a mess. It's a crime scene. We can't go in."

"Roger that," Morris said, dialing a number on his phone and walking away.

Pam stepped back. "Do you think he's all right?"

Jess looked over the apartment. "Hard to say."

"There's a bedroom and a bathroom…" Pam's words trailed off, leaving her fears unspoken.

Morris returned and peered into the apartment. "Cops on their way. I'm going inside, be sure we don't need an ambulance."

He stepped carefully between the mounds of debris on the floor, eased the bedroom and bathroom doors open with his elbow, and reversed his steps to back out. "There's no one in the apartment."

Pam breathed an audible sigh of relief.

Jess took several photographs, panning her cell phone camera across the studio. "This place was a mess before someone decided to search it."

She turned to Pam. "When did you last see Gotting?"

"Two days ago. He went out in the morning, came back mid-afternoon. Nothing unusual."

"Walking?"

"No. He drives an Audi."

Jess raised her eyebrows. It was a curious vehicle for a guy living in a low rent apartment.

"It looks nice, but it must be old. Kind of dirty. Don't think he ever washes it," Pam said.

"No job? He doesn't go out every day?"

Pam shook her head. "Not since he lost his job. It can be days before I see him sometimes."

"Where did he work?"

"Finger-Lickin' Fried Chicken. Half a mile south down the road."

Jess turned to close the door. Someone had been searching for something. She paused, the door still half open.

A short stubby bottle caught her eye. It had rolled against the wall in the kitchen. Probably when whoever was searching the apartment emptied the cabinets.

She leaned into the apartment without stepping inside, stretching to get her phone's camera as close to the bottle as she could. She fired off half a dozen shots to be sure she got a couple of good ones, and leaned back out of the apartment, closing the door behind her.

"What was it?" Pam said.

Jess brought up the picture on her phone and zoomed in. She knew what she had seen. But she had to look.

Pam tried to look at the phone's screen. "Was it important?"

Jess held the picture up. "It's a baby's bottle."

Pam frowned. "He doesn't have a baby. And I've never seen anyone visit with a baby. What would he need that for?"

Jess clicked her phone off and shook her head. She had the awful feeling she knew why, but she didn't want to voice her guess. As if saying it aloud would make it more likely.

CHAPTER TWENTY-NINE

Tuesday, November 28
11:00 a.m.
Kansas City, Kansas

A POLICE CRUISER WITH two officers arrived in the apartment parking lot. Morris went down the stairs to brief them on what they'd found.

Jess called Stephenson while she waited. When he answered, she said, "What do you know about Earle Gotting?"

"Not much. What have you found?"

"When we arrived at his place, a guy was here searching the apartment."

"Who was it?"

"Don't know. Male in a black BMW SUV. He got away."

Stephenson asked, "Any idea what he was searching for?"

"No. And he ransacked the place." She kept her voice down, just in case someone was around to overhear.

"What about Gotting? Any sign of him?"

"Not yet. Which is why I need to hear what you know."

"Right." She heard hunt and peck typing on an electronic keyboard before Stephenson continued. "I just sent you a report. He has priors for possession of drugs and illegal possession of a firearm. Not at the same time. Separate incidents. He spent five years at Humboldt prison on the last one. After you called earlier, I asked around. He received the maximum sentence because of the priors, but also because he was on the way to use the firearm when he was arrested."

"Any record of violence?"

"Nothing in what I have."

"Why was he arrested?"

Stephenson said, "Stupid thing. He ran a red light. Not speeding. But still odd since he had no prior traffic violations on his record."

"So, he might have been distracted and didn't notice the light. Anything else?" She asked.

"Yeah." A long pause followed.

"Spit it out, okay?"

He cleared his throat. "Looks like Gotting lived two floors down from your apartment in the same building when Peter was abducted—"

"Really?" She felt her eyebrows shoot north. She cocked her head and tried to recall Gotting, but she had no memory of him.

She'd lived in that building because she couldn't afford to live anywhere else. She'd always been careful, although events had proved she wasn't careful enough.

"Sorry. I guess I thought you knew," Stephenson said. "Police interviewed almost everybody at the time, including him. Nothing suspicious, according to the report. He moved out a month later."

"It was a big complex. There were a lot of people living

there and most of them were less than model citizens. By the time the cops quit and I started looking for Peter on my own, tenants had turned over several times." Jess nodded, although Stephenson couldn't see her. "Where did Gotting move to?"

"West Denver. Another apartment not much better. He's moved a lot in his lifetime."

"Always lived in Denver?" she asked. A shiver ran through her. A convicted felon. Not that there weren't plenty of them walking around. But still.

"Not hardly. He's been a regular gypsy. Iowa, Illinois, Arizona, New Mexico, and Missouri that I can find so far. And he's had more than one address in each state."

"And now Kansas City, Kansas."

Stephenson said, "That's where he was convicted. Like I said, he served five years in Humboldt. Released six months ago. Earlier parole denied. Served his full term."

"No reduction for good behavior?"

"Humboldt has a reputation as a tough place. Hard to serve a sentence without some kind of trouble there."

"It'd be good to know what happened. Can we identify his known associates, including friends and enemies?" she asked.

"The guy's a loner and a vagrant, mostly. Moves around, lives by his wits, based on what I see here." Stephenson clicked his tongue. "I'll see what I can do. But don't hold your breath."

Jess thanked him and hung up.

She found Stephenson's email with Gotting's details and forwarded it to Morris.

A minute later Morris came back up the stairs, his hands filled with sample bags, gloves, and face masks.

The officers followed and began to go from door to door, taking statements from the neighbors.

Jess held her hand out for a mask and gloves.

Morris grimaced. "I can't just let you walk in there. Evidence, and all that."

"I'm not going to plant evidence against the guy. If I had any to plant. Which I don't."

Morris sighed and offered no further objections. He handed her a face mask and pair of gloves. "Apparently, Earle Gotting both sells and uses drugs. We need to be careful."

"Just talked to Stephenson. When Peter was taken, Gotting lived two floors below me in Denver."

Morris's eyes widened. "That can't be a coincidence. Did you know him?"

"I was a kid. Overwhelmed. Exhausted. I've been wracking my brain to remember the guy, but—" She shrugged. "I sent you a list of Gotting's known addresses. Might correlate to other kidnappings."

"Maybe." He spoke as he typed email messages on his phone. "Kidnapping isn't rare, unfortunately. We have to be careful not to read too much into things."

She put on the face mask and gloves. "Are we going in?"

Morris nodded. "Local guys don't think this situation requires a crime scene team."

Jess scowled. "But we need prints. Confirm Earle Gotting really lived here. And there's BMW-man. And more."

"I get it, Jess." Morris pulled a small bag from his coat pocket. "But we don't know that a crime was committed here. We don't have any evidence of a robbery or a burglary even. Resources are stretched everywhere. I brought my own kit. We can take pictures and send them off."

"But—"

"They're kind of stretched, Jess. Unless we turn something up."

"Like what? We need a dead body?"

"Pretty much. They got two this morning. Like I said, they're a bit stretched."

Jess sighed and let her angst drain away. In a system that was always on the verge of overload, she was more than privileged to have the undivided attention of an FBI agent, and, she smiled, not just an agent, but the best agent.

Morris opened the front door. Jess made her way to the baby bottle. The manufacturer's name had worn off, and it had years of caked-on grime. She picked it up with a pen and dropped it in a plastic evidence bag.

She sifted through the clutter on the kitchen floor but found no other baby paraphernalia.

Morris scoured the inside of the upturned sofa before righting it. "Nothing," he said.

Using the fingerprint kit, he worked his way over the door that led to the fire escape and the window beside it.

In the living room, Jess found three more baby bottles, the first two were on the window ledge behind the drapes. The last one was on the floor under a crumpled sweater. Each bottle contained ash and cigarette butts. She bagged all three.

Behind the sofa, she found a phone charger. She held it up. "No-name brand with an odd shaped connector. Must be a burner." She turned it over. The plastic was faded from the heat of being used. "And an old one."

Morris took a photograph of the charger and sent it off for identification.

"There's no computer. No laptop, no tablet, no nothing," he said.

"Unless our friend in the BMW took it."

"Maybe."

She looked around the wreckage in the room. "But if that was what BMW-man wanted, why all this? I mean, I doubt a laptop was hidden inside the sofa."

"So, if there was a computer, that wasn't the only thing he wanted."

"Or he wasn't sure what he was looking for. So this was a fishing expedition."

"Maybe."

Morris gathered prints from the kitchen appliances and cupboard doors.

Jess righted the coffee table. Underneath were a collection of thick motorcycle magazines. She picked one up. It fell open awkwardly. The central pages had a large square cut out.

She flipped through several of the others, which had been similarly cut. She held one up to show Morris. "Looks like this could have been how he either sold or bought the drugs."

"Or both." He nodded, held open a large evidence bag, and Jess dropped in the magazines.

Morris's phone buzzed. He checked his email.

"The office is still correlating kidnappings against Gotting's address. However…" He held out the phone.

A police statement was on the display. The date was three years after Peter had been taken. A single mother's eighteen-month-old was abducted from a third-floor apartment while she collected her mail on the ground floor.

Jess scrolled down. The police investigation concluded the culprit had used a fire escape to exit the side of the building, well away from the main lobby and the mailboxes.

She scrolled back to the top to check the date. "Gotting moved out two weeks earlier. Could have easily kept a key though."

Jess handed back Morris's phone. "You think he's always been like this?"

"Like what?"

Jess rolled her eyes and gestured to the mess on the floor.

Morris pursed his lips in thought. "Probably. The neighbors say he's never been anything more than a drunk. Why?"

"Because he's a wreck." Her skin tingled. Chills ran down her back. "He's never cared for anything."

Morris's shoulders sagged and his eyebrows sank. He knew where Jess's thoughts were going. "So, if he did take Peter, and any other children…"

She swallowed hard. "This isn't a good sign for what happened to them."

CHAPTER THIRTY

Tuesday, November 28
11:05 a.m.
Kansas City, Kansas

HALLMAN AWAKENED WITH AGONIZING pain in his
neck from sleeping while slumped in the old desk chair. Bright
light made its way through filthy windows in the derelict room
and shined right in his eyes, from which he assumed it was mid-
morning.

He moved his frozen joints slowly, head in one hand, and
massaged the stiffness in his neck. When he could hold his head up,
he stood and walked circles around the room to get the rest of the kinks
out of his muscles. The debris on the floor crunched under his boots.

His stomach growled and his tongue stuck to the roof of his
mouth. He was dehydrated and hungry. But he felt worse than if
he'd enjoyed a wild drinking party the night before.

Hallman pushed the idea of food to the back of his mind. He
had work to do. He adjusted his coat and hat using the reflection in
a broken pane of glass.

Metcalfe had been watching Norell's house last night, but Hallman's instincts told him he couldn't wait any longer for Metcalfe to get out of the way. Metcalfe was up to something. Only one way to find out. Time to deal with Norell.

Hallman checked the street. Nothing much going on out there and certainly nothing alarming. He exited the building and walked a block in the wrong direction before he realized his mistake. He doubled back along a parallel street and headed northwest.

Norell's street looked the same in the daylight as it had last night. Trees lined the road, few vehicles were visible, and no one walked along the sidewalks. Worse, Metcalfe's BMW was still there, but he'd moved it a little closer to the Norell house. The darkly tinted windows did the job of shielding the driver from view even in the daylight.

This time, Hallman walked one street over and behind Norell's house. He saw no walkway across the lawns, and the house had a backyard full of kids. They'd spot him in half a second if he tried to saunter past.

While he studied the situation, looking for a way to get to Norell's without being noticed, he caught a flash of black in his peripheral vision. An SUV, moving fast. Without thinking, he stepped close to a tree and dropped to one knee, pretending to tie his boot.

The SUV roared past.

Hallman kept his head down, fidgeting with the laces on his boots. As the SUV swept down the street, he risked glancing at the disappearing vehicle. The windows were tinted and the tail lights were distinctive. A BMW. Probably Metcalfe's, but he couldn't be sure.

He retraced his steps back to Norell's street. Metcalfe's BMW was gone. A mixed blessing. Metcalfe might have had something else to do. Or he'd dispatched Norell and left. Only one way to find out.

Hallman straightened his back and strode purposefully along the sidewalk to Norell's house. A wrought iron fence ringed the property for decoration, not security. The gate had a latch but no lock. He grinned. Maybe his luck was finally changing.

The house looked unoccupied. The drapes were closed, but he could see light from inside around the edges. If Metcalfe hadn't killed him, Norell might have left for work already. His wife or children could be home.

The driveway led up to the house. A concrete walkway circled the building. A six-foot white fence that looked like plastic separated the front and rear lawns.

A two-car garage was detached, but a roof covered the walkway to the side of the house. Both garage doors were closed. He couldn't see inside.

If Metcalfe's BMW hadn't sped out a few minutes ago, he might have parked his SUV inside. He could be waiting.

Hallman approached the solid steel front door, his gaze darting from window to window looking for movement but saw none. He pushed the doorbell. A loud buzz sounded inside the house.

No one came to the door. A minute later, he rang again.

After another minute of waiting, he took the concrete path around the house.

Hallman tried the garage's side door. The handle turned easily, and he stepped inside.

High up on the back wall, narrow windows admitted enough light to reveal two small Mercedes SUVs.

A selection of hand tools hung on a rack on the wall opposite the side door. Hallman homed in on a series of screwdrivers. The eight-inch standard had a thick shaft. Long and strong enough to stab through flesh and muscle, short enough to prevent an opponent from ripping it out of his hand during combat. He took a hammer, too. Just in case.

A door clicked.

He whipped around. No one had entered. He paced to the door, taking care not to knock any of the tools to the floor.

He stood behind the door. He heard noises outside. Something heavy being dragged along the concrete. He adjusted his grip on the screwdriver.

"Is it okay there?" A man's voice asked. Norell. No question.

"It'll do," a woman replied, probably his wife.

Hallman heard footsteps crunching on the walk and then a door closing.

He listened hard, cupping his hand around his ear. After the door closed all right, with a solid thump of the wood and a spring latch clicked into place, he heard no secondary click to suggest that either Norell had locked the door.

They had either ignored the bell he'd rung at the front door or hadn't heard it. Since they were talking and behaving normally, Metcalfe was probably not inside the building.

Hallman redoubled his grip on the screwdriver. It was time to pay the Norells a visit.

CHAPTER THIRTY-ONE

Tuesday, November 28
11:30 a.m.
Kansas City, Kansas

JESS LEFT MORRIS AND the pair of officers to search
Gotting's apartment and went looking for Pam McGinty.

She spied the leasing agent with a couple of prospective
tenants driving a golf cart around the apartment complex. The
entire trip wouldn't take long.

Jess waited near the office until McGinty returned and
parked the golf cart in its assigned space out front. The couple
asked the last few questions and left.

McGinty approached Jess. "Find out anything else?"

Jess shook her head. "I was wondering if you had his license
plate number."

"Earle's? Yeah, I should have it. Come on in and I'll check."
McGinty unlocked the office. She retrieved a wad of papers from
a filing cabinet hidden in the pantry. She wrote out a number on
a Post-it and handed it to Jess.

Jess looked at the paper. "This is the Audi, right?"

"Definitely. He's only had one car since he's been here."

"Did he come here straight from prison?"

McGinty shrugged. "He made the deposit and hasn't been any trouble."

Jess nodded.

She said, "Actually, I felt a little sorry for him because of his limp."

"He has a limp?" Jess was still struggling to remember Gotting from thirteen years ago.

"Not real bad. Happened in prison. Doesn't seem to slow him down or anything."

"The guy who ran out the back didn't limp."

"I imagine Earle could run and you wouldn't see much of a limp."

Jess thanked McGinty and left.

As soon as she stepped outside, her phone rang. Stephenson's name appeared on the display.

"Jess," he said, "No luck on tracing Gotting's known acquaintances. Seems to be a bit of a loner."

"None at all?"

"None we can find. Or maybe none who will admit knowing him." Stephenson paused. "You need me to help in Kansas?"

"I'm good for now. I'm with Morris."

"Well, let me know if you change your mind. I can get there quickly."

She thanked him and hung up.

Morris was in the parking lot standing near the police cruiser. The cruiser pulled away as Jess approached.

He smiled. "I sent off about fifty prints. Mostly partials, but there were a few good ones. I did the baby bottles, but there was nothing on them."

She cocked her head. "I don't know whether that's a good thing or not."

"Hard to know at this point," he replied.

She handed him Gotting's license plate number. "Can you run it?"

"The local field office is already collecting background. In fact, I have a set of pictures. Take a look." Morris forwarded the email to her phone.

Jess examined the images. Gotting was thin. The height chart behind his mug shot showed him at five feet, ten inches tall. Typical male pattern baldness, but he'd had dark hair to match his eyebrows once. Dark brown eyes. His facial expressions suggested a sullen demeanor. Although no one ever looked happy in a mug shot.

She saved the photos and closed the email. "I got more background from McGinty. Gotting limps. Not bad, but noticeable."

Morris nodded. "The man in the convenience store didn't limp. Nor did the BMW driver."

"So we may have a gang."

"Or they could be unconnected. Either way, why ransack Gotting's apartment? What were they looking for?"

"And did they find it?" Jess asked. "Can you get a list of Gotting's associates from Humboldt?"

"We can get whatever information they know. We'll ask for enemies, too." He looked at his watch. "You up for chicken and a few questions for the manager?"

Jess nodded. "Questions? My favorite lunch."

Finger-Lickin' Fried Chicken was a large yellow and green

building with its name written in red neon flashing lights on the roof. Jess suspected it would be visible from space. The moon even.

The overwhelming stench of fried food hit her before she exited the SUV. By the time she was inside the store, she didn't think she would ever stop smelling of old chicken grease.

The man behind the counter took their request to see the manager without a blink. A woman in slacks and a white top appeared. Her name badge said "Chicky."

Morris held out his FBI ID and stared at her badge.

She held out her hand. "It's a joke. Evelyn Benton."

They shook hands with her and introduced themselves.

Morris asked, "Does Earle Gotting work here?"

Evelyn shook her head. "Used to."

"You let him go?"

"No. He quit."

"Why?"

"You'll have to ask him."

"You didn't ask him about it?"

Evelyn shifted her weight. "No."

Morris lowered his voice. "Really?"

Evelyn took a deep breath. "This is my one and only restaurant. I don't have the money to act like the big guys. I try to pay a fair wage and I keep a—"

"Evelyn, we're just looking for Earle."

"Right… Well, I didn't have any proof, but I was beginning to suspect he was doing something with drugs."

"Something?"

"Selling…them…here." She put her hands up in front of her. "I know, I know. I should have told someone."

"What made you think he was selling drugs here?"

"He used to bring in magazines."

"Motorcycle magazines?"

Her gaze flitted to Morris. "Yeah. He read them, but I caught him selling one, and who buys a used magazine?"

"Did you ever actually see any drugs?"

"No. But he knew I'd seen him, and he quit that afternoon."

"Has he been around since?"

"No."

"Did any of your staff know him?" Jess said.

Evelyn shook her head. "Earle was a loner."

"Did he ever mention any friends? Girlfriend? Family?" Jess said.

"Not to me."

"Anyone ever come to see him at work?"

"Not that I know."

"How well did he do the job?"

"No complaints. He just didn't like to mix, and…"

"He sold drugs."

"Yeah. I should have been suspicious from the start."

"Because he'd been in prison."

"No. Because of his car."

Jess frowned. "The Audi."

"Yeah. Most of the people who work for me don't own a car like that."

"Like what?"

"Well, expensive. A6. All the bells and whistles."

"It was an old one, right?"

Evelyn shook her head. "It was filthy dirty, but it was definitely this year's model."

Morris was on the phone before he left the counter at Finger Lickin' Fried Chicken. Jess thanked Evelyn and followed him out. He finished his call as Jess started the Ford's engine.

"She was right. Audi A6. This year's model," Morris read the information from his phone. "He bought the car two days after he was released. According to the tax records fifty-three thousand dollars. Cash."

Jess said, "Fifty-three thousand for the car and he works at a fast food place. That actually seems like a good fit for a drug dealer. But why did he live in that low-rent pigsty?"

"Cover, most likely. Or perhaps it's a good place for distribution. Parking lot's large and close. Easy to get in and out," Morris said. "But I'd like to know how he got so much cash only a couple of days after he was released from prison. Banks are required to report large cash transactions, but we haven't turned up any bank accounts or large withdrawals."

Jess cocked her head. "Where did he buy the car?"

"Private sale." Morris consulted his phone. "Seller's listed as some guy named Zander Norell. Lives here in the city. I have an address."

Jess put the car in gear.

CHAPTER THIRTY-TWO

Tuesday, November 28
11:00 a.m.
Rio Grande National Forest
Gunnison, Colorado

EARLE GOTTING DROVE WEST from Colorado Springs, heading toward the Rio Grande National Forest, following his route from memory.

He stopped at a small garage nestled on a staggered junction. A sign above the door read The Orange Mart. Perhaps to reinforce the name, the door was painted vibrant orange.

There were only two pumps, and he had to pay the cashier inside first. His weak right leg was stiff, so he used the short distance to the building to work it out a little. After he filled up the Audi, he went inside again, limping less the second time.

The Orange Mart offered an eclectic mix of food, alcohol, and DIY products. It wouldn't rival one of the big chains, but for people who lived in the area, it was probably the go-to place.

He found a couple of day-old sandwiches wrapped in

cellophane in a fridge. From the same fridge, he took a six-pack of beer and a two-liter bottle of water. On top of the sandwiches, he stacked a loaf of bread and a dozen cans of soda.

In the DIY section, he picked up a portable gas heater with a tiny propane cylinder, a flashlight, and a roll of black duct tape. At the checkout, he bought three pre-paid phones. He didn't know how his plan was going to work yet, but an anonymous phone was always a good idea for criminal activities.

He paid in cash. The man at the checkout raised his eyebrows at the stack of phones. Gotting shrugged. "Kids. Always losing the things."

The checkout clerk grunted and stuffed the goods in two lightweight plastic bags.

Gotting returned to his Audi, and continued on the mountain road, minding the speed limits. The last thing he needed was to be stopped by some local cop looking to raise revenue with fines for speeding tickets.

While he'd lived in Denver, he'd skied and snowboarded over much of the state. There were plenty of resorts that had hundreds of miles of well-groomed runs, but what he really liked was the backcountry.

He'd begun experimenting with what the French called off-piste sports in Vail, where he'd found large open bowls across the back of the main mountains. But they were over-used areas. He preferred places where the snow hadn't been touched, the kind of locations he'd found in nature magazines.

He wasn't an extreme snowboarder or anything. He wasn't the type to launch himself off giant drops or schuss straight down a steep mountain soaring thousands of feet in the air. What he loved was the isolation. He'd spent much of his life alone and being alone in nature felt good to him.

If his plan worked, his name and his face would become publicly known. He'd be required to hide out for a while. Maybe a long while. His mug shot and prints would be circulated to every cop in the country. None of that worried him. There were a million ways to flee to South America with barely a handful of cash, and he'd have much more than a handful to splash around.

Maybe he'd head down to Argentina. He'd heard about good snow there, and his prison cronies were always talking about Argentina as the ideal place to disappear.

The Audi carried him effortlessly all the way into the Rio Grande National Forest, south of Gunnison.

Snowboarding was how he'd come to find the perfect cabin. It had been a mainstay of his kidnapping career while he lived in Colorado. He'd also used the place after he'd moved his baby theft operation to Arizona and New Mexico.

He slowed at a road sign for US-149. The letters were faded and hard to read. The road was nothing but turns and switchbacks. On either side were rocks that stretched up into soaring mountains, mostly covered with white already. The snow had come thick and early to Colorado this year.

After fifteen minutes of hard driving, he turned off the road onto a rocky track. The Audi slipped and slithered. The track disappeared into thick pines. The snow was lighter under the tree canopy, but the track steepened. He figured the ruggedness was an asset. No one was likely to happen upon him here.

After five minutes of intense struggle, the Audi arrived at a derelict shelter. One of the walls had collapsed since he'd been here last, but the sides facing the road were mostly intact. The roof was practically non-existent.

He angled the Audi into the shelter, turned off the engine, and scrambled out into the cold. The air was bitter. He could see his breath with every exhale and breathing at this altitude wasn't easy, either. But the blissful silence was totally empty, which he'd only ever found in the mountains.

The shelter had not been built as a garage for a car. It had probably been constructed long before motor cars were common, he figured. But it prevented anyone traveling the road from seeing his car. That's all he cared about.

The nearest neighbors were two miles in either direction, but he wasn't taking any chances. He limped over to the side of the shelter, dug under the snow, and found the big garden rake he'd left there. It was lightweight plastic and thin strips of easily bent metal. He'd bought it a decade ago and it was still good enough for his purposes.

He used the rake's handle as a pole to steady his gait as he worked his way back to the road along the rugged terrain. From the turn-in point, he walked backward as he swept the rake across the car's path for fifty feet until the tracks extended far enough into the trees to be invisible from the road.

Satisfied, he returned the rake to its original place. He grabbed his Orange Mart purchases from the trunk and walked farther up the path to where the track stopped. He angled right, ducking through the trees and trudging past the undergrowth. The going was tough. His weak leg ached from the cold and the exertion.

After fifteen minutes of heavy struggle, he took the next step and burst out of the dense trees and thicket.

In front of him was a wide-open area. On the far side was a long, steep slope of solid rock. It stretched forty feet above him and only the occasional weed popped out from its nooks and crannies.

Centered in the rock was a building. It looked like it grew

out of the slope, which in many ways it did. Miners had built it long ago as the entrance to a network of shafts. Gotting didn't know what the miners had been digging for, but the building they'd left served his purposes perfectly.

He covered the open area with ease. The chemical by-products of the mining had killed off all growth in the area long ago and seemingly forever, as far as he could tell.

In the center of the building were ten-foot high, heavy wooden double doors. An outer frame was filled with thick, rough cut planks with gaps and holes, but no more than he remembered. The doors had no handles. Across the face of each door, the word Danger had been spray-painted in three-foot-high letters. The paint had almost disappeared, the outline of the letters marked now only by the faded wood.

The doors were too big to move, and after decades of neglect the hinges had probably seized. He walked around the side of the building. A three-foot-high hatch was the only other external feature.

His heart skipped a beat when he saw that two planks had been nailed across it. The planks were weathered, but recent. The nails had been driven in hard.

This was his safe house. If he couldn't use it, his budding plan would fall apart.

He debated returning to the Orange Mart to buy tools but appearing in the same place twice might make him more memorable to the clerk. Or more likely, the CCTV. Every space in America seemed to be watched these days. Why would the Orange Mart be any different?

He searched the area and gathered rocks. Collecting and piling them by the hatch was exhausting work. He wedged a rock into the gap between the new plank and the original hatch and pounded it with another rock. Gradually the rock sank deeper into the gap, widening it.

He repeated the procedure with a larger rock, gradually widening the gap. He worked his way toward the nails, maximizing the stress until finally, with one last solid crack, the new plank broke. He pried the remaining parts away from the hatch and dealt with the second plank in the same way.

He used one of the broken planks to lever the hatch open and stepped inside.

The air was damp and fetid, a choking smell of earth and decay. The rear wall was the solid rock slope. Slivers of light pierced through the gaps in the wooden structure, revealing far more holes than were apparent from outside. Holes that allowed the cold to enter.

He worked his way into the middle of the building where he found an open path, clear of the spars that held up the rest of the building. A one-time rail track that ran into the mine, the rails long gone.

Gone, too, was the inflatable mattress he had left there years before. He searched around to find it but had no luck. He grunted. He'd slept rough on enough occasions, he'd manage a few more nights. His payoff would be worth the discomfort.

Where the rail track's path met the escarpment was a rusty six-foot metal door that led into the mine. It was closed. He lifted a large handle. Metal scraped against metal. Fortunately, the lock mechanism hadn't seized, but when he pulled on the door, it didn't move.

He wedged one of the new planks into the frame around the door and leaned on it with all his weight. The plank creaked. The metal squealed.

He shifted all his weight onto the plank. The plank creaked

one last time and broke, throwing him on the floor.

He sat up. He needed the space behind the door. It was the only place he could be sure the boy would be contained. Leaving him in the rest of the building with its shafts of light would give him hope, and hope might enable him to escape.

He inspected the hinges. The lower one didn't move as he levered the door. After fifty years or more, it had finally rusted solid.

He found an old tin can on the floor and worked his way back to his car.

He opened the hood. The engine was still warm. He pulled out the dipstick and let the oil drip into the can. It was a depressingly small amount, but he had to open the door into the mine shaft. He threaded the dipstick back into the engine and ran through the process again. It took several minutes, but in the end he had a quarter inch of oil in the bottom of the can.

He returned to the metal door. The oil had thickened in the cold, but he managed to spread a good layer over the hinge. He let it penetrate for a few minutes then used his weight to lever the door back and forth. The metal screeched.

In the dim light, he was sure he saw the lower hinge move. He rocked on his heels then threw all his weight backward, pulling on the door handle. The metal scraped. He saw rust crumbling off the hinges. He pulled harder. The door jerked open.

The lower corner smashed into his right foot, tearing his boot across the top and scraping the tender flesh beneath. Pain burned his foot like a hot poker.

He screamed as if he'd been attacked by a grizzly and threw himself away from the door.

He dropped to the ground, writhing in pain, and grabbed his

toes, squeezing hard to numb the unbearable agony. Nothing worked.

He sat on the ground for a few minutes, cradling his foot. In the dim light, he could see the door had gouged a chunk of his skin and underlying tissues. Breathing hard, he waited for the torture to lessen, which took a good long time. If his right leg hadn't been damaged already, the pain might have been even worse. He shuddered.

Finally, the torment subsided to manageable proportions.

He was able to stand. Carefully, he tested his weight. He limped in a circle, walking not much worse than he usually did. Nothing crunched and no bones poked through his muscles.

He tucked the skin flap back over the wound and folded the leather of his boot into place. Each time he put pressure on the area, a fire raged in his right foot.

He tore off a strip of the black duct tape, and covered the rip in his boot, pressing gingerly to get a seal.

Confined inside the boot, with the skin flap in place, his foot throbbed, but the searing torment had lessened. He couldn't sit here forever. He had no choice but to keep going.

When he could confidently put his weight on his foot, he went back to the door. It creaked open with just a tug this time.

He shone his flashlight into the blackness. The tunnel walls glistened with dampness. The air had a different quality in here. He sniffed a couple of times to be sure. Less organic decay and more metallic chemicals, maybe.

He placed the cans of soda on the damp floor, and the bread on top.

The flashlight wasn't bright enough to illuminate all the way down, but he knew that fifty feet back there, the tunnel had been sealed up.

He stepped out of the tunnel and pushed the door almost closed.

He wasn't finished with his preparations, but the discomfort in his foot stopped him from completing his tasks. The rest would have to wait.

He was ready for the first stage of his plan, at least.

He'd never abducted an older child before. He figured it would be different from stealing babies, sure. But he was experienced. He'd know what to do.

Tomorrow, he would kidnap Peter Kimball.

CHAPTER THIRTY-THREE

Tuesday, November 28
11:40 a.m.
Kansas City, Kansas

HALLMAN GLANCED AROUND THE garage one last time. He saw nothing more useful as a weapon than the screwdriver and the hammer. Not that he really thought it would actually be necessary to use a weapon on Norell. He had the feeling the threat alone would be more than enough.

He gripped the door handle. The distance from the side door of the garage to the kitchen door was four or five paces. He needed to move quickly. If Norell or his wife were in the kitchen, his element of surprise would be lost.

Once he was in the house, he would go for the wife. Norell would be easier to manage after Hallman subdued her. Norell wouldn't have the guts to risk any harm to her. The guy was a wimp.

Hallman took a deep breath.

Before he could move forward, he heard metal scraping the driveway, and an engine revved as it approached the garage.

He ran toward the main garage doors. He dropped low and pried back the weather-stripping to see outside. A white Toyota was in the driveway. Henrik Metcalfe stepped out.

Hallman's blood ran cold. Had the Toyota been parked in the street? Had he missed it? Had Metcalfe swapped cars to con him? Probably. That was the sort of thing Metcalfe would do.

He raced around to the hand tools and grabbed a saw. It was unwieldy, but it would inflict a lot of damage. If forced to fight Metcalfe, he needed to inflict as much damage as possible and as fast as he could possibly deliver it.

He moved from the tools to the side door and pressed his ear against the wooden frame. Footsteps landed hard on the concrete. He gripped the saw with two hands.

The footsteps stopped. There was a click followed by a creak. He recognized the sound as the kitchen door opening. Were Norell and Metcalfe working together?

An indignant female voice called out, but Hallman couldn't hear any conversation. The kitchen door slammed, and everything went quiet.

He transferred the saw from one hand to another as he wiped his sweaty palms on his jeans. Minutes passed. He breathed hard, tense and ready. He was trapped but running would only draw more attention to himself.

The minutes dragged on.

The kitchen door opened and closed. Footsteps pounded the concrete again. A car door slammed, and the Toyota backed out of the driveway. Hallman ran to watch through the weather-strip. Metcalfe left alone. The Toyota pulled away.

A moment later, a flustered man ran down the driveway and

closed the gate. He had trouble keeping it closed, Metcalfe must have broken the latch. Eventually it held, and the man walked back toward the house, glancing along the street as he did so.

Hallman sank onto his haunches. Sweat stuck his clothes to his body. He breathed hard.

The side door opened.

He jumped to his feet. He ran headlong around the vehicles, the saw held out in front of him. When the man stepped into the garage, Hallman body-checked the door, slammed it closed, and held the saw inches from the man's neck.

"Zander Norell?" Hallman said.

Norell strained backward, away from the saw. His mouth was half open. His breaths came in short gasps. His eyes were so wide they looked like they might pop out. He nodded.

"What did Metcalfe want?"

Norell's gasps slowed. "What?"

"The man who was here. What did he want?"

"Nothing."

Hallman pressed the saw against Norell's neck. "Tell me."

"He wanted…he wanted the name…he wanted a lawyer."

"Why?"

"He…he must be in trouble. Yes… He needs a lawyer. You know?"

"No, I don't know."

"Please, let me go."

"Did he hurt your wife?"

Norell said nothing.

"Did he kill her?"

Norell shook his head. "No, no. Please—"

Hallman withdrew the saw from Norell's neck but kept it close, threatening. "Where can I find Peter Kimball?"

Norell's face froze.

"Is that what Metcalfe wanted?" Hallman said through clenched teeth.

Norell licked his lips and nodded.

"So, where is Peter Kimball?"

"I don't know."

Hallman pressed the saw against his neck and a thin trickle of blood flowed down his neck and soaked into his collar. "Where is he?"

Norell's eyes widened and he took a deep breath. "I don't know."

"You sold babies. Some scheme with Earle Gotting." He shook the saw in front of Norell's face. "Tell me and you'll never see me again."

Norell lowered his gaze. "Gotting brought me babies sometimes. I passed them on for private adoption. Good families. I never knew any names."

"You passed them on to who?"

Norell breathed hard and looked at Hallman. "A...a lawyer."

"The same lawyer you told Metcalfe about?"

"I don't want to get hurt...."

He pressed the saw blade against Norell's neck again and ran it lightly across his skin this time. A thin line of blood popped out on his neck. "Did you tell Metcalfe? Yes or no."

Norell closed his eyes. "I-I gave him another name. Someone who died a few years ago."

Hallman smiled. He'd dead-ended Metcalfe. Plausible deniability courtesy of the dead. Good thinking on Norell's part.

Then again, if Norell had lied to Metcalfe, he was probably lying now. He couldn't go to the police, but he could be buying time.

Hallman flexed the saw blade. "You got the keys to one of the cars?"

Norell nodded and held out a key fob. "It's all yours."

Hallman took the keys and shoved Norell toward one of the Mercedes SUVs. "Oh no. You're coming with me."

CHAPTER THIRTY-FOUR

Tuesday, November 28
11:45 a.m.
Kansas City, Kansas

NORELL LIVED IN A two-story modern home in a typical suburban area. Trees dotted the grassy apron adjacent to the sidewalk. Residents parked their vehicles in garages or driveways, not along the curbs. Only guests and lawn services parked on the street.

The drapes were closed. "Looks like nobody's home," Jess said as she parked the rental. They got out and moved around to the trunk.

"At work, probably," Morris said as he checked his firearm.

Jess's Glock was still in its case. She felt self-conscious loading and checking it while standing in the street, but she did it anyway. She tucked the gun in her bag, along with another magazine.

Morris watched her. "That's for defense, right?"

She scoffed. "If we find Peter, whoever took him is the one who'll need a defense."

He scowled. "Jess—"

"Relax. It was a joke." She wasn't joking, and he couldn't possibly have thought otherwise. But he accepted her statement at face value.

He continued to stare at her, and she wondered what she would actually do if they found Peter's kidnapper. She'd only know when it happened. If it ever did. Peter had been gone so long. Many days, she'd struggled not to lose hope that she'd ever find him.

Morris opened the front gate and Jess started up the path to the house.

The garage door opened. A small silver Mercedes SUV drove out with two men in the front seats.

Jess waved them to stop. The driver continued out of the driveway. She backtracked along the path, waving her arms in the air and shouting, "Wait, wait!"

Morris stepped to within a few feet of the vehicle as it turned right. The garage door remained open.

Jess dug her car keys from her pocket.

The front door to Norell's house opened. A woman stepped out. "Zander," she shouted at the departing vehicle. She turned to Jess and Morris. "Who are you?"

"FBI," Morris shouted. "Who was in the Mercedes?"

The woman frowned. "My husband. What's going on?"

"Who was with him?"

She shook her head. "Where is he going?"

"No idea," Morris said as he ran for the Ford.

Jess jumped into the driver's seat and punched the start button. She swung the vehicle across the road as Morris closed his door. Even with the steering hard all the way to the stopping point, the Ford's turning circle was too large. She rammed the gear lever into reverse, shot halfway across the road, she floored the accelerator.

The Mercedes had disappeared.

"Right," Morris said.

She braked hard for the junction and waited for three cars to pass.

The Mercedes was several blocks ahead. One of the intervening cars had a left turn blinker on and came to a stop, waiting for the oncoming traffic to clear.

"Why ignore us?" she said.

"Could be lots of reasons, but his wife's response suggests his leaving wasn't normal."

The Mercedes turned right.

"So, he's running away or he's running toward something."

"Reasonable assumption," Morris said.

Jess checked her mirrors. No vehicles behind her. The line of traffic in front of her wasn't moving. She twisted the wheel to get around the car in front, mounted the curb and drove past the congestion.

Morris looked around but said nothing.

She raced a few more blocks and took the right after the Mercedes. The next street was lined with small shops on one side. Cars were parked at forty-five-degree angles in a line out front.

She eased by, eyeing each one for the silver Mercedes.

Morris leaned forward, straining to see.

Past the shops, she picked up speed. Side streets whipped by.

"Stop," Morris yelled.

She slammed on the brakes. A car behind honked.

"The last street. On the left," Morris pointed.

She twisted around. The car behind her was too close for her to reverse.

Morris pointed forward. "The next road, then try and get over one."

Jess raced forward, the Ford's tires squealing as she hurled it through ninety degrees.

The road was quiet. She judged fifty to be the fastest she could drive safely.

She saw two roads on the right, but nothing on the left. The street ended at a divided highway. She accelerated and joined the flow of traffic.

They passed the road the Mercedes had taken. Morris stared. "No sign."

Jess blew her frustration out in a long stream of air.

Morris opened the sunroof and climbed on his seat to look out. A moment later he dropped back into his seat. "Silver Mercedes ahead," he said, buckling his seatbelt.

Jess squeezed between two trucks to change lanes and accelerated.

Morris phoned in a request for backup to stop the Mercedes.

Jess turned on the hazard flashers and honked the horn. Two cars moved over immediately. A large Cadillac SUV blocked her way. She weaved from side to side, her hand on the Ford's horn.

"Easy," Morris said.

As Jess eased off, the Mercedes accelerated.

The cars that had pulled over slowed. Jess whispered her thanks and dove into the space they created.

The Mercedes was ahead, traveling fast.

She floored the accelerator and the Ford responded dramatically. The engine roared and settled on its haunches as the speedometer climbed to ninety.

The Mercedes easily ran ahead. The road was clear.

Jess maintained a steady speed ten miles an hour over the limit.

Morris kept a running commentary on the phone.

The Mercedes slowed. The two men in the Mercedes seemed to be fighting.

Morris drew his gun.

Jess inched closer. The Mercedes braked and lurched to one side, smashing into her Ford and shoving her sideways, trying to push her off the road. Metal crunched and Jess wrestled the steering, fighting to keep the Ford in her lane.

She tapped the brakes, slowing enough to wrench the two vehicles apart.

The Mercedes rocked on its suspension. One of the men turned to look at her.

She backed off. The Mercedes lurched across the lanes and slammed into the guardrail, showering sparks in the air.

She braked hard and swung onto the shoulder, maintaining a twenty-foot margin between her vehicle and the Mercedes as it came to a stop in a cloud of dust and gravel.

The traffic behind them stopped, blocking both lanes.

Morris leaped from the Ford and took up a position by the rear wheel. Jess ran around the rear of the Mercedes to join him.

Police sirens sounded in the distance.

"FBI," yelled Morris. "Get out. Keep your hands up."

A man jumped from the passenger side and ran around the front, using the SUV to shield himself from gunfire.

"Hands up!" Morris repeated.

The man in the driver's seat climbed out, holding his leg. "Don't shoot. I'm Zander Norell. I was kidnapped."

Jess rose a fraction to look over the Ford's hood. The passenger was long gone.

Norell leaned on the hood of the Mercedes, apparently in pain.

"Keep your hands where I can see them," Morris said.

Norell collapsed on the ground and feebly held his hands up.

Morris kept his gun pointed toward Norell as he approached.

Jess crouched and moved toward the Mercedes.

She confirmed that the vehicle was empty, but thirty feet ahead she saw movement behind a tree.

She stayed behind the hood and trained her gun on the tree. "Stop!"

The passenger's face peered from behind the tree. He ducked back just as quickly.

"Come out," she called, but he stayed behind the tree.

The traffic on the highway began moving. Maybe the show wasn't all that interesting.

Morris came up beside her. "I cuffed the guy."

She pointed. "The other one is behind that tree."

Traffic rolled past.

The sirens grew louder.

"We can wait for backup." Morris swiveled his head to look at the passing cars. "Let's move out of the traffic."

He nudged Jess toward the guardrail. He grabbed Norell, still in cuffs, on the way.

Jess kept her gaze on the tree. She saw the man hiding behind the trunk.

The traffic gained speed.

A harsh staccato burst of gunfire split the air. Jess ducked and covered her head. A futile, automatic response.

Bullets raked across the Ford. Automatic fire. Tearing metal and splintering glass. Steam and smoke billowed. The air smelled of harsh chemicals.

Morris spun around and doubled over with a grunt, both hands clapped to his side.

A white Toyota rolled past, the passenger window down and a large gun barrel poking out.

Jess jerked up her Glock, leveling it on the Toyota a second before squeezing the trigger. She fired three times. Close and fast. Concentrating on the Toyota's window as the gun jerked in her hands.

The Toyota driver fired back. The muzzle veered in Jess's direction. Bullets hammered into the street on her left. She flung herself back and smashed head first into the guardrail.

Pain speared her skull. Multicolored spotlights bloomed across her vision. Her legs wobbled as she tried to regain her balance until her knees buckled.

Morris lay on the ground, his hands clutching his side. His clothes were soaked with the dark blood that dripped through his fingers.

The Toyota pulled onto the hard shoulder in front of the Mercedes, and she heard shouts coming from that direction.

She shuffled forward, her gun ready. Her legs didn't want to move. She rolled onto her side to see the Toyota, training her gun in that direction.

The Mercedes passenger jumped into the Toyota, and the car screamed off. She adopted a classic shooter stance and steadied her aim. She wanted to fire. She wanted to stop the man who shot Morris. But shooting at a speeding car on a crowded street was foolhardy.

Norell had crawled to the guardrail and used it to prop himself up.

She crawled to Morris on her hands and knees. He lay on his back, blood spreading into a widening pool on the street. She grabbed his wrist and found a pulse, but his hands were limp and his eyes were closed. He didn't speak or groan or make any noises at all.

She placed her hands over the bullet hole in his shirt and pressed down, attempting to slow the blood loss with pressure.

People raced from their cars to surround her and Morris. She heard frantic calls to 911. A man tucked his coat under Morris's feet and used his hands to help Jess staunch the blood flow.

After what seemed a century, sirens approached, and flashing lights lit the scene. The crowd parted and paramedics swarmed in. One man hoisted her away from Morris as two doctors ripped into sterile packs of IVs, tubes, and field dressings.

Morris didn't flinch as they jammed needles into his veins.

Jess sat back and stared off into the distance.

CHAPTER THIRTY-FIVE

Tuesday, November 28
11:50 a.m.
Kansas City, Kansas

HALLMAN THREW OPEN THE Mercedes door moments after the vehicle crashed head-on into the guardrail and the airbags deployed. The blast was numbing, but the adrenaline rushing through his body jerked him back to reality fast.

He jumped from the battered SUV and climbed over the guardrail.

Norell climbed out of the other side. A tall guy from the Ford shouted "FBI." Norell's hands shot up into the air.

The woman driving the Ford had a Glock in her hand when she got out. Hallman tossed the saw he'd stolen from Norell's garage over the guardrail and into the long grass beyond. The saw was a puny weapon against their firepower.

Police and ambulance sirens sounded in the distance.

His eyes scanned quickly for the nearest cover. He spied an established tree with an eighteen-inch trunk and hid behind it.

More shouting. Norell begged the FBI agent not to shoot. The agent moved to Norell and cuffed him.

Hallman looked around wildly for an escape route. The FBI agent would move in on him next. The highway's shoulder was a broad swath of unkempt grass which thinned out as it reached a side road. On the far side of the road was a wide gravel area running up to an industrial park.

The FBI agent didn't advance from the Mercedes. Probably a good idea. The open space between the SUV and the tree would have made him an easy target if Hallman had a gun, but he didn't.

The FBI agent moved closer to the guardrail.

Hallman fixed his gaze on the woman. He recognized her. She wasn't an FBI agent. Jessica Kimball. *Damn!* How had she tracked him down so fast?

The police sirens grew louder as the vehicles approached. Emergency lights danced over the cars stopped on the highway. His stomach clenched as his tension mounted. When more cops arrived, he'd be hemmed in. Not that his chances of escape were good now. The Mercedes was trashed, and the Ford would catch him in seconds if he tried to run.

The traffic began moving, rolling at first then picking up speed.

Automatic gunfire rent the air. He dropped to his knees and leaned into the tree for protection. Was the FBI shooting? There were a few single shots then more automatic fire.

Whoever was shooting, wasn't aiming at him. He peered around the tree. The FBI man was down, Norell was cringing in a fetal position, and Kimball was crawling toward the FBI man. She looked dazed like she might have been hit.

He twisted around. Who was shooting?

A white Toyota pulled over on the hard shoulder. The passenger window was open.

"Get in!" Metcalfe shouted.

A chill gripped Hallman, paralyzing his muscles.

"Get in," Metcalfe screamed.

Hallman's heart pounded in his chest. Had Metcalfe fired on the FBI? Was he trying to kill them all?

The Toyota's engine revved hard and the car jerked forward. The passenger door flew open. "Now," Metcalfe screamed again.

Hallman ran for the open door. He cleared the guardrail in one bound and dove into the car.

Metcalfe floored the accelerator and the Toyota lurched forward, which caused the door to bang shut. Hallman twisted around in the seat and wrestled the seatbelt on. The needle on the speedometer climbed past eighty.

"What's going on?" Hallman said.

Metcalfe glared. He weaved around slower traffic and took the next exit at seventy mph.

"You shot an FBI agent back there."

"I missed that scum Norell."

"You were trying to kill Norell?"

"Duh."

Metcalfe fishtailed the Toyota around a ninety-degree bend into a parking lot.

"Why?" Hallman said.

"Why!" Metcalfe shouted. "You should be asking why I didn't kill you, asshole."

Metcalfe parked beside a silver Volkswagen Jetta. "Wipe anything you touched."

Metcalfe leaped out of the Toyota and rammed a bent coat

190 | DIANE CAPRI

hanger down the Volkswagen's window and into the door's pocket.

Hallman grabbed the cuff of his jacket and wiped over the Toyota's seat and door handles as best he could, and hurried out of the car, glancing around wildly. He expected a horde of cops to land on them at any moment.

The Volkswagen's locks popped open. Metcalfe ripped a panel from under the steering wheel and plugged a small box into some electronics. The car burst into life.

Hallman ran around the Jetta and slipped into the passenger seat.

Metcalfe cruised out of the lot and doubled back the way he'd come.

Hallman took a deep breath. "So, tell me why you wanted to kill Norell."

Metcalfe growled, "Because we're partners now. Like it or not."

CHAPTER THIRTY-SIX

Tuesday, November 28
1:00 p.m.
Kansas City, Kansas

THE FIRST AMBULANCE TOOK Morris. The paramedics
loaded him onto a stretcher and one carried the IVs along beside
him. Jess asked to go in the same ambulance, but they said no.

Norell was taken next, with a squad car following.

They put her in the last ambulance after the police had run
through the preliminary questions. They bagged and took her
gun.

She had no strength to argue, but she was able to walk
thanks to the medics and a generous supply of oxygen.

At the hospital, she went through a series of tests. An hour
later she sat propped up on a bed, waiting for the results.

A man in a dark suit and short cropped hair stepped into her
room. His dark brown eyes looked almost black. "Jessica
Kimball?"

She nodded.

He offered his ID. "I'm Special Agent Emilio Fernandez. From the Kansas City field office."

Jess scrutinized his ID and nodded as she returned it. "How's Henry?"

Fernandez put the ID into his jacket and stuffed his hands into his pants pockets. "Not great. He lost blood, but the paramedics were there quickly. He should be okay in a couple of days."

"Is he awake?"

"He's sleeping right now, but he asked for you earlier."

Jess gave a flat smile. "Can I see him?"

"Once the doctors say it's okay. Couple hours or so, probably."

"When he wakes, will you tell him I... I asked about him, too."

Fernandez nodded. "I know you two are involved. It's in his file."

Jess frowned. "There nothing illegal about that, is there?"

He shook his head. "Not at all. I just want you to know I understand your concern."

"Sorry." She exhaled, looking at Fernandez. "Do you know who shot Henry and why?"

"Not yet," he paused. "And we don't know anything more about your missing son yet, either."

She nodded.

"That's why I'm here. Morris asked my boss for help and he cut me loose for a few days. See what we can turn up."

"We?"

"Henry filled me in on the case when he came into town. Unfortunately, we were too slow to provide the support we should have."

Jess shrugged. "We… I was too impatient."

"We are where we are. Can you tell me what happened?"

"Definitely."

"Good. Norell claimed he was kidnapped. Do you believe him?"

She sneered. "That he was kidnapped? Hard to tell."

"But the shooter in the Toyota was working with the passenger in the Mercedes?"

"Makes sense to me. He got into the Toyota of his own free will and then disappeared," Jess said.

Fernandez didn't argue.

"Has Norell said anything about why he was kidnapped if he was?" She asked.

"He claims he's in too much pain to talk about it," Fernandez frowned and looked down briefly as if he was thinking about Norell's excuses seriously. "Could someone have tipped Norell off? Told him you were coming to talk to him?"

"No. We didn't tell anyone about the link we uncovered between him and Gotting."

"Yet Gotting's partner does a drive-by and shoots at one of our agents." Fernandez's mouth worked for a couple of seconds before he remembered his manners. "Sorry, I didn't mean to be unfeeling."

Jess shook her head. "It's okay. You're right. The attack on us wasn't random. I didn't notice the Toyota following us."

"Understandable in the heat of the moment," Fernandez said.

A doctor entered the room. She flashed a broad smile, probably trying to put Jess at ease. She nodded at Fernandez then stood beside the bed. "You're very lucky. No serious injuries that we can find, aside from that large bruise. Still, I'd advise against driving or operating machinery for at least twenty-four hours. Forty-eight would be better." She signed a wad of papers on the patient chart. "You can dress and go."

"How's Henry Morris?"

The doctor glanced at Fernandez. He nodded.

The doctor cleared her throat. "Agent Morris was shot twice. Nine-millimeter rounds. They passed through his left side. One bullet hit a kidney, and the other struck his intestine. But both wounds were nicks, and we've dealt with them."

Jess exhaled, relief flooding through her. But the doctor wasn't finished.

"The impact tore away a large chunk of flesh and caused internal bleeding. Loss of blood was moderate, considering. He has been conscious, but we have him sedated now." She patted Jess's arm and offered a reassuring smile. "He's not out of the woods yet, but at this moment he is recovering well. He should be okay."

Jess closed her eyes and nodded. She swallowed to clear the lump in her throat. "Can I see him?"

"He's asleep, but sure."

Jess nodded her thanks. "What about Zander Norell?"

The doctor pursed her lips. "I can't give you those details. But we're keeping him overnight as a precaution."

"Can I talk to him?"

The doctor shook her head. "He's denied everyone access. We have to respect that. He has a police guard and called his lawyer."

The doctor handed a wad of papers to Jess before she left. "You're free to go as soon as you feel up to it. And good luck to you."

"I need to talk to Norell," Jess said to Fernandez after the doctor left the room.

"We're going to do that soon as his lawyer arrives."

"No, I want to talk to him now. He has information about my son. I have to find out what he knows."

"You're a private citizen. I can't tell you what to do." Fernandez shook his head. "But that's not a good idea, Jess. Let us do our job. We'll find Peter."

Jess shook her head. "I've waited far too long for someone else to find him. I'm his mother. It's my job."

He shrugged and didn't reply.

"I'm looking for my son no matter what you say. But I'd rather do it with your help." She paused and tried to soften her words with a gentler tone. "Look, you were too slow to provide the support you should have. You said so. Now's your chance to make it up to me."

Fernandez took a deep breath. "I'm sorry. Questioning Norell without his lawyer is off-limits. We can't do it, and you can't do it without us unless Norell consents. Which he's made clear he's not doing."

"It's not the questions I care about. I need to hear his voice. I'll know if he was the man who tried to blackmail me. And I want to see how he reacts when I ask about Peter. I'll be able to tell if he took my son, and if he knows where Peter is now."

"Technically, Carter Pierce is the blackmail victim."

She scowled. "My son and I are being threatened."

Fernandez nodded. "Fair enough. I'll arrange for you to watch. Do you feel up to walking?"

She rolled off the bed. Her balance seemed good. She nodded. "What about Norell's wife? She's got to be wondering what happened."

"She spent a while with her husband and left."

Jess walked cautiously to the door. Apart from a headache, she seemed fine. "Then let's pay her a visit before she gets defensive."

CHAPTER THIRTY-SEVEN

Tuesday, November 28
2:00 p.m.
Kansas City, Kansas

HALLMAN KEPT HIS HANDS to himself to minimize the chance of leaving fingerprints. He said little, thinking furiously while the gloved Metcalfe drove the Volkswagen and headed north out of the city.

"You have any idea how much trouble you're in now? Gotting took Peter Kimball and handed him over to Norell." Metcalfe shook his head as if Hallman was as dumb as a bag of rocks. "I persuaded Norell to give me the name of the lawyer who sold the kid."

"They sold him?" Hallman frowned. That was a new piece of the puzzle, but it made sense. Gotting hadn't abducted the kid because he wanted to be a daddy. No one who'd ever met Gotting would have assumed anything that stupid.

Metcalfe gave him a nasty glare. "What? You thought Norell kept the kid for himself? That's why you were hiding out in his garage? Hoping to find the kid at his house? Wise up."

Hallman held his breath waiting, but Metcalfe never mentioned Carter Pierce. Pierce was the only reason Hallman's plan would work. Which wouldn't happen if Metcalfe got wind of it.

Kimball made reasonable money working as a reporter, but she'd spent it all looking for her kid. She didn't own anything worthwhile that she could pawn, either. She couldn't raise enough cash. Kidnapping and transporting the kid across state lines would get Hallman thrown right back in prison. He wouldn't take the chance merely for the chump change Kimball could scrape together.

Pierce's net worth was more than half a billion dollars. His philanthropic causes were well known, as was his habit of taking care of the employees at his glitzy magazine like family. Not surprising since he was a workaholic with no family. Carter Pierce could pay millions, and he would if he was pushed hard enough. Hallman had every intention of shoving him until he paid.

Which left the question of Metcalfe, driving with a gun in his lap pointed straight into Hallman's leg. Once he was no longer useful, Metcalfe would dispose of him.

Which meant Carter Pierce couldn't be mentioned. Once Metcalfe knew about Pierce, Hallman would die face down in a gravel pit.

Metcalfe left the highway and worked his way through minor roads, finally stopping by a line of trees near a scrap yard where rusty old cars were piled in heaps. He drove slowly along the road and stopped near a group of newer vehicles to the scrap yard.

"You owe me, Hallman. Big time. Police had you nailed back there. Without me, you'd be in the slammer for the rest of your life. So, here's the deal. You're cutting me in. We're going to find Kimball's kid, and we're going to make millions." He put his gun in his jacket and cracked his knuckles. "Or I'm going to kill you with my bare hands."

Hallman forced himself to breathe evenly as his body twitched. "Snap" Metcalfe was big enough and strong enough to follow through on his threat. He'd broken many bones before. He'd do it again.

"You want your money, and I'm trying to get it. You want to help me, I've got no problem with that."

Metcalfe laughed derisively. "We're no longer discussing a miserable fifty grand. I'll take half."

Hallman stared. In an instant, his three million was chopped to one point five. His plan became their plan. His work became Metcalfe's reward. When the whole thing was over, Metcalfe would kill him and take all the money anyway.

Not a chance. Hallman nodded and held out his hand. "Deal."

He'd work out how to deal with Metcalfe. But no way would he give this thug half of his three million dollars. Not a chance in the world.

CHAPTER THIRTY-EIGHT

Tuesday, November 28
3:30 p.m.
Kansas City, Kansas

AGENT FERNANDEZ LED JESS through the hospital corridors to Morris's room. A policeman stood guard. He said, "Just a precaution."

Jess stepped into the room. Henry lay still, breathing softly. The usual medical paraphernalia surrounded the bed. An IV machine clicked every second, pumping fluid into the back of his hand. Wires snaked under the covers.

Fernandez pointed to the IV. "They knocked him out. It's not as bad as it seems. He needs rest."

She squeezed Morris's hand. He didn't respond. "What are you doing to get the guy who did this?"

"Everything we can. We're tracing CCTV, witnesses, forensics. We'll find him."

She nodded, watching Henry for any sign that he knew she was there. She saw none. She stood by his bed for a few minutes.

Finally, she swallowed hard. "Let's go talk to Mrs. Norell."

"Ready when you are."

She followed him to the parking lot.

Fernandez's car was a tired, old, dark blue Ford Crown Victoria. He laughed at her surprise. "There are times when a new Cadillac doesn't blend in. Besides, I juiced the engine and tricked out the brakes and suspension. This baby's better than anything rolling off the production line these days."

The inside of the car was as tired as the outside, but she crawled into the passenger seat and fastened her seatbelt.

"The police took my gun," she said.

Fernandez offered her a mock scowl. "Are you suggesting you want a weapon?"

"When he shoots at me again, I want to have the option of shooting back."

He nodded. "Once KCPD has a ballistics sample they should return your Glock."

Fernandez drove from the hospital to Norell's house without consulting the GPS. As he approached the house, he pointed at the glove box. "Put the light on the roof."

Jess found the large domed light. "You want to arrive with flashing lights?"

He nodded. "Helps convince people we're serious."

She opened the window and reached for the roof. The light clamped itself to the car's metal. "Magnetic," she said.

He grinned. "Nothing but the best."

A KCPD cruiser with steam trailing from its exhaust waited at the front curb in front of Norell's house. Fernandez stopped the Crown Vic behind it.

An officer stepped out of the cruiser. Fernandez flashed his FBI identification, and the officer climbed back into his squad car.

The garage doors had been closed after Norell's hurried departure earlier. The grass was cut and edged, the flowers had been pruned, and the leaves were mostly raked.

Lights glowed inside the house. Jess glimpsed a woman's face peering from behind an upstairs drape.

Fernandez rang the doorbell. He kept his finger on the button longer than necessary. The door opened a few seconds later.

The woman Jess had seen twice now offered a flat smile. She glanced briefly at the Crown Vic.

"Mrs. Norell?" Fernandez said.

"Who are you?" If she recognized Jess, she didn't act like it.

He held out his ID.

Mrs. Norell leaned forward and studied the words on his ID. "I've already given a statement."

"We just need a few minutes of your time. We're looking for a missing child."

Norell breathed out through her teeth with a hiss. "I have nothing to say. Really."

Fernandez gestured into the house. "Could we come in?"

Norell nodded and led them into the kitchen. A window looked out on a deck and the backyard. She sat down at a large oak kitchen table.

Fernandez sat down beside her. Jess remained standing.

"The doctors say your husband is going to be okay," Fernandez said.

She nodded hesitantly.

"You're worried?" Fernandez asked.

"Someone shot at my husband. Of course, I'm worried."

Jess fought back the desire to say that someone she cared for had been shot, too. She took a deep breath. "Do you know of any reason why someone would do that?"

Norell chewed her lower lip and shook her head.

"Has he argued with anyone lately?" Jess said.

Norell shook her head again.

"Any trouble at a restaurant or at the mall?"

Norell scowled at Jess. "No."

"Did he know the person who kidnapped him?"

"No."

Jess said, "Agent Fernandez, do you have a photo of the man in the SUV with Mr. Norell?"

Fernandez found the photo from the CCTV on his phone and showed it to her. "Do you know this man?"

She studied the photo and handed the phone back. "No. I've never seen him."

"What about your husband?"

"You'll have to ask him," she said, squaring her shoulders.

"We will when his lawyer arrives."

Jess said, "That's a little strange, isn't it? He's got a lawyer before he's even been discharged from the hospital?"

"He needs one, doesn't he? You never know what's going to happen. And Belk's done work for us before," Mrs. Norell said, thrusting her chin forward.

Fernandez said, "Belk?"

"Ammerson Belk. Our lawyer. Well, my husband's really," she said. "Contracts, legal stuff. He's in advertising."

"Who does your husband work for?" Jess asked.

She shrugged. "He got into internet advertising a few years ago."

"What does he advertise?"

"He helps startups. The food industry, mainly."

"Ever heard of Finger Lickin' Fried Chicken?"

Mrs. Norell nodded. "On the other side of town. We never go there, and I'm pretty sure he's never worked with them."

"What about Earle Gotting?" Jess asked. "Do you know him?"

Her eyes widened. "No. Was he the one who shot at my husband?"

"We don't believe so," Fernandez replied. "Did your husband sell a car recently?"

Mrs. Norell shook her head. "No. We bought new SUVs a couple of years ago. Traded in our previous pair."

"Has your husband ever owned an Audi?"

"No."

"Do you know anyone who owns a white Toyota?"

"I gave the police a list. Three people. The Hammonds, the Worlockers, and the Riveras. But I really don't think any of them would shoot anyone, let alone Zander. We've known each other for years."

"What work did your husband do before internet advertising?" Jess asked.

"Different things. Flipped houses for a few years until the recession. Then he owned a sandwich shop." She stopped for a deep breath. "He always says you have to work for yourself if you're going to make money. But that was years ago. I really don't think it was anything to do with the sandwich shop. Do you?"

Jess asked, "You don't work with him, I guess?"

She shook her head. "Zander is very particular. We agreed early on that we shouldn't work together. Spoils a relationship, you know?"

Jess paused. "Have you had any unusual visitors lately?"

Mrs. Norell's eyes narrowed. "What do you mean by unusual?"

"People you haven't seen before, people who live a long way away. That sort of thing."

She shook her head slowly. "No."

"You're sure."

"Positive." Norell pushed her chair backward. Her bottom lip quivered. "This has been very frightening. You always think these things happen to other people, but…"

"Yes." Jess stood. "One last question. Does your husband have an office?"

Mrs. Norell stood. "He works from one of the bedrooms upstairs."

"We'd like to take a look," Fernandez said.

Mrs. Norell took a deep breath. "Zander doesn't like people in his office. He likes to keep everything organized. He doesn't even like me to go in there. I'm sorry. No."

CHAPTER THIRTY-NINE

Tuesday, November 28
3:40 p.m.
Kansas City, Kansas

JESS AND FERNANDEZ SAT in the Crown Victoria. The heater blew a good stream of warm air.

"She's lying," Jess said, watching the house.

Fernandez nodded. "She's definitely had visitors she didn't want to tell us about."

"I don't think it was the man who kidnapped Norell." Jess cocked her head.

"She didn't know who was in the SUV with him. We could try the neighbors."

Jess nodded her agreement. "What about the Audi? Does she really not know who owns it now? Or was all that stuff about matching SUVs a bit of misdirection?"

"Hard to believe she doesn't know what happened to the Audi. It must have been stored somewhere. I'll run a check on rental garages." Fernandez scribbled in a notebook.

Jess cocked her head, thinking aloud. "Why did he sell the Audi to Gotting?"

"Might have been a payoff." Fernandez wrote in his notebook. "We'll check Norell's bank account. He owns his own business. Plenty of opportunity for financial creativity."

Jess thought aloud. "So Norell is blackmailed by Gotting and kidnapped by someone else? That's hard to believe. All of this is tied together somehow. But how does all of this relate to my son and the guy trying to blackmail me?"

Fernandez shrugged and opened his door. "Let's try the neighbors."

CHAPTER FORTY

Tuesday, November 28
3:50 p.m.
Kansas City, Kansas

METCALFE HOPPED THE FENCE at the scrap yard, found a car with an intact license plate, swapped it with the Volkswagen's, and minutes later they headed back into Kansas City.

"If you need a weapon, I'll give you one. But don't you go getting any ideas," Metcalfe said with a scowl. He held both hands out in front of him for emphasis. "I can wring your neck."

"I haven't forgotten," Hallman said. "We need to work as a team if we're going to get the money from Kimball and avoid the FBI."

"What do they know?"

"My crystal ball's a little cloudy," he replied. When Metcalfe frowned, he shrugged. "Nothing I guess. Otherwise we'd be in custody, wouldn't we? But Norell could have told them about the lawyer he used to sell the boy, I guess."

Metcalfe shook his head. "Not likely. He's not an idiot. He was selling babies. Takes a cold-hearted bastard to do that."

Hallman shrugged. "He didn't seem like a fighter. They lean on him and he'll fold like a step ladder."

Metcalfe scowled and fell silent for a while. "You got a plan for the handover?"

Metcalfe was beginning to think ahead, which wasn't a good thing. Hallman had spent six long months planning this. He wouldn't give up his hard work to Metcalfe unless he had to.

He shook his head. "Have to find the kid first. After that we'll work something out, depending on where and when we find him."

"You know the right lawyer?"

"I think so."

"What if the lawyer doesn't know where the boy is?" Metcalfe said.

"He's a lawyer. He can find him. Look him up on a database or something."

"And if he can't?"

Hallman shrugged. It was a stupid question.

"You got a backup plan?" Metcalfe said.

Hallman played dumb. "Use one of those online lookup places, maybe?"

Metcalfe changed lanes to go around an eighteen-wheeler. "We're going to need his Social Security number, and anything else we can get."

"The lawyer will have records. Lawyers are packrats."

"You better hope so," Metcalfe growled.

They drove on in silence. Hallman knew if they came to a dead end with the lawyer, the plan was finished. And if the plan was finished, so was he. He found himself hoping that the lawyer would be worth it, even as he knew lawyers never were.

The right lawyer lived in Mission Hills, an upscale area of the city. Tree-lined avenues, manicured lawns, houses tidy and ready for magazine features.

The home was a sprawling single-story building with a detached garage and a low, white picket fence.

The house walls were painted brick, a light cream that contrasted with the dark green fake shutters adorning the windows, and the large porch covering the front door.

The street was deserted. No one parked on the road. Probably something to do with the homeowner's association.

Metcalfe drove past, traveling the speed limit. Hallman looked over the houses and lawns on the street. He twisted to look behind the trees as they passed.

"Nothing," he said.

Metcalfe looped around the street behind the house and parked by the garage. A single small light hung over a side door with a frosted glass pane.

"One at a time," Metcalfe said.

Hallman knew what he meant. One stranger was less threatening than two, but once one was inside the second could enter easily.

Metcalfe stood against the wall, several paces away from the door, well out of sight when the owner opened the door.

Hallman put his ear to the door and rang the bell. A muffled tune rang out inside the house.

He stepped back and waited.

He saw no movement behind the frosted glass. He rang the bell a second time. Nothing stirred. He gave it a full minute before working his way along the windows, looking for some sign that the house was occupied. No luck.

"Norell told me the guy was single. Probably still at work," Metcalfe said. "Get back in the car."

He drove to the street behind the lawyer's house. The plots were large, the houses well separated. He parked by a hedge directly behind the residence they were watching.

They walked around to the garage. Hallman scanned the area. On foot, they were easy prey for the cops. His hands felt clammy and his shirt stuck to his back.

"Anything goes south and we exit through the rear," Metcalfe said, tilting his head in that direction as they walked up the lawyer's driveway. "Straight over the fence and into the car. By the time anyone around here notices, we'll be gone."

"We're going to sit here and wait?" Hallman said.

"You got something better to do?"

Hallman found a side door into the garage. He glanced over the neighboring houses before slamming his weight into the door. It creaked and cracked, but the lock held. He leaned against it until it gave.

There were no windows and the garage was dark. A Chevrolet Suburban filled one space, the other was empty.

Shelves lined the walls and garden tools hung in neat lines. A large wood and metal workbench was filled with empty plant pots.

On either side of the roll-up doors was a wide section of wall. Anyone standing there would be hidden until the car was in the garage. Metcalfe nodded his agreement.

They took up position, tucked in the corners, backs leaning against the wall. Metcalfe held up his gun and tapped it with his finger. Hallman wasn't sure if he was indicating he would use it to subdue the lawyer, but he gave him a thumbs-up.

CHAPTER FORTY-ONE

Tuesday, November 28
5:00 p.m.
Kansas City, Kansas

JESS ENTERED A SMALL room where a plainclothes detective and two FBI agents were already working. They acknowledged her when Fernandez ushered her to an empty seat.

A TV monitor showed Norell and his lawyer, Ammerson Belk, seated on one side of a small table in an interview room. The camera was high up in the corner of the room. Both men avoided looking into the lens directly.

Jess sent a text message to Morris, and stared hopefully at her phone, but received no reply. After a few moments, she put her phone away. Maybe he was resting, which was the right thing to do.

Fernandez entered the interview room and sat down on the opposite side of the table.

Belk straightened his chair and arranged a yellow legal pad on his knee to take notes.

Fernandez laid a sheaf of papers on the table and went

through the preliminaries. The clarity of his voice via the microphone and through the TV was startling. He questioned Norell about his recovery before diving into more serious issues.

"According to your statement, you entered your garage and a man attacked you."

Belk leaned forward. "Why are you holding my client?"

"We're not holding him. He was discharged from the hospital and agreed to provide a statement." Fernandez looked back at Norell. "Did you know the intruder?"

Norell shook his head. "No."

"Did you know he was in the garage before he attacked you?"

"How would I know that?"

"Was the door open? CCTV? Unfamiliar noises from inside?"

"No," Norell said.

"You said he forced you to drive your SUV, is that right?"

"Yes."

"Where did he want you to take him?"

"He just said to drive."

Fernandez nodded. "You headed downtown?"

"I thought it was better to be around other people, not miles out of town with no one around."

Belk leaned forward again. "He threatened my client with a sharpened saw. A dangerous weapon in an enclosed space. Mr. Norell was doing the sensible thing. This is all in his earlier statement to the police."

Fernandez nodded. "Why was he in your garage?"

Norell shrugged. "No idea."

"Do you keep anything special in your garage?"

"You declared the garage a crime scene and searched it

already," Belk interjected as he raised his eyebrows. "Did you find anything *special* in there?"

Fernandez ignored him and consulted his sheaf of papers. "Did you have any visitors the night before?"

Norell shook his head.

"You're sure?"

Norell nodded.

Fernandez waited.

"What?" Norell said.

Belk seemed to hear an internal alarm of some kind. He held up his hand. "My client—"

"I know my own house," Norell said, huffily.

Fernandez looked down at the papers. "Witnesses have confirmed a black BMW SUV was parked down the street from your house the night before you were attacked."

Norell snorted. "Nosy neighbors."

"The BMW remained on the street late into the night, they said."

"Do you have a point?" Belk said, seemingly irritated now. But Jess figured his reactions were all practiced and offered for show. He had to know they were being watched and the session recorded, even if his client didn't.

Fernandez kept his attention on Norell. "Do you know who was in the BMW?"

Belk shook his head. "Down the street? How is he supposed to know who visits his neighbors?"

"Mr. Norell was attacked. We're trying to find out who is responsible," Fernandez offered reasonably. "We need to be thorough, don't we?"

Belk waved the comment away. "Anything to help the police—"

"FBI."

"You haven't told us why the FBI is involved in this, anyway. Was this a federal fugitive or something?" Belk frowned, and Fernandez said nothing. "We have provided a statement—"

"And I only need a few clarifications. Just so I understand your statement. To help the FBI." He pronounced the bureau's initials slowly for emphasis.

Fernandez picked up the sheaf of papers. "The BMW was also seen earlier that morning at your house. Parked in front of your gate."

Belk pressed his lips into a thin line.

Norell stared at the table.

"Did you have a visitor last night?" Fernandez said, his voice cool and calm.

Norell took a deep breath. He glowered at Fernandez. "There was…there was someone. Bible pusher sort of guy. Trying to boost his congregation or something."

"Which church was that, sir?" Fernandez asked smoothly.

Norell shook his head. "I don't know. I wasn't interested. Sent him away. That was it."

"He didn't stay long?"

"No."

"Didn't come inside your house?"

"No."

"Okay. No one else?"

"No one."

Fernandez nodded. "Tell me what you know about Earle Gotting."

Norell took a breath before shaking his head. "Never heard of him."

"Interesting." Fernandez flipped through his papers, found the one he was looking for, and held it up. "According to county records, six months ago you transferred ownership of an Audi to him."

Norell glanced down at the table as if he was thinking really hard about the question. "I think I did sell that car around then. Maybe I did sell it to him. Sorry. Just forgot the buyer's name."

Fernandez shook the paper he was holding and leaned forward to pass it over to Belk. "According to the documents filed with the state, he purchased it from you for fifty-three thousand dollars."

Norell shrugged. "So."

"It was practically brand new."

"I didn't like it. It was…complicated."

Fernandez nodded. "Did he pay cash?"

"He doesn't have to answer that," Belk said.

"Of course, he doesn't, Mr. Belk. It's a simple enough question, though. Why wouldn't he want to help us find the man who attacked him?"

Belk leaned forward, his elbows on the table. "My client was assaulted by a madman. He was shot at and injured. He could have been killed. His vehicle was severely damaged. What we want to know is what you're doing about it?"

"We are looking for the man."

"It doesn't sound like it." Belk poked his chin out like a pugnacious bulldog.

"What does it sound like, Mr. Belk?"

Belk clamped his mouth shut a moment and made up his mind. "Mr. Norell has told you everything he knows. Unless you have anything else, he's tired. He'd like to go home."

CHAPTER FORTY-TWO

Tuesday, November 28
6:05 p.m.
Kansas City, Kansas

HALLMAN'S BACK ACHED. THE garage floor was the usual hard concrete. He'd been propped up on the floor, his back to the wall for more than an hour. He stood and stretched. His knees protested the movement. He was too old for this crap.

Metcalfe watched him. Sometimes he stared, other times he scanned the garage, but all the time Hallman knew he kept watch.

Metcalfe wore dark pants, a thick dark mid-length jacket, and heavy boots. The cold didn't seem to bother him at all. As they'd settled in their respective corners of the garage, he'd donned leather gloves and a black fleece hat.

Hallman paced the garage to get warm.

"Get back in the corner," Metcalfe said.

"I need to move. I'm seizing up."

Metcalfe stood. "Just keep your hands where I can see them."

Hallman glowered. "What kind of partnership is this? The lawyer might turn up with a friend. It's going to take both of us to get this plan done."

Metcalfe nodded slowly. "Just don't get any bright ideas, Hallman. I'd be more than happy to snap every bone in your body. Understand me?"

A car engine slowed out front and then revved. It was pulling into the driveway. The sound bounced off the walls.

Hallman pressed himself into the corner by the door and massaged the stiffness from his hands and knuckles.

Metcalfe drew his gun.

The engine stopped in the driveway. A door opened and closed.

Hallman felt for the seal around the garage doors and pried the rubber back a fraction. A Mercedes was parked by the back door into the house. A short, portly man was searching his pockets for his keys.

"It's Belk. He's not coming in the garage," Hallman whispered.

Belk let himself into the house. The lock clicked behind him.

Metcalfe hurried to the side door out of the garage.

"Wait," Hallman hissed.

Metcalfe had his hand on the door handle. "We've got to get him."

"It's too late. He's inside."

Metcalfe held up his gun with a hard glare. "We'll just knock on the door. Like we planned."

Hallman breathed out. His shoulders sagged a fraction. The adrenaline rush was fading. "Okay."

Metcalfe tucked his gun inside his jacket, they exited the side door, and took up the same positions as before, Hallman stood by the back door, and Metcalfe crouched several feet away out of sight.

Hallman rang the bell. The distorted outline of a man appeared on the other side of the frosted glass, the same heavyset guy that had climbed out of the Mercedes. Ammerson Belk.

Belk stopped a couple of feet from the door. "Who's there?"

"Is that Ammerson Belk?"

"Yes. Who are you?"

"Tim Hartly," Hallman lied.

Belk paused. "Who?"

"Zander Norell sent me."

"Who?" Belk said.

Hallman leaned close to the glass. "Norell. I have a message from him."

Belk unlocked the door as wide as the safety chain allowed. His fleshy face peered through the gap between the door and the frame. "What do you want?"

"Can I come inside?"

"No. What's the message?"

Hallman looked behind him. "Norell said not to tell you unless I was inside where no one could overhear me."

Belk scowled a moment. He slid back the chain.

Hallman stepped into a laundry room.

Metcalfe shoved Hallman into the room and darted in behind him, kicking the door closed, and pointing his gun at Belk's face. "One word and I'll blow your head off."

Belk staggered back against the washing machine, a horrified expression on his face.

"We're not here to hurt you, we just want some information," Hallman said.

Belk whimpered.

Metcalfe shook his gun in Belk's face. "Quiet."

Hallman eased Metcalfe backward and lowered his gun. "We want to talk. That's all."

Belk's lip trembled, but his whimpering stopped.

"Thirteen or fourteen years ago, Earle Gotting brought you a kid. A toddler. Not quite two years old."

Belk gave an unconvincing frown. "What is this?"

"I need to know where he is."

Belk breathed in and out with a loud hiss.

Metcalfe shoved the gun into Belk's face. "Answer the question."

Belk took a deep breath and pushed Metcalfe's gun arm back a bit. Now that he knew why they were there, he seemed to think he was in charge. "First, I don't even know who Earle Gotting is. And he certainly never gave me any kid. You've got the wrong guy. Sorry."

"Norell brought him to you. We know all about it. You and Norell." Hallman glanced at Metcalfe, who shoved the gun into Belk's pudgy neck.

Belk snorted and pushed the gun away again, trying to act cool. But Hallman saw his pulse jump at the vein on his right temple. "Okay. But I never knew the names. Another layer, you know?"

Hallman sneered. "Right. You arranged *private legal adoptions* without knowing the kids' names? Not a chance."

Belk pressed his lips into a thin line before he spoke. "What's this about? You can't blackmail me."

"We could blackmail you forever. But we won't. We want the kid. Then we'll go."

"Why now? After thirteen years?"

Hallman stared at him.

"Well it doesn't matter," Belk said. "I didn't have the names. I can't help you."

"It was thirteen years ago. June or July. You don't need the name," Hallman said.

Metcalfe waved his gun.

Belk sighed. "I don't have that information here."

"Then get it," Hallman said.

Metcalfe shoved the gun into Belk's hefty belly. "Now."

"Those records are in storage. Probably destroyed. It would take me a while to find them if they still exist." Belk shook his head. "I would have to go to the office. I don't keep things like that here at the house."

Metcalfe dragged Belk by the collar and shoved him toward the door. "Welcome to the wonderful world of overtime."

CHAPTER FORTY-THREE

Tuesday, November 28
6:40 p.m.
Kansas City, Kansas

METCALFE HELD HIS GUN in front of Belk's face. "You know what a 9mm round does to your body?"

Belk shook his head a fraction.

"It cuts a huge hole. The force of the impact from this range is like being hit by a truck. Rapid loss of blood." Metcalfe looked around. "Make a huge mess in here, for sure."

Belk stared at the gun.

"You do one stupid thing, and it'll happen to you. Bang. You'll be dead." Metcalfe pushed the barrel of the gun into Belk's forehead. "You understand?"

Belk leaned back, nodding, and swallowed hard. "I have a key. I can get in my office."

A broad smile spread across Metcalfe's face, and he stepped back, sweeping his arm in a wide arc toward the back door. "Then let's go."

Outside, Metcalfe pushed Belk toward the garage. "We'll take the Suburban."

"I'll have to move the Mercedes," Belk sputtered.

Metcalfe shook his head. "Suburban's four-wheel drive. Drive around on the grass."

They mounted the Suburban, Belk in the driver's seat. Metcalfe held the gun on him from the passenger seat. Hallman claimed the rear bench. The Suburban bumped over the drop from the driveway into a flower bed as Belk veered around the Mercedes on the lawn. The wheels scrabbled to climb back onto the concrete at the end of the driveway.

"Easy," Metcalfe said. "There's no emergency."

Belk drove downtown, stopping for the traffic lights and traveling below the speed limit all the way. In the midst of the towers in the center of town, Belk chose the entrance into an underground parking lot. He waved a card at the barrier, and after it lifted, he parked near the elevators.

Metcalfe put the gun in his jacket pocket. "One dumb move and you're dead. You got it?"

Belk nodded.

"Then let's go."

The elevator walls were metal plated, marked by gouges and scratches. Metcalfe stood behind Belk and Hallman.

There were only three buttons, two parking levels and a foyer.

Belk's finger hovered over the foyer button. "We'll have to change elevators. My office is on the eleventh floor. There might be people working."

Metcalfe poked the gun into Belk's back. "Make small talk. Like we're friends."

Hallman had the feeling Belk never made small talk because he looked like the concept was completely foreign to him. But he nodded anyway.

The elevator rose with a jolt and stopped the same way. The parking lot elevator opened in one corner of a large lobby. The front of the building was glass. Ficus plants dotted the space and water trickled down a fountain sculpture. The elevators to the upper floors were on the opposite wall behind a circular reception desk.

A security guard watched the group exit the elevator. He stood at the sight of Belk, his face showing some recognition. "Mr. Belk, everything okay?"

Belk cleared his throat. "Yes. No problem."

"You're working late?"

Belk made for the upper elevators and pressed the call button. "Actually, on our way to dinner. Just had to pick up some papers."

"Anywhere special?" the guard said.

Hallman watched a counter above the elevator doors click down. Eight, seven, six…

"Bergan's. The steak place."

"Nice." The guard shifted his weight. "And everything's okay?"

Belk nodded. "College reunion." He gestured to Metcalfe and Hallman. "We went to Cornell together."

"Right." The guard sat down. "Nice."

A bell chimed. The elevator doors opened. Hallman kept an impassive smile until the doors were closed.

Metcalfe rammed his gun into Belk's ribs and slammed him against the wall. "Why didn't you tell us there was a guard?"

Belk squirmed.

Metcalfe grabbed Belk's face, squeezing his fingers into his cheeks. "You think that's clever, don't you? Well, you think on this. Another surprise and I'm going shoot everyone in the room." He shook his gun. "Fifteen rounds. No chance I'll miss."

Belk twisted his head, unsuccessfully trying to free his face from Metcalfe's grip. "I didn't think. I—"

"No, you didn't think. Next time, everyone dies." Metcalfe shoved the gun into Belk's gut. Hard. "Got it?"

Hallman shifted his weight. The last thing he wanted was a murder on his hands. He wanted to collect his money and go. That's all. "We don't want anyone to die. Give us what we need and we're gone."

Metcalfe looked at him and Hallman's gut twisted. But Belk was alive. Right now, anyway.

Even as they all knew it wouldn't happen, Hallman said, "We just want to know where the boy is now, we drop you off back at your house, and we're gone."

Metcalfe nodded. "Yeah. Right… We're not going to hurt anyone unless you force us to." He let go of Belk as the elevator slowed.

Belk straightened his clothes. "There will be a few people around. Just follow me into my office."

The elevator opened into a small lobby area. Behind an empty receptionist's desk was a corridor. Belk walked down the corridor to a door with his name on it. He unlocked it with a key, and Hallman followed Metcalfe inside.

The office was long and narrow. A table and four chairs occupied the space by the door. At the far end was a large desk with a computer on the right side. One wall was lined with books.

Metcalfe took up a position at the door. Belk sat at his desk,

Hallman stood behind him to watch what he did with the computer.

Belk logged into the company's database tools. He brought up a file and copied a Social Security number onto a notepad. Then he put the number into another search tool. The cursor turned into a spinning beach ball.

"It might take a while," he said. He took a deep breath. "I can get a ride. You can take the Suburban. You can have it if you want. Get on your way."

"Our car is parked at your house," Hallman said.

"Oh. Right." Belk sighed. "Okay."

The computer screen flashed up a name and address. Belk wrote a Colorado Springs address on the sheet of paper. "That's the last known address. He probably still lives there. But it's not like I checked up on him or anything."

Hallman verified that the address Belk wrote down matched the one on the computer screen, folded the paper, and stuffed it into his pocket.

Metcalfe patted Belk on the shoulder. "If this works out, we'll never meet again."

"I sincerely hope so," Belk said.

"All you've got to do is walk out of here with us. Nice and easy."

Belk led the way back to the elevator. A woman in a dark blue pantsuit rode down in the elevator with them. She eyed Metcalfe and Hallman but didn't speak. In the reception area, she walked out of the front of the building.

The security guard stood. "All done?"

"Yep," Belk said.

"Enjoy your meal at...where was it?"

"Bergan's," Belk said.

"Right. Yes. The steak place. Should be good."

The security guard sat down.

Damn rent-a-cops, Hallman thought.

They rode the elevator down to the parking levels in silence.

Hallman scanned the area as they walked through the garage to the Suburban.

They left the underground garage in silence, Belk behind the wheel and Metcalfe holding the gun.

CHAPTER FORTY-FOUR

Tuesday, November 28
6:45 p.m.
Kansas City, Kansas

FERNANDEZ'S OFFICE WAS IN a line with a dozen other offices along one side of a downtown office tower. The furniture was standard metal and government-issue plastic laminate in a uniform gray. Non-descript and totally forgettable.

The office was separated from the workers' cube-farm by a glass wall. Weirdly, the door in the glass wall was wood. Or at least, something that looked like wood.

Jess sat with her back to the glass, aware that several eyes were on her back.

"Bible pusher," Fernandez said derisively. He sat on a low ledge by the window. "Can you believe that guy?"

"Norell? He lied the whole time," Jess said.

Fernandez nodded. "He knew the guy in the garage, and he knew where he was going."

"I agree. You gave up on the Audi. Why?" Jess asked.

He shook his head. "Simpler to get bank records. Criminals like Norell don't confess, regardless of how it works on TV."

Jess nodded. "And kidnapped with a saw? That's a new one on me. I figure the kidnapper wasn't prepared. The weapon was improvised."

"Norell surprised him?"

She shook her head. "In the middle of what? Robbing the garage? Stealing a car? A simple theft doesn't just turn into a kidnapping, does it?"

"Not usually, no." Fernandez drummed his fingers on the window ledge. "We're getting Norell and Gotting's bank records. Won't be available until tomorrow." He looked at Jess. "You should get some food and sleep. Nothing much will happen for the rest of the night. You'll need to be ready for tomorrow."

It was the last thing she felt like doing, but he had a good point. Jess stood to leave.

Fernandez's desk phone rang. Lines wrinkled his forehead as he listened. He put the phone down and stood. "KCPD just had a call from security at the office tower where Belk works. Apparently, he arrived with a couple of thugs. Belk said they were on their way to dinner at Bergan's. A fancy place downtown that requires a reservation, and a coat and tie. They were acting odd, so the guard called the restaurant and they don't have a reservation."

"Who were the two guys with him?" Jess asked.

"A KCPD officer reviewed the CCTV video. One of the thugs was Henrik Metcalfe. He's managed to evade jail time by dumb luck. And I mean dumb."

"Lawyers like Belk tend to meet a lot of criminals," Jess said. "Comes with the job, doesn't it?"

"He must have met up with these two right after he left here."

Jess nodded. "Either a busy schedule or dumb luck, as you said."

She fished out her phone and did a quick search for Ammerson Belk on the internet. Several pages of hits came up. He worked for a firm with a double-barreled name, Somersall-McCree. She clicked on the link for his biography. It was long. "This is weird."

She scrolled to the top of the page and clicked on the link for images. Definitely him. "Ammerson Belk practices family law."

"So?"

She scrolled up and down the page looking for anything that wasn't family law related and found nothing.

Jess cocked her head. "Remember Mrs. Norell said Belk represented her husband's business?"

"If you're thinking of questioning him, he's probably going to complain about harassment or police pressure if we haul him in again," Fernandez said.

"But he doesn't practice corporate law or criminal cases. There's no way he's going to dabble in cases like that," Jess said slowly. "And family law? Don't forget that I'm looking for my son. I can legitimately ask him for help."

Fernandez nodded his head sagely for a few moments. He grabbed up his car keys. "Okay. Let's go stake out his house."

CHAPTER FORTY-FIVE

Tuesday, November 28
7:00 p.m.
Kansas City, Kansas

BELK STEERED THE SUBURBAN up his driveway, bumped onto the lawn to go around the Mercedes, and into the garage.

Metcalfe pressed the button for the doors to close and waited until they hit the pavement to exit the SUV.

Belk got out after Hallman. He stood still by the driver's door. "You've got what you wanted."

Hallman nodded. "We're good."

Metcalfe picked up a roll of duct tape and a spool of green gardening twine. He unrolled a length as he walked around the big SUV.

Belk stepped back and dove for a tool chest. He yanked open a drawer and pulled out a gun.

Hallman stepped backward.

Metcalfe took two steps forward, grabbed Belk's arm and twisted it up and back, high and hard. Belk yelped in pain.

Metcalfe pried the gun from Belk's fingers. "All we're going to do is tie you up until we're on our way."

Belk shrugged and offered a single nod in surrender.

Metcalfe dropped the gun into his pocket and slapped a width of duct tape across Belk's mouth before he released his grip on Belk's arm.

"Put your hands out," Metcalfe said.

Defeated, Belk offered his hands, wrists touching.

With one swift flick, Metcalfe looped the twine over Belk's head.

Belk twisted and jerked back.

Metcalfe whipped the twine into a garrote around Belk's neck.

Belk swung his arms, grunting and choking as he landed ineffectual punches on Metcalfe's shoulders.

"No," Hallman said.

Metcalfe wrapped the twine around the spool, multiplying his leverage on the weak threads. He twisted the spool, tightening the twine.

Hallman stepped forward. "Stop. We can tie him up and take him with us."

Belk's fingers tore at his neck, digging into the flesh in a futile effort to get inside the band of twine and loosen it enough to breathe.

Metcalfe grunted with effort. "Don't be stupid. He knows us. Knows who we're looking for."

"Then put him in the Suburban," Hallman suggested. He'd done many things in his life, but he'd never murdered anyone. He hadn't counted on killing Belk, either.

Belk collapsed to his knees. His eyes bulged out of his head. His hands feebly patted at his neck.

Metcalfe shook his head, tugging tight on the twine. "Too much baggage. We have to cut off the trail. Stop anyone from coming after us."

"But he isn't going to tell anyone. He'll go to prison right along with us if he does. The guy's been selling babies. They'll never let him breathe free air again," Hallman said.

Belk's head lolled over. His arms fell to his sides.

"Don't be stupid," Metcalfe growled. "I traced you through Gotting and Norell. Cops are doing the same. The trail ends here. Now."

Hallman watched, horrified, as the life drained from the lawyer's body. He staggered back, knocking over the plants, pots, and gardening tools.

Belk's head hung forward, the twine buried inside a livid red line around his neck. His arms became limp and lifeless. Metcalfe held the body up against its weight, tugging the twine as hard as he could pull it.

"You don't have to do this," Hallman said, weakly, knowing Metcalfe wouldn't stop.

Metcalfe finally released the twine with a grunt. Belk flopped forward and crumpled face down on the concrete. His heart had stopped pumping. His nose smashed against the hard surface and a pool of blood drained by gravity onto the floor as another dribble oozed from the line on his neck.

Metcalfe rubbed his hands together, massaging where the twine had made deep purple grooves on his skin. "This is better. Trust me. Now we don't need to be concerned about him."

Hallman stared at Belk, the spool of green twine still wrapped around his fleshy, mottled neck. He'd died in a few seconds. Metcalfe had turned the harmless garden twine into a silent, unstoppable, deadly weapon.

With a soft click, the automatic timer on the garage door light went out.

Metcalfe's shoes thumped on the concrete floor as he dragged Belk's body deeper into the darkness behind a workbench.

Hallman worked his way around the Suburban in the dark, his hands on the side of the vehicle. His eyes failed to adjust to the faint light from around the side door, causing him to stumble over the pots and tools he'd knocked over earlier. He fell to the floor.

"Get up from there. Let's go," Metcalfe said, rubbing the dust off his hands and knocking the dirt off his coat. His voice suggested he was moving toward the side door, but Hallman couldn't see him.

Hallman's blood fizzed in his veins. He felt light-headed. Metcalfe was more than a thug. He was a cold-blooded killer. Part of the job. Belk was merely a task he could mark off his to-do list. The knowledge chilled him because Hallman knew his name was on the same list.

He swallowed hard. How long did he have to figure out a way to save himself from Belk's fate?

He ran his hands over the tools on the ground. He picked up a pronged garden fork with a long wooden handle and a strong plastic grip.

The thin light entering from around the broken side door revealed Metcalfe's shadow. "What are you doing? Come on. We've got to get out of here before someone shows up."

Hallman lunged. The fork's tines first. One hand guiding the wooden shaft, the other clamped on the D-shaped handle. He crossed the six feet of open space between them in a fraction of a second.

Metcalfe lurched to one side. He was too late. The spiked garden fork's tines struck him at waist height, scraping over the bones in his hip, and spearing into the soft organs under his ribs.

A grunting, squealing sound, part guttural anger, part high-pitched shock, pierced the silence.

Metcalfe's momentum and weight pulled at the fork. Hallman gripped hard to hold on, feeling the soft tissues give. One of Metcalfe's ribs cracked.

Hallman gawked at Metcalfe's doubled-up body, mesmerized by the gushing blood running down his side.

He twisted the fork.

Metcalfe screamed. Hard, loud, and powerful.

Hallman leaned into the fork, ramming it deeper into Metcalf's flesh.

Metcalfe found the strength to pull Belk's gun from his pocket.

Hallman shoved the fork hard to thrust him aside, smacking his head into the shelving along the wall.

Metcalfe's trigger finger jerked and the gun fired loud enough for the whole neighborhood to hear. The blast ricocheted off the concrete and rang in Hallman's ears.

The single gun flash seared the image of Metcalfe's grotesque grimace into Hallman's brain.

The fork was in Metcalfe's side. Deep. Unnatural. Terrifying. Blood soaked his jeans, splashed onto his shoes and ran onto the floor. So much blood. Pools of it, spreading everywhere.

Hallman fought back the urge to retch. He doubled his grip on the fork and twisted violently. Metcalfe groaned. *How could he still be alive?*

Hallman lashed out and kicked the gun from Metcalfe's hand with his boot. The weapon clattered across the bloody ground.

Metcalfe collapsed, the weight of his body pulling on the fork.

Still holding the fork with both hands, Hallman stepped to the gun, levering Metcalfe's body in an arc as he walked. Metcalfe screamed.

In one movement, keeping the pressure on the fork, Hallman knelt down, grabbed the gun from the bloody pool, and stood up.

Metcalfe stretched out a weak arm, his fingers twitching, too weakened to speak.

Hallman lurched backward, careful to stay out of Metcalfe's reach. He brought the gun up. Metcalfe's wound was horrific, the quantity of blood shocking, but he was a terrifying opponent.

He raised his bloody head and glared at Hallman, leaving no doubt Metcalfe would kill him, given a chance.

Hallman pulled the trigger. The gun bucked in his hand. The noise pounded off the walls. Light flashed long enough to blind him.

When his vision returned, he saw Metcalfe's blood splattered across the wall.

He choked back the bile rising in his throat. The handle of the fork twisted in his hand, as Metcalfe's dead weight levered it around.

Hallman let go.

Metcalfe's lifeless body slumped backward to the ground, dragging the fork with it.

Hallman's stomach churned at the mangled mess of what had once been human that was on the floor. In a reflective action, he twisted away and retched.

He staggered back, wiping his mouth and forehead, panting.

He hadn't planned for murder. Now he'd witnessed one and committed another.

He felt the cold sweat that bathed his entire body. The next thing he heard were several sirens approaching.

One of the neighbors must have reported the gunshots. The police would come in armed and pumped. He had only moments to get the hell out of there.

He stepped between splashes of blood, and around the fork jutting from Metcalfe's body. He bent and dug through the dead man's pockets for the Volkswagen keys.

The sirens grew louder by the second.

He had to clean his prints from the fork and gun. But how? He had no time to clean up anything.

He bent down, grabbed the fork, and yanked it from the lifeless body.

Without looking back, he wiped the side door's handle with his sleeve and stepped out of the garage.

The sirens were close. Red and blue lights were on the street, racing his way.

The only way out was across the back of the property like Metcalfe had said.

The first police car bounced up the driveway, braking on the other side of the Mercedes.

The headlight beam splashed over him.

He turned and ran before the squad car had a chance to stop.

CHAPTER FORTY-SIX

Tuesday, November 28
7:05 p.m.
Kansas City, Kansas

FERNANDEZ SPED ALONG THE freeway toward Belk's house. As he turned off onto the side street, he heard a flurry of cryptic talk on the radio. He turned up the volume just as the dispatcher repeated the address of a shooting.

"Belk's place," Jess said.

The dispatcher identified two squad cars responding. Fernandez cursed when he heard the sirens. "Nothing like giving the guy time to run."

He fishtailed the Crown Vic around a corner. "You're an observer. Got it?"

"You're not leaving me out of this," Jess said.

"I have no choice. I can't take you into an active shooter situation. I'll lose my job, at the very least." He braked to a halt.

Jess scowled. "Where are we?"

"Belk's place is two blocks away. Stay here until I tell you it's safe. Then you can walk over." When she made no move to get out of the car, he said, "You're wasting time."

She got out and slammed the door. He screamed away.

She heard the sirens approaching, but the echoes and distance made it hard to tell how far away they were.

The night air was crisp. The cold edged in through her jacket. Street lights lit the treetops, throwing strange shadow patterns on the sidewalk. She walked in the direction Fernandez had taken. She'd stay out of the line of fire, but she couldn't wait for him to come back. Hell, the shooter could be running toward her for all she knew.

At the corner, she looked in all directions but saw no sign of Fernandez's car. She turned left because she thought she'd seen him go in that direction.

The houses were large, set well back from the road. Lights glowed from windows or spilled around drapes. Occasionally vehicles passed by, turning into driveways and disappearing under automatic garage doors.

A shot rang out. She stopped in her tracks. More shots followed. The sound reverberated off the homes in the still night air. She couldn't pinpoint the location of the gunshots.

Jess jogged in the general direction of the noise. She took a right, picking up speed.

Ahead, she saw a man race down a driveway and across the neighbor's lawn.

Jess ran toward him, wishing she had her gun. Tackling a man running from the FBI would be too dangerous to try. If she could keep track of him until Fernandez arrived, that would help.

The man reached the fence at the edge of the backyard. He stood there briefly before he reversed direction.

Jess stopped. He was running directly for her, a garden fork waving in his hand. But she could barely see him in the dark. Maybe he couldn't see her at all.

She moved back, deeper into the shadow of a tree.

At the near side of the lawn, he reached a Volkswagen parked close to a streetlight. He ripped open the rear door and threw the big fork inside. He slammed the door.

She recognized him. She'd seen him before. Jess grabbed her phone and opened the camera. She clicked off a dozen pictures. He was the man she'd seen behind the tree when Morris was shot.

She gasped. He heard her. He swiveled his head and stared at her across the distance, as if he recognized her, too.

He pulled a gun from the belt of his jeans and ran straight for her. "Give me the phone." He waved the gun. "Give me the phone."

Fernandez shouted something in the distance. Flashing lights lit the rooftops behind her. The lights and sirens spooked him.

Instead of shooting her, he shook the gun at her. "Get the money. You want your kid alive, get the money."

He didn't shoot her because he wanted her alive. He still thought she'd pay him for Peter. And he was right.

Jess cocked her head and raised her phone to take a video this time. He turned and ran for the open door of the Volkswagen.

She ran after him, holding the camera on her phone aimed his way.

The car door slammed shut before she reached it. The engine roared to life and he drove off, the front wheels scrabbling for grip.

"Fernandez!" she screamed, holding the camera steadily aimed at the Volkswagen's retreating tail lights.

Two officers ran toward her, weapons drawn.

She pointed down the road. "Volkswagen Jetta. That way!"

One uniformed officer stopped and voiced a short radio report. The other officer ran farther down the road.

Fernandez's Crown Vic screamed around the corner. She stepped onto the side of the road, waving her arms. Fernandez stopped and she jumped in.

A squad car raced by, tracing the direction the Volkswagen had taken. Fernandez followed.

At the end of the street, they saw no sign of the Volkswagen. The squad car went right, Fernandez turned left.

The radio crackled with messages and reports.

"He was the man from the drive-by," Jess said, breathing hard and gulping air between sentences. "The one behind the tree. He knew who I was. He told me I should get the money. He must be the blackmailer."

Fernandez slowed as they passed an intersection. She scanned the streets on either side, looking for the Volkswagen's tail lights.

"He had a garden fork," Jess said. "Blood all over it."

Fernandez raced to the next intersection. "There were two corpses in the garage. He probably killed one of them with it, from the looks of the body."

Jess inhaled sharply.

Two squad cars crossed in front of them at the next intersection.

A burst of chatter on the radio indicated the Volkswagen had been spotted heading east, the opposite direction from their search. A squad car raced by on the other side of the road, siren on and lights blazing.

Jess found the portable light and attached it to the roof as Fernandez hung a U-turn and raced after the squad car.

CHAPTER FORTY-SEVEN

Tuesday, November 28
7:20 p.m.
Kansas City, Kansas

JESS BROUGHT UP A map of the area on her phone. The chatter on the police radio was confused and confusing. After a few moments, she scrolled her map north and found the last street named by the dispatcher.

"Left," she said.

"The cruiser's going straight," he replied.

"Left is quicker."

Fernandez swung through the intersection and floored it along a wide street. The shops were long closed and the sidewalks deserted. Street lights whipped by.

The road ahead forked at a traffic light. "Right," Jess said.

Fernandez slowed and rolled through the light waiting and watching the other traffic until everyone was aware of his presence. The road narrowed. Fernandez stayed clear of the cars lining one side of the street.

The radio crackled with the dispatcher identifying a new intersection name.

Jess scanned her map. "Straight ahead."

"Where's he going?"

"Hard to say. Interstate 435 maybe? Onto 35?"

"If he takes a freeway, we've got him."

"He's a mile from 435."

The dispatcher issued another update.

Jess scrolled east to find the location. "Second left."

Fernandez crossed the intersection at full speed. The Crown Vic's tires squealed in complaint. Red and blue lights reflected off the buildings on all sides of the street.

A block ahead, the Volkswagen raced across the street. A trio of cruisers in pursuit.

Fernandez hammered the brakes and angled the Crown Vic to follow.

Civilian traffic weaved as the Volkswagen tore by and police lights filled their rearview mirrors. Fernandez stayed close to the last cruiser.

With most of his escape routes blocked, the Volkswagen driver jinked into oncoming traffic. Cars swerved in all directions. The Volkswagen reached the opposite side of the road.

"Left now," Jess said, breathlessly, hanging on to the dash.

Fernandez turned hard, the tail of the Crown Vic sliding until it bounced off the curb. The car fishtailed as he raced for the next junction.

"Right," Jess said, more urgently.

Fernandez took the corner without question.

The Volkswagen raced toward them on the wrong side of the road. Fernandez grabbed the handbrake and slewed the rear of the car around. He floored the accelerator and the big car lurched forward, matching the speed of the passing Volkswagen. He eased away at the sight of pedestrians running for shelter in doorways and alleyways.

The Volkswagen blew through the next light. It hit the curb on the far side, bouncing hard and almost coming to a stop.

Farther down the street, road construction zones were ringed by orange cones and striped barriers. Fernandez raced past the Volkswagen. He wedged his foot hard on the brake pedal. The Crown Vic rocked on its suspension and blocked half the road.

Smoke drifted from the Volkswagen's front wheels as the driver floored the accelerator, angling to go around the Crown Vic.

A cruiser whipped by and threw itself in the Volkswagen's path.

The Volkswagen scrabbled onto the sidewalk.

The cruiser reversed to cut off the Volkswagen's escape, but the cruiser's wheels bounced against the curb and cut off the Crown Vic.

The Volkswagen bounced off the sidewalk onto the road, engine racing.

Fernandez reversed to go around the cruiser.

Orange cones and striped barriers scattered across the street as the Volkswagen tore through them. The Volkswagen disappeared, its engine screaming.

The next thing Jess heard was a heavy impact pounding through the air. Instantly, the crushing of metal and glass assaulted her ears.

The Volkswagen's engine ground metal before coughing to silence.

Jess leaped from the Crown Vic and ran full out for the road construction zone.

The Volkswagen was on its side in a hole, six feet down. The hood was crushed. Roof staved in. Windows nothing but jagged shards of glass around the edges. The flaccid airbags flapped in the swirling air.

KCPD cops surrounded the wrecked Volkswagen. Two of them climbed down into the hole. One was able to reach through the Volkswagen's crushed windshield. After a moment, he stood up and shook his head. "No pulse."

"ID?" Jess called, yelling to be heard over the sound of approaching sirens.

The officer looked briefly at her before reluctantly leaning in through the windshield. A moment later he appeared with a handful of papers, which he must have pulled from the driver's pockets.

He stuffed them into a plastic evidence bag. "A lottery ticket. A hundred and forty dollars, and…"

"What?" Fernandez said, breathlessly.

The officer held up a pink paper. "A Humboldt Prison release form. Shane Hallman. And get this, it's dated yesterday."

Jess felt the hairs rise on the back of her neck. *Humboldt? Where Gotting served time recently, too?*

"He was released from Humboldt yesterday?" Fernandez asked.

The officer nodded. "Monday. Ten a.m."

Fernandez took the evidence bag from the officer.

Jess whispered and nodded toward the body. "He knew me. He threatened me. He kidnapped Norell, and he was at Belk's."

"And now he's dead," Fernandez said matter-of-factly.

She breathed out hard. Hallman dead? The closest she'd come to a direct link to Peter in thirteen years? Gone. Just like that.

Everything Hallman knew died with him. Wiped out, right before her eyes. She could do nothing but stare at the Volkswagen as she struggled to find another angle. Surely, he wasn't the only one who knew where Peter was. Because she felt all the way to her bones that Hallman didn't have Peter now. Perhaps he never had.

Maybe she was engaged in wishful thinking, but Gotting had to be involved in this somehow, didn't he? Gotting was the one who lived in her apartment building. Not Hallman. At least, as far as she knew now.

She turned to Fernandez. "We need to talk to Belk and Norell."

Fernandez grimaced. "No chance of talking to Belk."

Jess stared. She shook her head in disbelief. "He's dead, too?"

"Just heard." Fernandez held up his phone. "He's one of the bodies back in the garage."

Jess gritted her teeth. "These guys are killing each other off. We've got to get over there before we lose the trail for sure."

"Or we could just wait for the last man standing," Fernandez suggested.

"Yeah. But it's hard to interview the dead ones."

CHAPTER FORTY-EIGHT

Tuesday, November 28
7:40 p.m.
Kansas City, Kansas

BELK'S HOUSE WAS COVERED by a sea of flashing lights. Four police cars, two ambulances, and a couple of unmarked Fords with dome lights blazing lit up the night sky like a carnival.

Fernandez parked half a block from the other vehicles. "Let's stay out of the way until we see what's going on."

They left the Crown Vic and walked toward the driveway. Fernandez stopped at one of the cruisers and suggested they might want to cut the lights. A few moments later, the scene was eerily dark.

Officers covered all entrances to the house and grounds. Fernandez flashed his badge and pointed at Jess. "She's with me."

They walked along the side of the driveway. A Mercedes SUV was parked between the detached garage and the back door to the house.

Fernandez produced a small flashlight bright enough to be visible from the moon and shined it into the vehicle's interior, which was unoccupied. Jess put her hand on the hood. It was slightly warm. "The engine was used recently, but not too recently."

"I saw Belk drive away from our office in this SUV," Fernandez replied.

Deep tire tracks ran on the grass and flower beds, suggesting a heavy vehicle had backed out of the garage and driven around the Mercedes.

"Put your flashlight beam over here," Jess said as she knelt beside the ruts. "Large wheels. Could have been a truck, I guess."

Fernandez nodded. "Probably a full-sized SUV. Security at his firm, Somersall-McCree, said Belk arrived there in a Suburban."

"Why did he drive around the Mercedes and mess up his lawn like that?" Jess wondered aloud. She stood and dusted the dirt from her hands. "So, he comes home in the Mercedes, and they're waiting for him. He's promptly forced to leave again, this time in the Suburban?"

Fernandez said, "Makes sense. Could have happened that way."

"Have you been in the house?" Jess asked.

"Not yet. Haven't had a chance." Fernandez shook his head. "After I dropped you off, I parked in the driveway behind the cruisers, heard shots, saw the man running out the back. I circled the block and picked you up."

A uniformed KCPD officer approached. "We've called the alarm company to send a tech before we go in the house. But the garage is open. You can take a look, but it's an active crime scene."

"Understood," Fernandez said. "Thanks. What's in there besides the two bodies?"

"I want to see them," Jess said.

He replied, "One's mangled badly. You'll need a strong stomach."

Jess flashed back to the moment she saw Morris shot and all the blood on his clothes. Her skin tingled, but she squared her shoulders and marched forward.

She nodded to the officer and followed Fernandez to the side door of the garage. The frame was smashed and the door hung half-open. Fernandez handed her a pair of gloves and paper booties. She gloved up, slipped the booties over her shoes, and stepped through into the garage.

The officers had set up some lighting inside the garage. Jess saw a dark gray Suburban parked on one side and two bodies sprawled on the concrete floor. One was Belk, the other was face down in a large, congealing pool of blood.

Fernandez circled the second body, careful to stay out of the blood. "Multiple stab wounds to one side and a gunshot to the head."

Jess turned her eyes away from the horrific sight on the floor. She asked the officer, "Any ID?"

"We're waiting for a full crime scene team before we touch anything," he replied. "But I'm pretty sure it's Henrik Metcalfe. Local thug with a reputation for violence."

On the far side of the Suburban, flower pots and garden implements were piled in a heap on the floor.

"A garden fork could produce the kind of results we've got over there," Fernandez said, jerking his thumb in that direction. "And you saw Hallman running away with a garden fork. Put two and two together, Hallman was probably responsible for this."

"He didn't seem like a cold-blooded killer, though." She nodded toward the bodies. "What happened to Belk?"

Fernandez shrugged. "The marks around his neck suggest he was garroted."

"Garroted? That's an intense and close physical act. Requires a lot of guts, not to mention strength, to do something like that face-to-face," Jess said. "I don't think Hallman had it in him, either physically or mentally. He didn't seem like that kind of man to me."

"Okay." Fernandez looked at the bloody body for almost a full minute. "So the dead guy here kills Belk. And then Hallman kills Metcalfe?"

Jess cocked her head to think about it. "Hallman was definitely hiding behind the tree at the drive-by shooting. When this guy, Metcalfe, drove up in the Toyota to pick him up, he hesitated."

"So you're thinking Hallman was improvising. Making it up as he went along."

She nodded. "Gotting, Norell, Belk, and Metcalfe were connected somehow when this whole thing started. But Hallman, the one who called to blackmail me, is at the center of all of this."

"You think blackmailing you was Hallman's plan alone?" Fernandez asked.

"Makes sense, doesn't it?" she said. "Gotting had baby things at his apartment, but he doesn't have a baby. Belk was a family lawyer, an obvious link in the chain to make my son a part of another family."

Fernandez replied, "I guess it makes partial sense. Quite a few missing pieces, though."

Jess nodded. "The important thing is that Hallman was

trying to blackmail me. He wanted three million dollars. He didn't claim to have Peter. Which probably meant he knows where Peter is."

"Or thought he knew," Fernandez said.

"Or thought he could find out," Jess added and knew she was grasping. "Which means we could find out first. We have more resources than he does. Hallman might have learned about all of this from Gotting while they were in Humboldt Prison. With Hallman dead, we need to get into their backgrounds. Gotting, Belk, Metcalfe, and Norell. All of them. Work, finances, family, friends, everything. Find the connection, we'll find Gotting. Then we'll find Peter."

Fernandez said, "We're already on it. We've got guys on the way to Humboldt, too. Nothing yet."

"But there must be a connection. We just need to find it. We've got a trail of bodies. All of these men who were probably involved in Peter's kidnapping." She heard the desperation in her own voice that she'd felt every day in her heart for years.

Fernandez shook his head. "Seems like a lot of muscle for one baby."

"If it was only one baby. This seems like a broader criminal enterprise to me." She raked her hand through her hair and took a long breath. Despite the grisly scene behind her, she felt a spark of hope lighten her heart.

Fernandez nodded but didn't reply.

"Regardless, this is way more than I've ever had to go on before." She stepped out of the garage and waved to Fernandez to follow as she hurried toward his Crown Vic. "Come on. We've got a lot of work to do. Peter's waited long enough."

CHAPTER FORTY-NINE

Tuesday, November 28
8:05 p.m.
Kansas City, Kansas

FERNANDEZ CALLED TO GET a contact at Belk's offices, Somersall-McCree, and persuaded the office manager to meet him there without explaining much. He parked on the street in front of the building's entrance, which was a wall of glass. A security guard let them in when Fernandez showed his badge and directed them to the desk to wait.

A tall, thin man in a dark suit and vivid blue silk tie walked out to join them when the elevator doors opened. "Jasper Quinn. Senior partner with Somersall-McCree."

"Emilio Fernandez, FBI, and this is Jessica Kimball." They shook hands. "I'm sorry to bring you the bad news. Please keep this confidential until next of kin has been notified. Your colleague, Ammerson Belk, has died."

Quinn looked down as he paused to compose himself. He

cleared his throat. "Sorry. He's been a friend and colleague for twenty years."

"I understand." Fernandez nodded. "I'm afraid he's been murdered."

"What?" Quinn's eyes widened, and his lips pinched. "Someone killed him? But why?"

"That's what we're trying to find out. Do you have any idea who might have done this?" Fernandez asked.

Quinn shrugged. "No. But it's safe to say that lawyers rarely make all sides happy if we're doing our jobs well. Family matters like we handle here are especially difficult. People are very emotional about personal issues. You've probably seen plenty of evidence of that, yourself."

Fernandez nodded.

Jess couldn't argue, either. She'd reported way too many cases of domestic homicide to doubt the truth. "Does your firm handle family law matters exclusively?"

"Yes, but that covers a lot of ground. Family law extends to marriage, divorce, wills—"

Jess said, "Adoptions?"

"Certainly," Quinn nodded. "All the time. Across the country and the world. Adoptions are one of the happier types of legal work we do."

"Do you represent corporations?"

"You mean in adoptions? I'm not sure corporations can adopt children in this country."

"In any type of matter."

Quinn frowned. "Sure. Family owned corporations and other types of business entities. Prenuptial agreements, trusts, that sort of thing."

"I see," Jess said.

Quinn gestured toward the circular guard desk. "I understand you wanted to see what happened when Mr. Belk arrived here tonight."

The guard played recorded video of Belk arriving and leaving not very long ago. The recordings showed him in the parking lot, the foyer, and on the landing in front of the doors in his office. Two men were with him. One was Metcalfe. The second one was Hallman. Jess had seen him twice and believed he was her blackmailer. The three men talked with each other, but the recording lacked sound.

"You don't have cameras in the elevators, or in the office area?" Fernandez asked.

"The camera in the elevator isn't working," the guard said.

"And we don't believe in spying on our employees," Quinn added with a frown.

"Do you recognize either of the two men with Belk?" Jess asked.

The guard shook his head. "Never seen them before."

"I work on the top floor, so I don't generally see Mr. Belk's clients," Quinn said.

Fernandez pointed to the elevator. "We'd like to see his office."

Quinn seemed unsure. He paused briefly before he made up his mind. "You'd better come this way."

They rode up the elevator in silence. The doors opened onto a small but well-appointed reception area. A young man sat behind the receptionist's desk playing games on his phone. In one of the client chairs, a woman was reading a book. Both jumped to their feet.

Quinn introduced Barbara the receptionist and Jeremy from IT. From his tone and their terrified faces, Jess figured their employment would be terminated in the morning.

Fernandez shook his head and held out his FBI badge for Barbara and Jeremy to see. "Mr. Belk returned to the office a couple of hours ago with two men. Did either of you see them while they were here?"

Barbara shook her head. "We left to grab dinner at five-thirty. We came back twenty minutes ago because Jeremy had to check some software upgrades or something."

Jess asked Jeremy, "When Mr. Belk and the two men went into his office, can you tell us what they were doing?"

Barbara shook her head. "We don't have cameras or anything in the offices, I'm afraid."

Jeremy said, "If he used his computer, we could find some things. A keyboard logger might help, but we don't have one. It's against company policy. What we can do is find anything he looked at on the company servers. We can also track outside websites he visited. But it'll take a day or so to do any of that."

"Why so long?" Fernandez asked.

"We don't have the passwords we'd need for the routers. The guy who does is on vacation. Hiking in the Appalachians. No cell coverage for most of the time." Jeremy shrugged.

"No one else knows the passwords?" Jess asked, incredulously.

Quinn said, "They're locked down. For security. We never imagined anything would be so urgent that we'd need a backup system."

"Can you tell us what cases Belk was working on?" Fernandez asked.

"We can't disclose our clients' names or their confidences. Surely you know that would be unethical. Get a warrant, and we'd be happy to comply," Quinn said, starchily.

"He always had a lot going on," Barbara said, helpfully. "Workaholic, I thought."

"We need the names," Jess replied.

Quinn shook his head. "Sorry. Like I said, not without a warrant."

Jess spun around to face Quinn. "Belk was just garroted, minutes after he left here. One of those two men with him was murdered with a garden fork. Another man died in a traffic accident. We suspect they were all engaged in the interstate kidnapping of at least one boy. We need facts. Now. Before anyone else dies."

Quinn squared his shoulders and raised his chin to look down his patrician nose. "And you shall have the facts. When you get a warrant. It's not a matter of failing to cooperate, Ms. Kimball. I'm ethically and legally obligated to protect our clients' privacy. Ammerson Belk would certainly understand that. He wouldn't give you that information, either."

Jess turned back to Barbara. "We need to see Belk's office."

Barbara led the way down the corridor to the door. She opened it and stood aside, allowing them to enter.

The office was long and narrow. Golden tan carpet and dark, fine-grained wood furniture. A table for meetings was closest to the door, and farther back was a large desk with a computer. The office smelled musty as if the door was closed most of the time, which it probably was.

Fernandez told the employees to stay out of the room.

Jess walked in and began to look around. She didn't touch anything because she didn't have another pair of gloves.

One wall was lined with neatly arranged books. Large collections bound in matching covers with long titles that she'd never heard of. She skimmed over them but saw nothing out of place.

The room was immaculate, no pens or paper anywhere. "Why is there nothing on his desk?" she asked.

"The firm's policy. To protect client confidentiality." Barbara said from the doorway.

The computer was cold. Jess looked at Jeremy. "You can't find anything in his browsing history?"

Jeremy shook his head. "It gets deleted every twenty minutes. Privacy."

Jess sighed. "Let me guess. The firm's policy."

Jeremy offered a restrained smile.

"Do you know what cases Ammerson was working on?" Jess asked Barbara.

Barbara nodded.

"Do the names Gotting, Norell, or Hallman mean anything to you?"

"No," Barbara said.

"Kimball? Peter Kimball?"

Barbara shook her head.

"Can we see the records for his cases from thirteen to fourteen years ago?"

Quinn said, "Not without a warrant."

Jess wanted to throttle him.

"Even if you had access to the records, they wouldn't tell you much," Jeremy said. "Years ago, the firm had a big server. Kept everyone's work in one place. When it died, they discovered the backup system wasn't working."

"What do you mean, wasn't working? As in everything on the whole server was lost?" Jess asked.

Jeremy shrugged. "I wasn't here then."

"We have the paper records in the basement, though," Barbara said.

"Can we see them?" Fernandez asked. Before Quinn spouted off about the warrant again, he added, "We'll need to describe what we want for our warrant."

Quinn nodded, but he didn't look happy about it.

They rode the elevator to the lobby. Fernandez put his hand on Quinn's arm. "I have something to discuss with Mr. Quinn and Jeremy. You go ahead with Barbara, Jess. Make a list so we'll have what we need for the judge."

Jess nodded and followed Barbara through a door and down two more flights of stairs. The last flight was an open staircase with a handrail on either side.

When they reached the bottom of the stairs, she realized the basement was huge. It must have occupied at least half the area of the building. Stacks of bookshelves were lined up and disappeared into the distance.

Barbara saw her staring at the stacks. "Somersall-McCree has more than a hundred lawyers. We generate a lot of paper. You'd be lost down here for days if you tried to find those old files on your own."

Barbara led her to a table surrounded by filing cabinets. She worked her way around the cabinets and found the one she wanted. She opened the third drawer down and pulled out a thick handful of papers from the rear.

"I know who you are. I've followed your search for your son for a long time. I'm so sorry." She gave Jess a knowing, sympathetic look. "Is it your boy you're looking for, Jess?"

Jess nodded, surprised when tears welled in her eyes. She was tired. That's all. She'd cried all the tears she had in her body for Peter long, long ago. She blinked the tears away.

Barbara sifted through the papers on the table, finally pulling out a couple dozen pages. She held them out. "Here's a list of Mr. Belk's cases from thirteen to fourteen years ago. They're listed alphabetically by client."

Jess asked, "Can you write down the title of these documents, the dates, and where they're kept in the files, so we can get the right information to the judge when we request the warrant?"

Barbara pulled out a chair and found a legal pad. She spread the pages on the table. "I'll do that now. Have a seat while I work through these."

She started at the back end of the pile, leaving the documents close enough for Jess to read. She'd scanned only half a page when she gave Jess a knowing look. "Shoot. I have to find a pen. You stay here. I'll be back."

Jess understood Barbara's motives perfectly. She nodded but said nothing, teary again at the younger woman's kindness.

Barbara placed a pad of sticky notes on the table and moved into the stacks out of sight.

Jess pulled out her phone and scanned the relevant pages quickly. Every time she saw a matter listed as "adoption," she took a photo of the entry. After several minutes she had marked nineteen adoptions.

Almost two a month.

Barbara came back with her pen. "You know, you'll also want the full files, won't you? These documents are just a list of the clients and matters during that time frame. Come this way."

Jess followed her as she navigated between the rows of bookshelves.

The shelves were stacked with cardboard boxes, labeled with numbers and dates and names on the ends, one matter per box.

The shelves towered over Jess. She ran her finger along the top of one of the boxes, revealing a thick layer of dust.

Barbara stopped twice at intersections, checking the numbers on the end of the shelves before deciding which way to go. Moments later, she stopped in the middle of a row and pointed out several different boxes.

She pulled a ladder over and climbed up to find the relevant boxes on the upper shelves, while Jess found the ones she wanted lower down. They arranged the boxes in numerical case order on the floor.

Barbara winked at Jess and said, "I'll be back in a few minutes. I need the list to get these organized."

Jess sorted quickly through the contents of the boxes. Several of the file numbers were missing from their boxes. Paperwork is always unreliable. Not like computer records. But fully twenty-five percent of Belk's cases from the relevant time frame was missing.

When Barbara returned, Jess asked about the missing files.

"Huh. That's odd." Barbara pulled out her phone. "I don't have the actual case files, but I can search the financial records."

Jess beamed at her. The woman was an angel.

She worked her phone quickly while Jess looked over her shoulder. The screen was covered in names and numbers that meant nothing to Jess. After a bit of sorting, Barbara found one of the missing case numbers, all of which were listed as *consultations* and the fees were always $150.

"What sort of consultation was Belk doing for $150 each?" Jess said.

Barbara shrugged. "Hard to say. A hundred fifty dollars used to be our standard fee for an hour's consultation before we took on a client. If we didn't take the case, they never paid anything more. So it could be anything, I guess."

Jess felt her hope collapse. These files were another dead end.

Barbara's face lit up. "But there wouldn't be a record in the file for a consultation. Because there's a case number, that means we actually did take the case. We should have more documents. I don't know why they're not here."

"Do you have any information on how the bill was paid?"

"Sure." Barbara brought up another page. "Cash. I'd show you the invoice, but it's confidential, too."

Jess nodded. "Who signed for receipt of the money on behalf of the firm?"

"Hang on." Barbara scrolled to the bottom of the page. "Looks like Tanya Norell."

Her blood ran cold. "Norell."

Barbara smiled. "Tanya was our bookkeeper forever. Did all Mr. Belk's finances. She left about five years ago. I'll bet she could answer all of your questions. Do you know her?"

Jess shook her head. "But I'm going to."

CHAPTER FIFTY

Tuesday, November 28
8:45 p.m.
Kansas City, Kansas

FERNANDEZ DROVE TO THE Norell house. He was quiet, and so was Jess. Her phone buzzed. Barbara had sent the invoice with Tanya Norell's name on it, even though she shouldn't have and she'd be in trouble if her bosses found out.

Still, Jess was grateful to her. With Hallman dead, the Norells were another link to Peter, and she wouldn't waste the opportunity to talk to them.

The police radio crackled with almost constant reports. Officers called in an accident on Interstate 435. The dispatcher called for assistance with a robbery in Glenaire. A jogger had collapsed in Sweetwater Park.

KCPD officers responded with methodical precision, mere seconds between a report on the radio and a car dispatched to assist.

Fernandez stopped the Crown Vic in front of Norell's place, exactly where she and Morris had stopped earlier in the day.

The Norell house was dark. She noticed a fine line of light around the drapes in one window on the ground floor.

She followed Fernandez to the front of the house. The doorbell played a tune that seemed to run forever. The door opened a fraction.

Mrs. Norell peered through the gap. "Yes?"

Fernandez held out his badge. "We'd like to talk to you."

"Could you come back tomorrow?"

"No. Unless you want me to bring an arrest warrant."

"We're getting ready for bed." When they didn't leave, Mrs. Norell stared a few moments before releasing the chain and opening the door. "You better go in the living room."

Jess plopped into an armchair. Fernandez remained standing.

Mrs. Norell sat on the sofa. "My husband is resting."

Fernandez nodded. "We have some bad news. Ammerson Belk is dead."

Mrs. Norell's eyes widened and her mouth hung open. "What? I don't.... I don't believe it."

"I'm afraid it's true. He was killed about an hour ago," Fernandez said.

She shook her head. "No. How?"

"We're waiting for a coroner's report, but it looks like he was strangled."

Mrs. Norell turned white. She swallowed. "I mean...who...do you know?"

"What's your connection to Belk?"

She wrapped her arms around herself. "Just... He's my husband's lawyer. Was his lawyer."

"Did you know him?"

She shook her head.

"Personally?"

She scowled. "No!"

"Did your husband have a lot of business with Mr. Belk?"

"Well, some. He was running a business. You always have to have a lawyer."

"A family lawyer? Was your husband in some sort of family-related business?"

Norell's gaze flipped to Fernandez then back into the middle distance. "I think… I guess he just got to know Belk. You know? Hit it off."

"What about Earle Gotting?" Fernandez asked.

She shook her head. "I don't know him."

"He bought an expensive Audi from your husband six months ago."

"I don't know anything about that."

Fernandez frowned. "Earle Gotting has disappeared, and Ammerson Belk is dead. Two people connected to you have had a very bad day. You think that's a coincidence?"

"How would I know?"

Fernandez's phone rang. He stepped out to take the call.

Tanya Norell glanced at Jess.

"We found several old baby bottles at Gotting's apartment," Jess said.

Norell screwed up her face. "And what's that got to do with me?"

"To our knowledge, Gotting never had children."

She huffed. "Maybe he looked after other people's kids?"

Jess leaned forward. "That's exactly what I think, Mrs. Norell. He looked after other people's children."

"So, good for him," she nodded.

"I don't think he was kind. I think he stole children while your lawyer, the man you worked for, Belk, sold them in a phony illegal adoption scam."

Mrs. Norell screwed up her face. "Good grief. No. I don't know what you're talking about."

"I don't believe Gotting paid you fifty-three thousand dollars for your Audi, either. I think you gave it to him."

"What's this about?" She puffed her chest, indignantly.

"Perhaps Belk helped you sell the babies Gotting stole."

"No." Mrs. Norell shook her head vigorously. "Of course not."

"You paid Gotting off. Back payments, maybe? Or hush money? Perhaps he knows enough to get you locked up?"

"That's ridiculous."

"Maybe you and your husband killed Belk because he knew everything."

Mrs. Norell stood. "We didn't kill anyone. And certainly not Mr. Belk. You're not pinning that on me."

Jess stood up. "I don't need to pin anything on anybody. The truth will come out. I'll make sure it does. That's what I do. Count on it."

Tanya Norell's face had turned a sickly shade of green.

Jess pulled her phone from her pocket and held it out, Barbara's spreadsheet on the screen. "I'll be looking much more closely into the financial records at Somersall-McCree. You can count on that, too."

Norell leaned forward, adjusting her glasses to see the spreadsheet clearly. She jerked back. "I don't know what that is."

"It's a list of Belk's cases." Jess pointed out a line. "This one is for consulting."

Norell shook her head slowly. "I don't know—"

"You know what consulting is, Mrs. Norell," Jess said. "It's when a lawyer meets with someone to assess a case or provide advice. These are Belk's cases from thirteen years ago."

Norell shook her head more vigorously.

"A case number was assigned at the firm for each of these consultations. That means work was done and a file opened."

Two cars drew up close to the house and cut their engines.

Norell uttered an exasperated sigh. "I don't know anything about that."

Jess scrolled to the bottom of the page. "Really. Because you signed this page."

Norell's lower jaw trembled. She forced her lips together and shrugged.

"You were the bookkeeper," Jess said. "Bean counters know everything."

Norell frowned and swallowed. "I was a clerk. I don't know what Belk did."

"Two minutes ago, you didn't know Belk at all. Now your name is all over his business finances." Jess cocked her head. "And I've only been searching your background for about an hour. Imagine what I'll find once I get serious."

Tanya Norell crossed her arms and sat down, her mouth clamped shut. Which is what she should have done from the beginning. Jess smirked.

Fernandez opened the front door. A KCPD officer walked in, a torn and charred plastic bag in his hands. The two had a mumbled discussion as Fernandez rummaged in the bag.

"What's that? What's going on?" Mrs. Norell said.

The officer left the bag with Fernandez and stepped into the living room.

"They found the bag in a park nearby," Fernandez said quietly to Jess. He handed her a latex glove.

The bag was stuffed with damp and charred paper. Jess used the glove to pull out the remains of a page. She saw names and addresses, and an official-looking stamp cut off at the bottom of the page.

"An adoption record," she said.

Fernandez used another glove to pull out a small piece of paper. It was half a check made out to Somersall-McCree, dated eight years earlier.

Jess pointed to the name. "The name's misspelled. It's missing a letter."

Fernandez turned it over. The back of the check was endorsed by T. Norell.

Mrs. Norell stood. "What's going on?"

Jess pulled another check from the bag. It was dated six years earlier and had the same spelling mistake.

"These are checks reflecting payments going back over several years," Fernandez said, riffling through them quickly.

Jess looked at the adoption record. It looked like any other formal court document to her. The payments were most likely made by people who didn't realize they'd been given the wrong spelling. All a part of the scam, no doubt, since the checks had been endorsed and cashed.

Mrs. Norell stepped toward them. "What's going on?" she asked again.

The officer held his hand out, keeping her back.

Fernandez closed the bag. "There's a lot of evidence in this mess. Lots of large checks flowing back and forth. We need to get this to forensics."

Mrs. Norell's face contorted, her eyebrows pressed down

and wrinkles creased deeply around her nose. "What is that? I've never seen that."

Jess forced her anger back. "It's all the evidence any court will need of the illegal adoptions you conducted. You made a lot of money selling stolen babies. And you're going to prison for a very, very long time."

"No! I did no such thing!"

Jess shook the adoption record in front of Mrs. Norell's face. "This is proof!"

"We didn't sell any stolen babies. That's crazy! We never—"

"Really? Because your name is on the checks." Jess took a deep breath. "Good luck explaining that."

"But...but, we just handled the paperwork. The...we helped to match up parents with kids who needed a good home." Norell whispered, "I swear. That's what we did."

Jess lost her patience. "Earle Gotting took my son. A baby. Not even two years old. He brought the babies to you and your husband. Then your lawyer, Belk, sold the children."

Norell shook her head. "That is not true. It's not!"

Jess shook the adoption papers in Norell's face. "You knew what was going on. You collected the money. You're going to rot in prison."

"I didn't," Norell whispered, a horrified look on her face.

"Oh, hell yes you did." Jess grabbed the plastic bag. "All these kids? These parents? The pain and anguish. The suffering you've caused? You, your husband, and everyone else involved. If it was up to me, you'd all get the death penalty. As it is, you're going to prison forever. I will never, ever, allow you to breathe free air again."

Jess leaned so close to Norell's face she could feel her breath.

"Jess." Fernandez put his hand on her shoulder. "Step back."

When she did, the officer placed Tanya Norell under arrest, read her her rights, cuffed her, and led her out of the house.

Jess pointed to the upstairs bedrooms. "We need to get him, too."

Fernandez shook his head and held up the papers. "Another lie. Her husband was out there burning those documents. KCPD already took him in."

CHAPTER FIFTY-ONE

Wednesday, November 29
7:30 a.m.
Colorado Springs, Colorado

THE AIR WAS DRY and bitter. Tiny flakes of snow blew over the windshield of Earle Gotting's Audi, dancing and curving in the wind, touching the glass briefly before they twirled away.

He struggled to suppress his overwhelming cravings for drugs in order to keep his mind as clear as possible. He hadn't slept much because of his throbbing foot. And he was cold. He started the engine and switched on both the heat and the heated seats. His clothing wasn't warm enough. He had limited cash to buy warmer ones, and he was reluctant to take more chances that might cause people to remember him anyway.

He'd flipped through the news but found nothing worrisome reported from Kansas City. Which could have been okay, but he feared not. Thirty-six hours ago he'd escaped from Metcalfe. Plenty of time for Hallman or Metcalfe to locate Peter Kimball and steal him before Gotting had the chance.

He had one big advantage. He knew Colorado. He'd skied and snowboarded many of the resorts around the state before he'd started using and selling drugs in Kansas City. He knew back routes to get onto trails and the easiest ways to steal passes and avoid suspicious security staff. He loved the mountains. He'd never felt better than the times he'd spent here.

He grinned. Peter Kimball's new family had moved back to Colorado, which was a bit of luck he hadn't dared to count on.

The clock on the dashboard indicated it was time. He drove a mile along the minor roads to Peter's school, caught in school traffic. In the last couple of blocks, the line of cars peeled off, and he headed directly to the back of the school.

He parked by the industrial buildings two blocks from the school's rear exit, which was the one Peter normally used. If his mother dropped him off at the front door today, he'd need a backup plan. He didn't have one.

Choosing a different time to kidnap the boy would have required extensive surveillance. The sort of thing he'd been able to do when he lived in apartment buildings and stole babies. It could take weeks to confidently nail down a kid's schedule. He didn't have the time here. This whole job had been a rush. This plan had to work and it had to work today. Right now, in fact.

He rolled his car too close to the corner to prevent any parents from parking in front of him. An immediate right turn would shield his license plate from Good Samaritans, should there be any. This spot also gave him a pretty straight run to the right highway. He could get out of here fast.

He watched via the rearview mirror. Peter wore a dark blue coat yesterday. Maybe he'd wear the same coat today. But maybe not. Gotting watched the faces of the boys carefully. He needed to get the right boy on the first try.

A pair of girls walked onto the street and passed him by without so much as a second glance.

A white panel van appeared behind him and blocked his view. The driver jumped out and jogged across the street with a parcel under his arm.

Gotting stepped out of his car and walked around the van to peer down the street, watching for Peter.

The van driver returned and pulled away. The rear of the van slid on the snow as he raced around the corner.

Gotting returned to the Audi's warmth and kept watch using his rearview mirror.

Two kids wearing matching yellow jackets came into view, pushing and shoving each other as they ambled down the street. They eyeballed Gotting as they walked by his car.

He looked down and fiddled with the radio. No reason to give them a clear view of his face. Bad enough they'd noticed him and his Audi. He heard them talking about him as they moved on, but he didn't look up until they passed.

He glanced into his mirror. His breath caught.

Peter was approaching from the other side of the street. He wore the same dark blue coat and no hat.

He had the same curly blond hair as his mother. He had her eyes, too. Big, brown, ringed with dark lashes. Gotting might not have remembered Jess Kimball's features from years ago if he hadn't seen her on that damn *Denver PM* interview. Her face had burned itself into his brain.

Gotting slammed his palm on the steering wheel. He was parked on the wrong side of the street. He stabbed the button to open the trunk and rushed to the rear of the car.

The two kids in the yellow jackets turned and watched Gotting's burst of activity. He lifted the trunk lid to block the view.

The Audi's trunk was both deep and wide. He'd removed the emergency release handle, just in case. Kids were too smart for their own good these days. Inside the trunk, he'd struggled to store a heavy, three-foot section of tree trunk.

He wrapped his hands around the tree and hefted one end up and out past the edge of the car's trunk.

He glanced behind him. Peter was twenty yards away, walking purposefully in the cold.

Grunting and groaning, he dragged the trunk another few inches from the car. He panted heavily and put his hand on his back.

He raised his hand and waved.

"Excuse me," he called. "Could you lend me a hand?"

Peter slowed his pace and looked across the street.

Gotting gingerly stretched his back. "I just need to get this out of the car and I'll be okay."

Peter stopped walking. Nice kid. Too bad.

"It's kinda heavy," Gotting shrugged. "If you wouldn't mind?"

Peter jogged across the road. Gotting pointed to an empty space in the trunk. "You can put your backpack down there."

Peter pushed his backpack deeper into the Audi's trunk and patted the tree. "Where are you taking this?"

Gotting smiled. Man, this kid was gullible. How had he lived to be fifteen? "The place behind us. I can probably manage once it's out of the car."

Peter rocked the tree trunk, judging the weight. "It's pretty heavy."

"I think we'll manage it together."

Peter nodded. "No problem." He looked at Gotting. "You sure you're up to it?"

Truth was, his leg hurt and his foot throbbed as if he'd scraped the skin off within the past hour. Still, he grinned. "I'm not that old, kid. I just need a little hand here. Hurt my back is all."

Peter grabbed his end of the tree trunk and Gotting did the same on the other side. "One, two, three."

He lifted. Ironically, his back actually twinged. He grimaced and grunted.

Peter lifted his end clear of the car and stepped back. Gotting shuffled quickly to keep up.

"Down?" Peter said.

Gotting nodded, unable to speak. Man, the damn thing was heavy.

They lowered the weight to the ground simultaneously.

He panted, trying to catch his breath. "Any chance you could move it another couple of feet?"

"Sure. You take it easy." Peter offered a concerned smiled and bent down, adjusting his grip on the bark.

Gotting checked the street quickly, seeing it was all clear. He pulled a smooth rock from his pocket, gripped it hard, and swung for the side of Peter's head. The blow was a solid whack. It contacted above his ear, slightly back from the thin skull at the temple. He didn't want to kill the kid. Just knock him temporarily senseless.

Peter's knees gave way, dropping his body straight onto the tree trunk.

He looped his arms around the kid's torso and yanked him up and into the trunk, head first. Peter moaned. He folded the kid's legs and jammed him into the Audi's trunk.

He dropped the stone on the ground, yanked off one glove and pulled a syringe from his pocket. He removed the needle's cover with his teeth, eased the needle under the kid's skin, and mashed the plunger all the way down.

No time to find a vein. But the boy wasn't a hardened addict. He'd get enough into his system to render him unconscious for a few hours.

Gotting closed the trunk lid, stepped into the car, and drove away. He didn't waste any time eying possible witnesses. What for? Nothing would cause him to stop at this point.

Besides, witnesses, if there were any, were usually too shocked to help police much. Only a few minutes later, self-doubt would set in. They began to convince themselves they hadn't seen anything at all. Of course not. How could they have witnessed a kidnapping and not reacted immediately? Every second of indecision increased his chances of a successful escape.

Gotting made the planned right turn immediately, and pressed the accelerator, ignoring the throbbing in the top of his injured right foot. The Audi squirmed on the road's thin layer of snow and then straightened out.

A car passed in the opposite direction. It seemed to slow. He kept moving and never looked back. He kept his speed slightly above the limit, as much as he dared without attracting attention.

Two miles down the road, he checked the rearview mirror. No one was following. No sirens. No noise from the car's trunk, either. So far, so good.

He took the entrance ramp onto US-24 west and settled into the middle travel lane. He bumped his speed up and set the cruise control.

He slapped the steering wheel. Hot Damn! He did it!

"Screw you, Hallman!" he shouted. "You, too, Metcalfe!"

And then he laughed.

Gotting was running on pure adrenaline now, his own speed control. The Audi easily handled the inclines. US-24 led into the mountains, on the way to easy street.

After an hour, he found the gated lane. Whatever house lay beyond the gate was hidden far into the trees. He got out to open the gate.

He reversed the car and backed up the lane to point the trunk away from the road when he parked. The kid was probably heavier than the tree trunk had been. No reason to carry him any farther than necessary.

He shoved a roll of duct tape in his pocket and pulled the cover from the needle of another syringe.

He stepped out into the crisp morning air again. The snow had stopped. He listened for passing vehicles and heard none approaching. He opened the trunk.

The kid's head rolled toward him, eyes open but vacant and glassy. He was a long way from real consciousness. Gotting put the syringe back in his pocket. Nothing more was necessary yet.

He put the boy's hands together and curled the duct tape around them, trapping his fingers, and running the duct tape down past both wrists. He taped his ankles next and then closed the trunk.

The boy offered no resistance. His eyes hadn't even tracked Gotting's movements as he secured the tape. The kid wouldn't come around for hours. Which was good. Because Gotting had a phone call to make.

Jess Kimball would be waiting for news. But first he had to find a better cell signal.

CHAPTER FIFTY-TWO

Wednesday, November 29
8:05 a.m.
Kansas City, Kansas

JESS SAT IN FERNANDEZ'S office, her eyes boring into him incredulously. "After everything he's done, he wants *what*? To make some kind of *deal*? Sure. Great idea. Why don't we all swim naked together in a cesspool while we're at it?"

Fernandez pursed his lips and ignored the sarcasm. "It's not a terrible suggestion. He wants to trade information we need for some kind of leniency in sentencing."

"Just him? What about her? He's throwing her under the bus?" Jess shook her head. These people were all scumbags as far as she was concerned.

"He hasn't shown much inclination to include her, and she hasn't come to grips with her situation yet." Fernandez shook his head. "They're both in custody, but we're still gathering evidence. We don't know what we'll be able to prove, after all this time. And we need to know where these kids are now.

Directly and voluntarily from the Norells may be the only way
we can get the information we need."

Jess shook her head. She'd been around the criminal justice
system a long time. She understood the realities. But she didn't
have to like it. Not one bit. "What does he claim he's got to
bargain with?"

Fernandez sighed. "He says he knows where your son is."

Jess stood up and walked around her chair. "How does he
claim to know that?"

"We haven't heard the specifics."

"But think it through. Say Gotting kidnaps the children. Belk
organized the private adoptions. Mrs. Norell handled the
paperwork at Belk's firm to hide the money. What did Norell
do? What was his part in all of this? Middleman? Salesman?"

Fernandez said, "That's our conclusion."

Jess nodded. "Okay. So how does the middleman know
Peter's location now? Thirteen years later?"

"Trace the paperwork. He knew who the adoptive parents
were. He's got the kids' Social Security numbers." Fernandez
shrugged. "This is the twenty-first-century western world.
Surveillance Nations and so on. Everyone can be tracked down
these days, given a good starting point, enough time, and some
applied energy. Might not even take very long."

"Right. So we check the search history on his computer. We
seize all of his documents. We search everything they own,
down to their underwear," she said, jutting her chin forward.
"You're the damn FBI, Fernandez. Act like it."

He wiped a palm across his face and sighed. "Already done
all of that. No sign of anything useful. Likewise, on his phone.
No suspicious name searches. Nothing."

"Exactly as I thought," Jess nodded. "He has nothing we want. No information to offer. Does he?"

Fernandez shrugged. "We'll never know unless he tells us, will we?"

She sat down, out of steam. "Maybe Belk told him. Hallman went from Gotting to Norell to Belk, right?"

"Right."

"That most likely means Belk was the one who found Peter, doesn't it?"

Fernandez nodded. "And Belk probably told Norell when he was called in as Norell's lawyer."

"So Norell *could* know? Maybe."

Fernandez nodded again. "Seems possible."

Jess rested her forearms on her thighs and hung her head. All of these scumbags were as low as they could possibly get. Monsters. They stole babies. Sold them to unsuspecting people desperate to be parents, in illegal private adoptions. Maybe they'd even faked international adoptions to fleece more money from them.

She mashed her hands together. How many times had they done this? Left mothers, fathers, and families to suffer one of the worst possible agonies, a lost child. A child they'd borne, nurtured, intended to love and protect from harm of every kind.

Exactly like Jess. On the day Peter was born, and every day since, he'd been her entire world. She could not forgive these people. Make a deal with them? No chance in hell.

She ground her teeth and looked up. "No."

Fernandez frowned.

"That's why you told me, right? You want me to agree? No." She stood up, shook her head, and leaned forward over his desk to get right in his face. "No. Definitely not. Never. No."

He sighed, but he didn't flinch. "Jess, we have no idea where Earle Gotting is. So we have to assume he's alive. We haven't been able to confirm that Hallman is the one who called you. Could have been Gotting just as easily. We know Gotting's a killer. He's going after Peter. We have to assume that, too. Speed is important here. You know that."

"It's not just Peter and me, though, is it?" She gestured outside his office. "They kidnapped so many children. Of course, I want my son to be safe. I want him back. I've been looking for him for thirteen years."

Fernandez nodded as if she'd finally come to her senses. He was wrong.

"No. We can't make a deal. Not until we've exhausted everything we can do." She stepped back from his desk.

Fernandez sighed. "You know we don't need your approval or your permission. We have to do what's best here. Whether you like it or not."

She nodded. "Give me one day. If we can find Peter in that time, we'll also know how to find the others. We can nail these creeps to the wall *and* get all the kids back."

Fernandez didn't reply. But he didn't disagree, either.

"Gotting will call. He wants his money. We're the only way he can get it." She paused. "And in the meantime, we keep looking for those adoption records. Use them to find the kids."

Fernandez folded his hands together on the desk. "Okay. I'll get us twenty-four hours. After that, my bosses will do the deal. I'll have no control over it."

"Good. Let's get to work. We don't have much time." She set a twenty-four-hour timer on her phone. "Do you have any good news?"

"The second body in Belk's garage was definitely Metcalfe. He was stabbed with a garden fork before being shot. Most likely Hallman killed him, but it could have been Gotting or any one of his other enemies. Metcalfe wasn't a popular guy."

Jess nodded.

"He had deep marks on his hands, probably made by a lot of tension applied to a wire or cord. We suspect that means he killed Belk."

"And then Hallman killed Metcalfe. They did us all a favor," Jess said.

CHAPTER FIFTY-THREE

Wednesday, November 29
9:00 a.m.
Kansas City, Kansas

JESS HEADED OUT OF the FBI offices toward her rental. The air was damp and cold. A blanket of gray clouds stretched to the horizon. She pulled her coat closer around her neck.

She might have time to stop by and see Henry in the hospital. He'd be awake. He was an early riser. Maybe she should call first.

Her phone buzzed before she had the chance. The display showed a transferred call from her office number. Probably her assistant, Mandy. She put a smile in her voice. "Hello."

"You Jessica Kimball?" said a man's voice.

Her skin tingled and her smile died quickly. "Who is this?"

"Just answer the question."

"Okay. Sorry. Hang on." First thing, keep him on the line as long as she could. She found a quiet spot and breathed a moment. "This is Jess Kimball."

"Good. You still remember your little boy? Or have you forgotten him?"

Her heart skipped a beat. Like any mother would ever forget her son. "Who is this?"

"Peter Kimball? You remember him, don't you?"

She didn't recognize the voice. Morris would compare it to the earlier calls, but Jess felt sure this wasn't the same guy. "You're going to have to tell me your name."

"Yeah, right. Like that's going to happen. You just listen good." Jess remained silent.

"You want your son to ever see the daylight again, you get me five million in cash. Used bills. Nothing larger than fifties. No trackers. No magic dust that glows in the dark. Nothing like that." The man's voice was rough and harsh. He sounded lucid. Under control.

A car drove past with a radio blaring. She missed a couple of words.

When she could hear again, he was still talking. "I know what to look for. Don't screw around with me. Because if I find anything like that, if you try to trace the money in any way, you'll never see your beloved Peter. Never."

Jess turned around and headed back to the FBI office. "You're the second person to make that demand this week."

The man screamed, "You're trying to mess with me!"

"Not at all. I received a similar call on Monday afternoon. So, the question is, do you really have my son?" Traffic was picking up along the street. A few pedestrians walked by.

He raised his voice again. Now, he was angry but controlled. "Yes, I have him. The little puker has turned into a dumb jock. Are you proud of him?"

Jess gripped her phone harder. "Let me talk to him."

"Like I'm that stupid. Waste of time, anyway. You wouldn't know him if he spoke to you."

"What makes you think that?"

"Because he was a toddler when I took him. He's never spoken to you. You've never heard him say a whole sentence. Baby words is all. Ma-ma. Crap like that. Nothing more."

Jess pressed the phone harder against her ear, trying to hear over the increasing traffic noise. "You're the one who took him? Personally?"

He laughed. "I let myself into your apartment that night while you ran down to the laundry in that crappy old basement. Easy to take him. He was sleeping. Didn't even wake up. Not even two years old. Ain't no way you're gonna recognize his voice now he's fifteen. Hell, he don't look nothing like that picture you've been showing on TV."

"*Denver PM*?"

"Yeah. I guess."

She nodded. Maybe he was bluffing. "I've had plenty of people make the same claim you're making. They just want the reward money. They don't really know where my son is."

The man scoffed. "You doubting me?"

"As I said, I've heard other people make that claim."

After a silence so long, she thought maybe he'd hung up before he spoke again. "The building you were living in was cheap. Flimsy doors, flimsier locks. I bumped the door open. Just leaned on the door frame and, poof, it opened. I walked out with him. Easy as pie."

"That much has been on the news. You said you saw me on TV. That's exactly what I said happened."

"You were wearing jeans and a Rolling Stones T-shirt, and flip-flops that squeaked on the stairs."

"But why would you take my baby?"

"This ain't twenty questions, lady. Get the money. Just like I said. Get it and wait. I'll be in touch," he growled.

He was about to hang up, so she took the chance. "You're Earle Gotting."

He laughed. "Whoever the hell that is."

"It's you. I know what you did. I know how your scheme worked."

"You don't know crap. That was always your problem. Thought you were so damn smart."

She said, "Belk is dead. Murdered. Both Norells have been arrested."

"Means nothing to me," he said, but she heard his voice hike up a notch. *Liar.*

"The guy who called on Monday to blackmail me was your friend, Shane Hallman. He's dead, too."

He snapped. His voice turned low and clipped and mean. "Don't know what you're talking about. All I want is money. If I don't get it, I'll be very sad. But no biggie. I've been unhappy before. I can always get more money. There's lots more mommies like you out there, ready to pay. But you? You don't get your boy? How you gonna get another one? Huh? Ain't so easy. So get my money while you still have the chance."

"I'm going to need more evidence."

"Oh, sure," he said sarcastically. "Five million. Twenty-four hours. Bye."

The line went dead before she could utter another word.

CHAPTER FIFTY-FOUR

Wednesday, November 29
10:00 a.m.
Vista Hermosa, Colorado

GOTTING CRUISED AWAY FROM Vista Hermosa, obeying
every road sign and sticking firmly to the speed limit. Small
towns used visitors to top up their tax revenue. A modern-day
form of highway robbery, as far as he was concerned. But a fact
of life.

Was anything Kimball said true? Or was she just trying to
rattle him? Belk and Hallman both dead? Not that he'd mourn
them, anyway. Good news, actually. Dead men can't talk.

But both Norells arrested? More of a problem. He'd been a
weasel. She was a bitch, plain and simple. Penny pincher, too.
Had to watch her like a hawk or she'd cheat him every chance
she got.

Kimball said nothing about Metcalfe. Where was he? That
bastard was as mean as any rattlesnake Gotting had ever
encountered. With any luck, maybe he was dead, too.

His thoughts returned to the Norells. She thought she was so smart. She figured out how to get money from those fancy clients at the law firm where she and Belk worked. She put the whole business in motion. He had to give her that much.

The two were useless for implementing the whole plan. Sometimes they'd meet the new parents if Belk couldn't do it. And she did the finance trick. Apart from that, they took no risks. Gotting never could figure out why they got paid at all.

He was always the one who took the biggest risk. He scoped out new adoption candidates. Most times, he found the babies on his own. He shuffled new identities all the time so police couldn't trace him to the apartments where the babies had gone missing.

And the brats he had to put up with? He shook his head. New babies. Up to two years old, that was the rule. The worst. Once he found a reliable drug he could dose them up with, things got better. But the first bunch had been hell. Even watching them for a few hours was miserable. Man, he was glad that part was over.

Belk had taken risks, too. He had a nice house and a good job at that swanky legal firm. Tough to run away from that if things went south. Course, now he wouldn't have to worry about it, Belk being dead and all.

Gotting noticed a sign on the side of the road. He'd entered another small town and checked his speed. He definitely couldn't risk being stopped.

The boy had been making moaning noises in the trunk for a bit. Despite the Audi's luxury construction, the sound still seeped through to the cabin.

He shook his head. It was ironic, really. After all this time, the thing was finally unraveling. Yet here he was, with a teenager in the trunk. The same kid he'd abducted as a baby years ago. A wry grin settled on his lips. He was pulling victory from the jaws of failure. How good was that?

He turned left and followed the road as it curved upward.

Peter moaned. The drug and the motion were probably messing with his senses. Gotting hoped the kid didn't vomit in the trunk. That would be more than inconvenient. He shrugged. Nothing he could do about it.

Belk and Hallman were dead. Huh. He had a thought. Did Jess Kimball kill them? Maybe she did. He might have, in her shoes. And hell, Hallman he could understand. What a scum bucket. Belk wasn't that bad.

He shook his head. He couldn't see Kimball killing them before she found her kid. Must have been Metcalfe. Yeah, that made more sense.

Metcalfe caught up with Belk and Hallman. He'd killed them, and the resulting investigation had led the police to Norell. Yeah, he could see it happening that way. Snap Metcalfe was a *mutha* and a half. Always had been.

So he had Hallman and Metcalfe to thank for his five-million-dollar payday. Sure. Why not?

A smile spread across his face. Even if Metcalfe was alive and coming after him, Peter Kimball was already gone. Metcalfe's killing spree would end at Peter's address. Because Metcalfe would never find him. Gotting laughed heartily visualizing the rage on Metcalfe's face. He'd pay money to see that, but no way was he going back there. Not even for the satisfaction of seeing Metcalfe rot in prison.

A fine dust of snow was blowing in the wind as the Audi climbed altitude. He turned on the windshield wipers. The trunk would be cold. The boy had grown silent. Either the drug had overwhelmed him, or he had regained consciousness. Gotting doubted the latter.

He slowed for the track leading to the derelict mine. The wind and the snow had erased his earlier tracks. As the Audi bumped its way over the rocky track, he considered skipping his rake routine, but the risk was too great. He was too close to his millions now to screw up like that.

The car slithered into the shelter. He cut the engine and stepped out. His weight caused his right leg to cramp and revived the throbbing burn atop his injured right foot. He walked the length of the car and back, trying to ease himself into the movement and deal with the pain.

The wind and snow together delivered the biting cold. He bowed his head to shield his face and eyes. He found the rake and swept the Audi's tracks away. The wind would do the rest. He put the rake where he could easily find it next time.

He pulled his gun and opened the trunk.

The boy was curled in a ball and pressed up against the back seats. He didn't move as the cold air swept over him. Gotting nudged him. The kid groaned. Gotting nudged him again, and he twisted around.

Peter's lips were pressed together. His eyes were only half open. With slow deliberation, he moved his duct-taped hands to shield his vision from the glare off the light and snow. He moaned.

Gotting held out the gun. "One stupid move and I shoot. Got it?"

Peter moaned. Not a yes or no, just an automatic response from the human submerged under the drug.

Gotting dragged the boy's legs out of the trunk. He pulled until his torso was halfway out, then levered him up under his arm. Gotting's foot screamed in agony with the extra weight. He shuffled Peter forward, testing to see if the boy could stand, but he grabbed the kid again as he collapsed. The last thing he needed right now was to wrestle him off the ground, and it was too cold to leave him there.

Gotting gritted his teeth and steered Peter up the track. They slipped and stumbled on the rough ground hidden by the snow blanket.

When the track ended, Gotting backed into the bushes, pulling Peter forward by his taped hands. The boy blundered his way through scrapes and scratches from the vegetation without flinching. He was beyond pain.

Gotting breathed normally again when he made it to the clearing. The last fifty feet was easy going. He dragged the boy through the hatch, past the metal door, and into the tunnel. He left Peter lying on the floor next to a wooden tabletop where Gotting had placed bread and soda. The kid rolled over onto his side and moaned.

He left a dim flashlight resting on top of the bread and closed the door. He wedged a wooden beam under the handle. When the boy came to, he'd likely panic. The light would at least allow him to get control of himself. Didn't matter whether he did or not. He couldn't escape the tunnel.

CHAPTER FIFTY-FIVE

Wednesday, November 29
9:15 a.m.
Kansas City, Kansas

THE MOMENT GOTTING ENDED his call, Jess reentered the FBI offices.

The receptionist frowned. "Forget something?"

Jess shook her head. "I need to talk to Agent Fernandez, immediately."

The receptionist called his office.

Thirty seconds later, Fernandez burst into the reception area. "You got my message?"

Jess shook her head. She held up her phone. "I got a call. You should be able to hear it. Morris has you guys tapping my phone."

"Threatening?"

"He wanted five million for Peter."

"Did you recognize the guy?" Fernandez asked.

She shook her head again. "How could I? Hallman is the one

who called me before and he's dead. I'm pretty sure this guy was Earle Gotting."

Fernandez said, "Let's see what we've got."

Jess raced up the stairs behind him. They stopped at an office cube outside his door, told an agent to get the recorded call, and walked into Fernandez's office to wait in silence.

The agent came in shortly afterward, handed Fernandez a note, and left.

"The call came from Vista Hermosa, Colorado," Fernandez said, reading the note.

Jess frowned. "I live in Denver, but I know the place. Up in the mountains."

"Locals are on their way to check it out."

"Did the call actually come from there? Or is he faking it somehow to confuse us?"

"Looks like a cell phone. Probably a burner. But we'll have a better idea after we hear from the locals."

She frowned when she remembered what he'd said when he saw her in the lobby. "What did you mean when you asked if I'd received your message?"

Fernandez handed Jess a sheaf of papers. "These are copies of adoption records for cases handled by Belk's firm from the month after Peter was taken. We got them from the court files."

Jess sifted through the pages. There were lists of names and addresses, more than she'd seen in the basement with Barbara. Case numbers, too. "Are these real people? Any of this verified?"

"Still checking. However…" Fernandez pointed to a line on the sheet. "We believe this is the couple who adopted your son."

A chill ran though Jess's veins. She read the names aloud and they felt strange on her tongue. "Ross and Lynette Tierney?"

Fernandez nodded. "He was at Higgins AFB at the time.

Thirty minutes north of here. It's closed now. The wife was a dental hygienist. Worked on the north side of Kansas City back then. The dentist she worked for died a while back. Husband's career Air Force. They've moved several times in the past thirteen years."

Jess swallowed. "Why do you think they're the ones who adopted Peter? And how could they, anyway? Legally, I mean."

"They couldn't. But they did. Which was probably accomplished with forged documents. We're still running that down." Fernandez pointed to the boy's new name.

"Steven," she whispered.

Fernandez nodded. "We can't be certain without a thorough DNA test. You understand that, don't you?"

"You think this is Peter, though." She couldn't move her gaze from the names on the paper.

Fernandez said, "We do. Timeline fits. He's the right age. In fact, he's the only boy on the list that might fit. If this isn't Peter, then we're at a dead end here."

Jess felt her stomach churning. She'd hit so many dead ends over the years. She knew what the disappointment felt like. She'd lived through it before. She could survive again.

Still, she stared at the paper. The words blurred through the tears that settled in her eyes. She cleared her throat. "Where are the Tierneys living now?"

Fernandez took a deep breath. "Colorado Springs."

Jess stood up. "Colorado? Then if Hallman was the blackmailer who called me on Monday, he never did have Peter here in Kansas, did he?"

"Probably not. It's impossible to say right now." Fernandez shook his head slowly. "We've already been in contact with the Colorado Springs Police."

She heard a new note of concern in his voice, which couldn't be good. She was almost afraid to ask, but she managed to croak, "And?"

Fernandez frowned. "They already knew the Tierneys. Lynette Tierney dropped their son off at school this morning, but a couple of kids reported that they thought they saw him talking to a suspicious-looking man. He never made it into school."

"Today? This very morning?" Jess sank into her chair and looked at the call log on her phone. She whispered, "Gotting called me after he abducted Peter from school."

"Seems so," he said gravely.

She shook her head. She knew who and how Peter had been taken now. Some of the people involved in the abduction were dead, some were in custody. But Earle Gotting, the original kidnapper, had survived them all. That made him either the luckiest bastard in the world.

Or the most ruthless.

A moment of total clarity shot through her veins. Gotting would kill Peter this time if it suited him. She knew it as well as she knew every last tiny thing about Peter's body. The little mole under his left arm. The broad, flat fingers that were so like his father's. The dark brown eyes and curly blond hair that matched hers. Even the freckles across his nose that his half-sister shared.

"Do we have a photo of Steven Tierney?"

Fernandez pulled a copy of a photo from a folder and handed it across his desk. Jess noticed her hand shaking as she took it from him.

She glanced at the photo. One quick look was all she needed. She gasped. Her entire body began to shake. She tried to speak, but no words came out.

Fernandez noted her reaction. He walked out of the room, saying, "Let me get you some water."

She barely heard him. Her gaze was fixed on the boy's picture.

Steven Tierney looked like the computer generated, age-progressed photo of her baby. Except the boy in this photo was so obviously alive. Vitally alive. He might almost be breathing in her hands.

He'd acquired a couple of small scars on his chin, probably from childhood hijinks. His earlobes were rounded, as they'd been from birth. He still had his father's lips. Strangely, she remembered the shape of Richard's mouth, after all these years. And she was looking at it again now.

DNA tests would prove what Jess already knew. Steven Tierney was her son. She'd found him. Finally.

Fernandez returned with the water and a box of tissues. "Are you okay?"

Puzzled, she cocked her head and realized she was crying. She smiled, took both from Fernandez and wiped her tears. "I will be. It's hard to express how I'm feeling right now. Happy. Relieved. And yet, terrified," she laughed. "On so many levels."

Fernandez smiled and joked, "I know what you mean. Hey, teenagers terrify me, too."

She laughed and cried again. She sipped the water. After a while, she managed to stop crying. For now, anyway. She shoved her emotions out of the way. They still had to find Peter and now that bastard Gotting had him again.

"Hallman's crime was blackmail. Now, we've got a kidnapping," she said.

"Exactly." Fernandez nodded.

"My son's life is at stake." She checked her watch. "I have less than twenty-four hours to get five million dollars and turn it over to Earle Gotting."

"Don't panic, Jess. There's a lot we need to—"

"You do what you need to do. What I have to do is call Carter Pierce," she said calmly as she threw the crumpled tissues along with the empty water bottle into the trash. "I'm the farthest thing from panicked. There's no time for panic."

"We have to go through the steps. We have a protocol for dealing with kidnapping. Thorough investigative—" He paused when he saw the steady look she gave him. He took a deep breath. "There's a flight to Colorado Springs in three hours."

"I'll talk to Carter, and I'll be ready when Gotting calls again," she replied.

"There's a lot to do before we think of handing over money," Fernandez said. "We want to get Earle Gotting out of the shadows and Peter back in one piece."

She nodded, but she'd already pushed the speed dial on her cell phone. Thelma answered Carter's phone and put Jess straight through. She told him what she needed. Before she finished the request, he told her she'd have the money instantly.

"And where are you? Kansas City? I'll have a jet waiting for you at the airport," Carter said. "What else?"

"That's more than anyone could ask for. I can't thank you enough, Carter." Jess's eyes began to tear up again. What had she done to deserve such a friend? Before the uncontrollable blubbering commenced, she said thickly, "I'll call you again as soon as I can."

CHAPTER FIFTY-SIX

Wednesday, November 29
11:00 a.m.
Kansas City, Kansas

THE PRIVATE CHARTER FLIGHT was scheduled to depart from Charles B. Wheeler Downtown Airport. The facilities were considerably better than the coach class arrangements Jess was used to on commercial flights.

Her phone rang. She recognized the Colorado area code.

"Where are you?" he said.

"Earle Gotting," she replied.

There was a long silence, which was all she needed to confirm his identity.

"Where are you?" Gotting asked again.

She waited a moment. "Kansas City."

"Get yourself to Vista Hermosa. It's a town in Colorado. There's a regional airport there. You can change planes in Denver."

"Why Vista Hermosa?"

308 | Diane Capri

"Because you're bringing me five million dollars to exchange for your son, I assume." He paused. She heard a big sigh. "Don't be stupid, Jess. Get the money ready. Bring it with you. You'll be with Peter before the end of the day tomorrow. Otherwise, you'll never see him again."

"I don't have five million. I work for a living. You must know that. You saw me on *Denver PM*." She paused. "I've got fifty thousand. I've saved thirteen years to pull that much together."

"Don't mess around here," he growled. "Get the money from your boss."

"I tried. He can't. He's rich, but it's all tied up."

Gotting laughed harshly. "No, it isn't. He's always giving it away to charity."

"He makes big donations, but it's all stocks."

"That's your problem."

"Even if he does pay, it's just a loan. I'll have to pay it back."

"Not my problem."

"But, five million dollars? I'll never be able to pay that back."

"You're not listening. Five million or he dies. Doesn't matter to me. I'll move on." Gotting grunted. "But it matters to you. Just tell me if it doesn't and I'll stop wasting my time."

Jess waited. Listening. Gotting breathed softly. He wasn't angry. She figured he was the sort of person who thrived on conflict.

"You have him? Peter's with you?" she said.

He growled. "Get the money."

"Listen. Wait. What if I can raise half?" She begged because she figured he was a man who'd like knowing she suffered. "Maybe I can get three."

"If you can get three you can get five."

"I can't. Even if I put up everything I have as collateral, it's not three million. I live in an apartment. I have a job. I'm not rich. You know that, Gotting."

There was a long silence. Gotting's breathing was still steady. He was thinking about it. She could tell. Thinking took time.

"One dollar less than three million, and your son dies," he said finally. "You won't get a better deal or a second chance. No more pleading or begging. Three million and we're done. Make your choice. Now. Stop wasting my time."

Jess gave a sigh of relief as if she meant it. "Okay. Right. I think I can do that. I think… Thank you."

"We'll do the handover at eleven tomorrow morning. No police, no FBI, no helicopters, nothing. Just you and my money. Be ready. I'll tell you where and how tomorrow."

"But I need—"

"All you need is the money. In a suitcase. And I'll be wanding you when we meet. Like at the airport. I find a wire or a gun or anything and poof, your chance of seeing your son goes out the window. You got it?"

"Yes."

"Good," he paused. "Don't screw with me, Jess. I know you've been to the police and the FBI. And I know they'll be all over this case. But I see one hint of them anywhere, one whiff even, and your son is gone."

CHAPTER FIFTY-SEVEN

Wednesday, November 29
11:30 a.m.
Vista Hermosa, Colorado

GOTTING SWITCHED OFF THE burner phone. He wiped the handset clean of fingerprints, pulled it apart, and tossed the pieces from the window a few hundred yards down the road. Even if the cops eventually found it, he wouldn't care.

He circled out of Vista Hermosa and back into the south end of town. Vista Hermosa was more of a small city than a town. It boasted three hotels, a hospital, and a regional airport with an instrument approach that could accommodate the jet.

The town grew up because of an abundance of good skiing within an hour's drive in several directions. Which made it a convenient location that would reduce the options for tracking him down.

He stopped at a sandwich shop then parked on the upper level of the airport parking garage. He ate his sandwich and watched travelers come and go.

When a space opened up on the side of the lot overlooking the runway, he raced around to claim it. He parked straight in where he had a clear view of the taxiway and the arrival area.

Kimball could fly a commercial jet to Colorado Springs or Denver, but from there, she'd need a puddle jumper into Vista Hermosa. That meant a prop aircraft, which would stop out on the tarmac. No fancy jet bridge. She'd walk across the open area to the arrival lounge. A medium height blonde woman with short curls. Possibly with a bunch of FBI suits in tow.

He settled into his seat. She shouldn't be too difficult to spot.

CHAPTER FIFTY-EIGHT

Wednesday, November 29
11:10 a.m.
Kansas City, Kansas

THE DENVER FBI OFFICE'S trace picked up on Jess's call. They called Fernandez while she was still talking to Gotting. By the time she hung up, a police car was on its way to a location identified by the phone company. Eight minutes later, the officer reported to the scene, which was a deserted road in the mountains outside Vista Hermosa. No sign of Gotting.

Jess and Fernandez were ushered onto a gleaming Gulfstream G500 by a man in a sharp pinstripe suit who introduced himself as Lawrence. The seats were roomy and supremely comfortable. She leaned back as the jet pushed into the sky, the engines a barely audible rumble behind her.

She connected to the aircraft's Wi-Fi network and brought up maps of the area around Vista Hermosa. Main roads led out in five directions, one to Colorado Springs, the others to ski valleys through the mountains. She'd visited several of the areas in the past. Most were rugged and busy this time of year.

In a short space of time, Gotting had made two phone calls from Vista Hermosa, which meant he had to be within about fifty miles. For the most part, he'd been cool and collected on the phone. But staying in the same town when the police would be searching for him? That was a significant risk. Which probably meant he'd hunkered down in another location.

She surveyed the places accessible within an hour's drive of Vista Hermosa. It was a big area, not so much the size, but the effort to get everywhere. The roads were narrow and winding, often snow-covered, and the mountains slowed all progress.

If Gotting had holed up in the mountains, where would he have chosen? Would he hide in the crowds, such as one of the busy ski areas? Or would he go for seclusion? The problem with Colorado was that there was an endless supply of both.

Then there was the question of the handover. If he wanted to get away after he had the money, he'd need a location with plenty of exits. A valley location was far from ideal. He'd be trapped there.

She drummed her fingers on the seat's soft leather. What made sense was to hold Peter in a secluded location and arrange the money exchange in a busy place.

Lawrence placed a small speakerphone on the polished wood table that separated her from Fernandez. "Mr. Pierce would like to talk to you, Ms. Kimball."

Fernandez leaned forward when Jess answered the call.

"Hi, Jess." Carter Pierce's voice resonated through the speakerphone as it did in person. "I'm making progress on assembling the money. Bills, unmarked, just as he said."

"I argued him down to three million," she said.

"Argued?"

"Talked. We discussed it and he agreed."

"That was a risk. Please don't do that again. The money means nothing to me. He knows you're working with the authorities." Carter paused as if he remembered she was not alone. "It might only take a little more pressure for him to walk away. Who knows where that would leave Peter?"

"If he thought I was a pushover, he'd be more suspicious and more dangerous, too. Anyway, he agreed, and three million will be easier to pay back than five."

"There's no payback for this, Jess. When I offered, I meant it. If this gets your son back, it's a small price to pay."

"This is not just a payoff for Peter. We have to keep both our focus and the pressure on Earle Gotting," Fernandez said. "If we're right, he's responsible for a long string of child abductions. That's a lot of children and a lot of families he's harmed. Both the birth families and the adoptive families have been crushed by his actions."

"Don't forget, he said no police and no helicopters," Jess said.

Fernandez shrugged. "Denver office says snow tomorrow. Helicopters are probably out of the question anyway."

"So, how are you going to stay focused on Gotting? Do we need more support on the ground? I can bring in a private agency," Pierce said.

Fernandez shook his head. "Definitely not. We have plenty of boots on the ground here."

"Then how about equipment? Even if Jess isn't wired or carrying a gun, I assume the car will be monitored," Pierce said.

Fernandez scowled. "We're not amateurs."

Pierce was quiet a beat. "Right. I'm sorry. I just want to be sure you have everything you need."

"You're doing a great job by supplying the ransom money, Mr. Pierce. We'll handle the rest. You can help by letting us do our job."

"And what do you want me to do?" Jess asked.

Fernandez looked at her intently. "As long as your life isn't threatened, follow his instructions. Don't get close enough for him to grab you or hurt you."

She nodded. "Okay."

Fernandez said, "Under no circumstances put yourself in a situation where he could take you hostage, like he did with Peter."

"Absolutely not." She shuddered.

"Once you have Peter, leave the area. Immediately," Fernandez continued. "Head in the opposite direction. Get as far away as you can as swiftly as you can. But be safe."

"No speeding. Got it." She grinned.

Fernandez frowned. "Do not try to take Gotting on in any way. We'll deal with him. We want to arrest him. We need to know where those other kids are, and we need him fully debriefed. Any questions?"

Jess shook her head. "Any idea what he's going to do?"

"Bluntly, no. But we're prepared. We'll have a couple of cars at every exit. We'll be able to follow you and him. If we can launch a helicopter we will. Keep it airborne but well away from you. We'll have vehicles ready to follow on the main routes. We'll be in radio contact. All of us. Including you."

Jess nodded.

"We'll rig a mic to hear you in the car at all times. He's probably going to use a phone, so we'll have lines to the major phone companies open the moment we start. If he uses a cellphone, we can get an approximate location quickly."

"How approximate?" Jess asked.

"A few hundred feet. Maybe less because of the mountains. You're going to be wearing international orange. He'll hate it, but we're not going to lose you."

"Won't that alert him?"

Fernandez shrugged. "He's slow-rolling us on the details. Wants to keep us as far away as possible. That's because he knows we're involved. Not much point in hiding that. As long as we can make him feel safe enough to go through with the handover, then we get Peter back."

"And after that?" she said.

"After that, the gloves are off." Fernandez shrugged. "Within reason, and consistent with the goals of the operation, of course."

Lawrence walked down the aisle again. "We need to end the call. We'll be landing in Colorado Springs in ten minutes."

"Good luck, Jess," Carter said. "I'll be sitting right here until it's over. Keep me posted."

"Will do. And thanks again, Carter. I can't tell you how grateful I am," Jess replied.

"Just come home safely. And bring Peter with you. I can't wait to meet the young man I've been hearing about all these years," he said and rang off.

CHAPTER FIFTY-NINE

Wednesday, November 29
2:00 p.m.
Colorado Springs, Colorado

THE TIERNEYS' HOUSE WAS a split-level on a sloping street. The front porch was rustic brick and the rest of the house was skinned with cream painted wood siding. A dusting of snow covered the front lawn.

Jess and Fernandez arrived in a taxi. She rang the doorbell. A man with square shoulders, weathered skin, and a buzz cut answered the door.

"Ross Tierney? I'm FBI Special Agent Emilio Fernandez." He held out his badge.

"They told us you were coming." Tierney nodded as he studied the badge. He turned to Jess. "Where's your ID?"

"I'm Jessica Kimball."

"She's working with us," Fernandez said.

Tierney said, "You're a reporter."

Jess nodded. "*Taboo Magazine*. But that's not why I'm here."

Tierney eyed her for a moment. "What are you here for?"

Fernandez gestured toward the house. "Can we discuss this inside?"

Tierney moved aside to let them enter. "My wife is in the kitchen."

The hallway was lined with pictures in a variety of frames. Many photos were of Peter and a slightly older girl, at various ages. Halloween costumes, sporting events, birthday parties. Normal events in a child's life. Events she'd missed. Years she'd never get back.

In every photo, Peter was happy. Laughing, smiling, well nourished, eyes glinting with joy. Whatever had happened to her son, he'd been loved. Jess could see that, even from the photographs. He'd had the kind of life she would never have been able to give him. How could she take him away from the only family he'd ever known?

"That's our son, Steven," Tierney said.

Mesmerized, Jess nodded and swallowed the lump in her throat so she could reply. "And you have a girl."

"Michelle. Started college this year. We checked on her. She's safe. And she's got a buddy system going with her friends. She won't be alone at any time until we get this all resolved." Tierney was a military man. He wasn't the kind to sit around wringing his hands. All problems called for action.

"That's good," Fernandez said.

The kitchen was a galley style with a breakfast table at the far end. A woman with dark hair stood by the table. Her eyes were puffy and red-ringed from crying. Her makeup was streaked from tears.

Jess held out her hand. "Lynette? I'm Jess Kimball."

She grasped Jess's hand and held it in both of hers. "You're the reporter."

"Yes. I'm assisting the FBI." Jess cleared her throat. "I'm so sorry you're going through this."

Lynette nodded, dubiously.

Jess and Fernandez sat at the table, the Tierneys sat on the other side, holding hands.

"What have you found out about Steven?" Ross asked. Lynette whimpered and blinked away more tears.

"Let me explain a little about where we are." Fernandez waited until both distraught parents nodded. "We've been investigating a lawyer in Kansas City."

Lynette frowned. "How can that be related to Steven? We want our son back. What are you doing about finding him?"

Ross shifted in his seat. "What lawyer's office?"

"Somersall-McCree," Fernandez said.

Ross leaned forward on his elbows. "We used them. You know. For our adoptions."

Fernandez nodded.

"Adoptions? More than one?" Jess asked.

"We couldn't have children. We tried for years." Lynette nodded. "Steven and Michelle are both adopted."

"So, what about the lawyer?" Ross said.

Jess looked down at her hands. "There is some evidence that the lawyer involved in your adoption wasn't entirely…ethical."

Lynette frowned.

These were such good people. They deserved to know the truth. Jess took a deep breath. "Thirteen years ago, my son, Peter, was taken. He was twenty-three months old. That was when you adopted Steven," Jess said.

Lynette gasped. She clutched her husband's arm.

Ross shook his head. "You think our Steven is your son?"

Jess said, "We're not sure. Not yet. But it seems like that could be true."

Ross jerked forward. "Did you take him?"

"Of course not. But when you hear the rest, you might wish I had," Jess said quietly.

He jumped up and his chair tipped over backward. The clatter as it hit the wood floor was deafening in the quiet room. "Is this why you're both here? You want Steven?"

"Not exactly," Fernandez said. "Please, Mr. Tierney. Sit down. We have a lot of ground to cover and not a lot of time to tell you everything."

Tierney stood, fists balled by his sides, nostrils flaring. He was willing to fight for his son. He loved Steven. That much was clear.

Lynette began to cry again. Softly. Tears flowed down her cheeks as she looked ahead, heartbroken, horrified.

"Please. Let us tell you everything we know. Then we'll answer your questions," Jess said.

Lynette looked at her husband, and he put a hand on her shoulder. She covered his hand with her own. After a few more tense moments, he bent to right his chair and sat next to his wife again.

"Thank you," Jess said.

Tierney said, "He's our son. We adopted him. Legally. We went to court. We have orders. Even if you're the biological mother, you can't just come back after all these years."

Lynette whispered, "We did everything right. A private adoption. We met the bio-mom."

"Please. Let us explain first. It will save a lot of time and heartache." Fernandez held up his hand. They both nodded.

Jess watched as these good people, parents who obviously loved their children, had their hearts ripped out. She remained quiet until Fernandez said his peace.

"The evidence we have so far shows that your lawyer, Ammerson Belk, operated an illegal private adoption scam within an otherwise legitimate law firm. It was a sophisticated operation. A great many people were deceived."

Ross's face was lined with confusion. "Why are you telling us now? Our son is missing. What are you doing to find him?"

"I-I can't even imagine what you've been through." Lynette sagged back in her chair, her mouth half open, staring at Jess. "You've been looking for him? All this time?"

What a kind, generous woman. Jess nodded. Tears welled in her eyes and she blinked them away.

"We had him with us. We took such good care of him. He's a wonderful boy." Lynette put her face in her hands and burst into tears.

The husband hugged her. "I don't understand this. We're terrified about our missing son. You come here to tell us something that might be completely wrong... Why? Why now? Can't this wait until we find Steven?"

Jess looked steadily at him. "The man who took Peter from me thirteen years ago is the same man who took Steven from you this morning. He's blackmailing me. He wants three million dollars for our boy's safe return."

Both Tierneys stared across the table, wide-eyed, shocked. Temporarily speechless.

After a while, Ross said, "Why you? Why not contact us?"

"Because he doesn't think you have three-million dollars. And he believes my employer will pay."

"That's insane. This can't be happening," Lynette said.

"It's the truth," Fernandez replied.

Ross opened and closed his mouth, but nothing came out.

"Your employer?" Lynette said. "Will he pay the ransom? I mean, if Steven's life's at stake?"

"He will. He's already agreed." Jess nodded. "He's a very generous man."

Lynette cocked her head, bewildered again. "You've been talking to the kidnapper?"

"Yes."

Lynette gestured to herself and her husband. "You've been talking about our son? Without us? We're his parents."

"He contacted me. Not the other way around," Jess said.

Fernandez leaned forward, both forearms on the table. "We only uncovered your names three hours ago. We came here directly from Kansas, as soon as we found out who and where you were. We couldn't possibly have included you any earlier."

"Ross, Lynette. Please. We're here now. I understand your position, believe me. And if we'd known about you earlier, we would have contacted you before. I've been looking for my son for thirteen years. I'm more than a little shocked to have found you now," Jess said as sincerely as she truly felt.

Lynette Tierney wrapped her arms around herself. "Steven was taken because of you."

"Twice." Jess pursed her lips and nodded. "I'm afraid so."

Lynette waved her hand in the air and dissolved in a puddle of tears again.

Her husband put his arm around her shoulders and hugged her close. "The ransom. That's… It's… I can do the delivery. I've had a lot of training. I can handle myself."

"I wish you could. Or the FBI," Jess nodded toward Fernandez and sighed. "The kidnapper has asked for me."

Lynette's lip trembled.

Ross shook his head. "But I'm his father. And I'm bigger. Stronger. No offense."

"I know. But that's exactly why he's asked for me. He thinks he's more powerful than I am. He thinks it's safer for him if I do it."

"But what are you going to do? I mean, if…"

"Mr. Tierney, you don't know me. Your concern is understandable and appreciated. Truly." Jess swallowed. "But I'll be fine."

"How do you know?" Lynette Tierney whispered.

"I've been kidnapped before and escaped. I've brought criminals to justice, and I've been shot at before. Several times," Jess said.

Lynette stared at her, wide-eyed.

"I don't relish all this adrenaline. No one with any sense does. But he wants me because he thinks I'm weak. I'll do everything I can to convince him he's right. Because I've trained for this for thirteen long years." She cleared her throat and put much more conviction into her voice than she actually felt. "I'm more than ready. And the FBI will be right there for backup."

She glanced at Fernandez. He said, "Absolutely."

Jess nodded. "I'm every bit as motivated as you are, Ross. Trust me. This guy won't beat me again. I'll bring…our son back."

No one spoke for a good half minute.

Ross looked hard at Jess and then at Fernandez. "You're going to get this guy, right?"

"Once the handover is done. We give them time to separate, so Peter and Jess are clear. After that, we close in."

Lynette sniffed back tears. "Steven. His name…the name he knows, is Steven."

Jess nodded. "Steven, yes."

"When's the handover?" Ross asked.

"Eleven tomorrow morning."

"Where?"

"Somewhere around Vista Hermosa. That's all we know."

"It's supposed to snow tomorrow."

"Hurts him as much as us, if it does," Fernandez said.

Ross thought for a moment. "You can't fly a helicopter in those conditions."

"We'll have as many people on the ground as we need," Fernandez said.

"Any aerial surveillance at all?"

Fernandez shrugged. "Helicopter is all we've got. Assuming we can get it into the air."

Ross pursed his lips. "I may be able to get something."

Jess frowned.

"Half our training these days is drones," Ross said.

"If he sees or hears anything…"

Ross shook his head. "Night Crow RQ-88. Light gray, twenty-foot wingspan. Ten hours flight time at twenty thousand feet plus. No chance."

Fernandez leaned forward. "Is that legal?"

"This is my son." He took a deep breath. "Look. We're a training base. We have to train somewhere." He ripped the top from a box of cereal, wrote on it, and handed it to Fernandez. "My cellphone. The weather doesn't matter at twenty thousand feet. We'll be up before dawn anyway. Call me. I'll be there."

Fernandez said, "Okay. Thanks."

Jess and Fernandez said their goodbyes and returned to the taxi and then to the Gulfstream. Ten minutes later they were in the air for the five-minute hop to the tiny Vista Hermosa Regional Airport.

Jess had no time to process the feelings she'd experienced at the Tierneys'. She shoved them aside, for now, knowing the time was coming when she'd need to face everything.

But not until Peter was safe.

CHAPTER SIXTY

Wednesday, November 29
3:00 p.m.
Vista Hermosa, Colorado

VISTA HERMOSA REGIONAL AIRPORT'S schedule couldn't be called busy. Only twelve inbound and outbound commercial flights in a day. There were only two airlines, one an independent and the other a sub-brand of a major carrier. They shared the same facilities, including the luggage trucks and orange cones that guided passengers between the aircraft and the terminal.

From his place on the upper level of the parking garage, Gotting had a clear view of the orange cones. Passengers disembarked the aircraft, either walking casually with their hands free, or struggling with overstuffed carry-on luggage.

The aircraft sat while a tanker refueled the plane. Then the process would happen in reverse. Passengers boarded, which was slower than deplaning. Eventually the aircraft door was closed, and the ground crew walked the aircraft out to the taxiway.

The plane rolled straight onto the runway and took off. The sound of its propellers carried through the cold air.

To pass the time, Gotting used an old map to write directions for a route into the mountains. The route was pretty simple, he just needed to get the road numbers down.

Another aircraft came and went. He watched the process happen three more times before a private jet came in.

The jet engines roared. Small puffs of smoke came from the tires as it touched down. It rolled to the far end of the runway before taxiing to the terminal.

The fuselage boasted the image of a multicolored scarf waving in the breeze. Gotting recognized the logo. ShareJet, a business jet taxi service for the rich. He grinned.

He leaned forward as the aircraft came to a stop. A door behind the cockpit opened. A man lowered steps from the aircraft. The rich didn't wait for the rickety flight stairs ordinary people used.

Jess Kimball stepped out. Gotting stared hard. He gripped the steering wheel like a vise. She'd begged for three million instead of five, and now she was traveling in a private jet.

She walked down the steps. A man followed her. In his crisp, dark suit he could have been a banker or a lawyer, but Gotting knew he was FBI. The G-man scanned the tarmac from the moment he exited the plane until they disappeared into the terminal.

Gotting backed out of his parking spot and headed around to arrivals. He parked two cars back from the airport's only rental car location. A few minutes later, Kimball and the G-man headed out to a Ford Explorer and drove out of the airport.

The Explorer was big enough that Gotting didn't have to get close to follow it. He watched them all the way to the Faversham

Hotel. It was one of those new places, mostly made of sheetrock, paint, and glass.

Large windows offered a good view into the lobby. He watched them check in separately and take the elevator.

Once they had disappeared, he drove back down the road and stopped at a parcel delivery place. He picked up a mailer with the word Express on it. He put the directions he had written earlier inside, sealed the mailer and wrote an address in the small box designated for the purpose.

The girl behind the counter paid him no attention when he handed over the padded envelope. She typed the address into a computer and frowned. "You know this place is just down the road, right?"

"Yeah."

She pointed. "Opposite the Faversham."

"I want a record of the delivery," he lied.

She shrugged. "Six dollars for delivery by ten a.m."

Gotting paid cash. She gave him a receipt with a twelve-digit tracking number.

Two doors down from the parcel delivery place was a sports store selling ski and snowboard gear. He checked his cash. He grimaced. He was running out of money just as he was about to get three million for the kid. The irony was painful.

He browsed the sports shop. He hadn't skied since his leg was mangled in prison. Snowboarding would allow both legs to work together. The boots wouldn't force him to walk like a robot.

He tested a couple of pairs of boots before settling on a pair that had a rough, crepe-like sole that he knew gripped well on snow. He bought the cheapest pair of goggles and a backpack. After he paid the bill, he was left with eleven dollars. Not enough for a ski jacket or a board, which left him with another task.

He joked about the sad state of his closet, and the checkout clerk was happy to give him a handful of metal hangers left over from the summer sales.

He sat in the parking lot thinking about what he'd seen. It shouldn't have angered him that Kimball arrived in a private jet. After all, she'd arrived in Colorado much more quickly. But he shouldn't have agreed to three million. He felt used and conned.

After a few minutes, he decided. She thought she'd got the upper hand. She thought he could be pushed around. Maybe she thought she was going to get her boy back without paying the money at all.

He grinned.

Time she learned how weak she really was.

CHAPTER SIXTY-ONE

Wednesday, November 29
4:00 p.m.
Vista Hermosa, Colorado

JESS STOOD IN THE Vista Hermosa police transportation garage, a large metal building in an industrial park on the outskirts of town. High windows allowed light in and a roll-up door provided access. A couple of police vehicles were on ramps being repaired.

The FBI and the Colorado Bureau of Investigation were well prepared. Fernandez had briefed her on the number and location of personnel from both agencies. But no large meeting of the entire team was scheduled, in case Gotting was watching.

Three times, Fernandez had offered to replace Jess for the handover. He introduced her to a female agent with a medium build and curly blonde hair who had volunteered.

Jess turned them down. An FBI agent was much better trained to deal with whatever happened, but Gotting knew exactly what she looked like. The smallest detail might push him to abort the exchange or hurt Peter. She couldn't take the chance.

Besides, Peter was *her* son. She'd spent thirteen long years searching for him. She was no vigilante, but she was prepared to pull out all the stops to rescue him. Certainly, more than she would ever expect someone else to do. She was Peter's mother. This was her job. She wanted to do it herself.

Even as she knew that preparation and planning would make the operation successful, she fought impatience. Tension tightened all of her muscles. She moved to a corner to work through a series of stretches. She was so close. Closer than she'd been to her son in way too long. Tomorrow seemed an eternity from now.

The FBI vehicle for the handover was a dark blue Jeep Wrangler with a muscular V8 and hardtop. She walked over for her training.

A man in coveralls and a black fleece cap introduced himself as Phil Collins. "Like the famous singer, except more hair and less money," he said, grinning and patting his head.

Jess gave a weak laugh. She knew everyone was trying to get her past the anxiety over Peter's safety. She appreciated their efforts, although they didn't seem to help much.

Collins grimaced and turned his efforts to preparing Jess instead of trying to relieve her stress level. He walked to the back of the Jeep.

"There are two guns. Glocks, since you're familiar with them. One under the driver's seat, the other under here." He showed her the outside gun first. He patted under the right rear wheel arch. "Try to grab it."

Jess knelt and reached under the Jeep's flared arch. She fumbled to locate the gun's grip.

"Dead center of the arch," Collins said, but he didn't reach in to guide her.

Jess found the gun. It was wrapped in something slippery.

"Keep your finger away from the trigger and give it a firm yank."

She did as he instructed and pulled the gun free. It was stored in a thin, transparent plastic bag.

"Rip the plastic off if you have time. You'll have better aim. Or fire immediately if you need to," Collins said. "Not elegant or clean, but it'll work fine. And you have seventeen rounds. Same as the Glock you're used to."

"Not that we're expecting you to fire at all," Fernandez said. "But just in case you need it for self-defense."

She nodded.

Collins took the Glock from her and opened the driver's door. "Try the under-seat gun."

She settled herself in the driver's seat. Without bending at all, she reached underneath the front of the seat between her knees and found it in one motion.

"Easy," she said.

"The same type of gun, the same number of shots," Collins said.

Jess returned the Glock to its place under the driver's seat. She closed her eyes and rested her hands on the steering wheel. In one smooth movement, she reached down, grabbed the gun, and aimed at the roll-up door, all without looking.

She could confidently assure Henry that she could reach the gun with her eyes closed.

Collins shook his head. "Don't try to shoot through the windshield. The bullet will go wild and you'll end up covered in safety glass. On top of which, in these temperatures, you'll freeze after only a minute or two of driving time. Better to fire through the side windows."

Jess nodded. "Got it."

Collins patted the dashboard, identifying locations as he explained each piece of equipment. "We've mic'd the interior. We'll try to listen, but reception isn't always the best in the mountains. We have a recorder on board, which won't help in the moment, but we'll have it for evidence against Gotting when we're done. The screen has navigation. Since you probably won't know where he's leading you ahead of time, leave it set to follow your location instead of trying to predict the route. Keep an eye on it all of the time. Pay attention to the roads around you, so you have an immediate idea of escape routes."

He pointed to a pair of gear levers. "Leave it in 4H, which means four-wheel drive, high range. It'll be good on the roads in this snow, and if you do go off-road, it'll work there, too."

"Manual transmission," she said, with her hand on the shifter knob.

"Six gears. You okay with a stick?"

"Haven't driven one in a while." She grinned. "One of the benefits of being a penniless student. I couldn't afford an automatic."

"Ah." Collins smiled, too. "We don't think you'll be going off-road, but if you do, manual transmission is best."

"I understand."

"One last thing." He stepped back from the door and gestured toward the Jeep. "This vehicle will cover all sorts of terrain. Big rocks and frightening slopes. But the kind of things you see on the internet? Leave that stuff to the professionals. If you're faced with a thirty-degree incline or steeper, you need to be looking for a different route. It'll do way more than that, but the margin for error will be overcome in a heartbeat. Roll this Jeep and you'll be in a world of hurt."

"Got it," she said again.

Collins settled into the passenger seat. "Let's go for a drive. Make sure you can operate everything."

She nodded, started the engine, and they put the Jeep through its paces. When they rolled back into the parking lot, Collins gave her two thumbs up.

"Thank you, Phil. I'll never listen to Genesis again without thinking of you." She smiled, and he laughed as he waved and walked away.

She stayed in the Jeep for a while, familiarizing herself with all the instruments, checking the position of the Glock, practicing her draw and aim with her eyes opened and closed.

Fernandez came over to check on her. "Any questions?"

Jess gripped the steering wheel, checking her sight lines through the windows, and practicing reaching for the gun one last time. Muscle memory and instincts were two invaluable weapons she couldn't take for granted.

This was it.

After thirteen long, long years she would exchange millions of dollars for her son, armed and prepared. She'd worked every day investigating crime for *Taboo*. She'd been in tight places and up against ruthless killers before.

But confronting Gotting was different.

He'd lived in her building all those years ago. He'd watched her for a period of time and she'd never noticed him at all.

He'd watched her for a long while. Long enough to know her habits and routines. Coldly, he'd identified her as an easy target. He'd found a way to steal her son and knew when and where to sell the baby.

He'd planned the perfect crime. And he'd pulled it off.

She hadn't found him. All the best investigators, the best agencies, the sharpest tech available had failed.

In the end, he'd exposed himself.

Only greed motivated him. He cared about nothing else. He wanted the money. He'd do anything to get it. Of that, she was certain.

He wouldn't be satisfied for very long. If his extortion scheme worked, if he lived, he'd want more money.

He'd find more victims. He'd blackmail another mother. And another. And another after that.

Nothing would make him stop. Not as long as he drew breath.

She squeezed the steering wheel. Whatever happened tomorrow, Peter would be saved. He'd always meant everything to her and he always would.

But Gotting meant even less to her than she meant to him.

Her never-ending manhunt was almost over. What would she do then?

"Jess?" Fernandez prompted again, louder. "Any questions?"

She shook her head and squared her shoulders. "I'm ready."

CHAPTER SIXTY-TWO

Wednesday, November 29
4:10 p.m.
Zuma Loda Ski Area, Colorado

GOTTING PARKED IN THE most remote parking lot at the Zuma Loda ski area, near the exit. The slopes had already closed and the daylight was fading fast. The looming mountains brought darkness much earlier out here.

The remote lot was mostly used by locals who valued cheap parking more than convenience. Skiers had to walk to the main area but could ski directly back to the car through the trees at the end of the day.

The locals were almost all gone now. Unlike tourists, once locals finished skiing, they didn't waste time in the bars. They had to drive back to their homes in the towns and cities across the snowy roads. Navigating in the dark while under the influence of alcohol was nothing but a disaster waiting to happen.

He ripped the labels off the snowboard boots he'd bought

340 | DIANE CAPRI

earlier. They fit him well enough and gripped the snow. He selected one of the coat hangers, straightened out the wire triangle and kept the hook.

He locked the Audi and walked along the road away from town. Lights from houses, chalets, and apartments glinted through the trees.

Ten minutes later, he found a chalet he could use set back off the road, up to an unpaved lane. Heavy drapes covered the windows, but there were people inside. He heard music and laugher as he walked quietly up the lane, which was even better.

Six SUVs were wedged into the small parking area. The snow around them was undisturbed, indicating they hadn't been moved today.

Farthest from the chalet was an old, light brown GMC Yukon, solid and heavy with bull bars and four-wheel drive. The front end pointed down the slope of the lane. Even better, it was at least twelve years old and wouldn't have an immobilizer.

He looked in through the windows to confirm no blinking red lights or other signs of an aftermarket alarm.

He hid behind the bulk of the vehicle and pushed the coat hanger through the weather-strip on the passenger door. He was about to pull up, hoping to open the lock, when he noticed the door wasn't locked.

He pulled the coat hanger out and lifted the handle. The door opened with a tinny metal clang. His heart jumped and he stared in the direction of the chalet. The music didn't stop. No one opened the drapes or came out of the front door. He breathed again and crawled into the vehicle.

Not only was the Yukon unlocked, but the keys were in the ashtray. Which wasn't surprising. People were pretty trusting around here, which he'd forgotten about. Leaving the doors unlocked with the keys inside was not only convenient, but it was also common practice.

He engaged the key and released the steering lock. He didn't start the vehicle. He released the parking brake and rolled the Yukon downhill along the lane. He used the vehicle's momentum to turn onto the main road without stopping. When he was a hundred yards from the chalet, he started the engine and switched on the lights.

The Yukon coughed into life. He light-footed the accelerator to keep the engine noise down and headed into the Zuma Loda resort.

There might have been a small town there long ago, but any sign of it had been obliterated by corporate investment. The resort was built for skiers and intended for profit.

Four ski runs converged in a big open area in front of pricey shops that sold trendy snow gear along with useless but expensive trinkets. Restaurants lined up for business, and several hotels faced the slopes, making the most of their ski-in/ski-out positions.

Away from the base of the ski runs, the buildings were less grand. Vehicles packed in along the streets because the public lots were full.

He found a bar illuminated by neon lights that he recognized and circled the block to the road that led out of Zuma Loda. He parked the Yukon and locked it when he stepped out, just in case someone else wanted to steal it.

He heard the noise from the bar at the end of the block. The après-ski crowd was going strong, which suited his purposes perfectly.

Outside the bar, they'd lined up their skis in a snow bank. The potential for theft was obvious, so they tried to split up the skis, mixing lefts and rights, but the colors were so bright that it took only a moment to match them again.

Snowboards were locked to a rack, though. He searched until he found an old one wedged in the snow bank. He rocked it in the snow to make sure he could break it free easily when he needed it.

Inside, the bar was packed. The air was humid because the snow on the boots mixed with warmth from the heaters to infuse the air with moisture. Coats were heaped in piles, on tables near groups of revelers, or hanging three deep on nearby racks. Even in the dim light, he could tell light blue coats were this year's color.

Beer flowed freely and a lot of it spilled. At the back, a local garage band thrashed through Tom Petty songs. He listened briefly on his way through. He wasn't there for entertainment, but he wanted to fit into the crowd and not draw too much attention.

Which was also why he went into the restroom and waited a few minutes. Walking in and straight back out of any bar in Colorado would put a spotlight on him for sure.

When he returned to the bar, the band was belting out "American Girl." Fortified with alcohol, guys and girls crowded the center of the room writhing in what might have passed for dancing.

He glanced around. Everyone seemed preoccupied. A light-colored jacket hung on the rack, a black fleece cap poking from the pocket. He lifted the jacket and slipped it on as he walked out.

Over his pounding heart, he heard no shouts, and no one ran after him. He didn't look back.

He found the unlocked snowboard again, pulled it from the snow bank with one swift tug, tucked it under his arm, and walked toward the Yukon, speed increasing with every step.

In two minutes, he was on the road and the neon lights faded in his rearview mirror.

CHAPTER SIXTY-THREE

Wednesday, November 29
8:00 p.m.
Vista Hermosa, Colorado

JESS LOOKED OUT OF her hotel room window, holding her phone to her ear while talking to Morris.

He said, "Fernandez has a good reputation."

"He's doing everything he can, Henry." She smiled so he could hear it. "He's not you, of course. But that can't be helped."

He wasn't mollified. "You're doing the handover?"

She could hear his disapproval all the way from Kansas. "It'll be okay. I want Peter, he wants his money."

"I don't like it, Jess. We have people who are trained for this work. Can't you let us do our jobs?"

Jess didn't reply.

He sighed. "I know it's a waste of breath to argue with you. But be careful. Please."

"Of course." She resisted the temptation to offer some sarcastic teasing. Partly because he was truly worried. And partly because it was nice to have someone who worried about her, finally.

"I talked to him. He's wired the car for sound and rigged two guns," Henry said, probably to reassure himself more than her.

She smiled, although he couldn't see her. "One under the driver's seat, one in the rear wheel arch."

"Have you practiced reaching for them? On no advance warning at all?"

"We ran through everything at the police station. Several times."

"But you can reach them? Quickly? With your eyes closed?"

"I practiced. A lot. No problem. I promise."

Henry sighed. "Weather will be our biggest obstacle. We all have four-wheel drive but don't get too far away from easy access. They can't help you if they can't get to you in time."

She was about to tell him she wasn't going to do anything stupid, but she paused, remembering who she was talking to.

He was the best FBI agent she'd ever met. He was genuine, sincere, and as brave as they came. He'd risked his life to save hers in Italy. He'd even relocated to her city so they could be together. He'd been shot helping her track down Peter. And he was lying in a hospital bed six hundred miles away because of her. He'd probably never sat out anything out in his life. Reading emails and listening to secondhand plans couldn't be easy for him.

Whatever happened tomorrow would happen. She was as prepared as she could be. They all were. There was nothing else she could say.

So she told him she loved him. He seemed stunned to silence.

"I do love you, Henry. Please don't act like you didn't already know that," she said.

"You've never said anything before." He drew a deep breath. "Promise me you're not planning some stupid grand gesture against Gotting tomorrow, Jess."

She shook her head and grinned. "I know lawmen are skeptical by nature. But the customary thing to say when a woman says she loves you is that you love her back. Not 'please don't commit suicide.'"

He paused for a long time. She heard him breathing, so he hadn't died. She waited.

After a while, he said, "I swear, if you die tomorrow, I'll never forgive you."

She laughed heartily and it felt really good to let go. When she finally could speak again, she said, "Good night, Henry. See you soon."

CHAPTER SIXTY-FOUR

Wednesday, November 29
11:00 p.m.
Vista Hermosa, Colorado

JESS SAID GOODNIGHT TO Fernandez when he got off the elevator on the floor below hers after dinner. Her room was a suite with a small kitchen and a tiny desk and chair that allowed the budget hotel chain to claim it offered a workspace for the busy professional.

She called room service to order a glass of Cabernet. While she waited, she dashed off an email to Stephenson apologizing for not having updated him with the rapidly changing events. He'd been her go-to guy for a long time while she searched for Peter. He'd become emotionally invested in the search, and she couldn't wait for Peter to meet him when they got home.

The wine arrived a few minutes later. She sat on the bed, sipping her wine to relax. Her nerves were fizzing. The handover was tantamount to a life-and-death game of chicken. Whatever happened, the first and only thing that absolutely had to happen was to get Peter away safely.

Even if it meant Gotting escaped. Not that she intended to let that happen. But if it did, Morris would track him down later. Peter came first.

She finished her wine, no more relaxed than when she started. No way could she sleep. But she had to. She had to be one hundred percent ready when Gotting called tomorrow. Fatigue was the enemy.

Maybe a warm shower would help relax her. She pushed off the bed and padded barefoot into the small bathroom.

She started the shower, testing the water with her hand. The mirror began to fog from the steam. The hotel provided small bottles of shampoo and conditioner. She placed them on the edge of the tub.

She'd seen a bathrobe in the closet. She walked into the bedroom and grabbed it. She tossed it onto the bed and reached to unsnap her jeans.

A blindingly bright light flashed high up in the corner of the bedroom.

A fire alarm sounded.

Deafening *whoop, whoop, whoop* blasted from speakers in both rooms of the suite and from the corridor. A mechanical voice said, "Please proceed down the stairs. Do not take the elevator."

She turned off the shower, dried her hands, and grabbed her coat. She slipped on her shoes. She put her palm flat on the interior door. It was cool to the touch. She pulled it open to step into the corridor.

She never got the chance.

Earle Gotting waited until she'd opened the door. He pushed

against her chest with both arms, leaning his weight into it. The force slammed her backward into her room.

She fell against the wall.

He walked inside and kicked the door closed with his boot.

All in one motion, he stepped toward her, grabbed her throat with his gloved left hand, and rammed a gun against the side of her head with his right, driving the muzzle into her skin.

He growled, "Don't think I won't shoot you."

The first thing she noticed was he smelled of sweat.

He was only a few inches taller than her. The hair she'd seen in his mug shots was fading fast. What was left dangled down the back of his neck in unwashed clumps.

Her head throbbed from the impact with the wall, but she ignored it.

"What do you want?" she said levelly. The fire alarm continued its ear-splitting volume, but he stood so close she didn't need to raise her voice.

"You know who I am?"

She shook her head. Playing dumb might make him talk as much and as long as possible while she figured out what the hell to do.

He relaxed his grip on her throat and shoved her toward the middle of the room, keeping the gun pointed at her face. "You're lying."

"You're the man on the phone."

"Forget it. Take off the coat. Slowly."

Jess slipped off the coat and laid it on the bed. The noise and the flashing lights were disorienting. She couldn't think.

"Turn around," he said.

Her heart skipped. "You kill me and you'll never get your money."

"You're mouthy for a woman who wants her kid back," Gotting grunted. "I think your boss is made of weaker stuff."

"You're wrong."

"I don't think so. I think I'll kill you, and he'd still pay up. Now turn around."

She turned but kept her head twisted toward him and his gun in view.

He grabbed the desk chair and shoved it at the back of her legs. "Sit down."

She sat slowly while keeping her head twisted around and her eyes on him.

He secured her silence by placing a length of duct tape over her mouth. She fought back her gag reflex.

He wrapped the duct tape around her wrists and secured her ankles to the base of the chair.

She couldn't talk. Her heart rate rose, pounding painfully against her sternum. She struggled to keep her breathing under control.

He ripped the tape off her mouth and applied it again. Looser this time, giving her room to breathe and to speak muffled sentences. "Don't want you dying too soon."

He sat on the bed, the gun leveled at her stomach.

The lights stopped flashing, and the alarm ceased. The noise still rang in her ears even as the silence overwhelmed her senses.

"What do you want?" she grunted, barely able to form words with her tongue.

"You know what I want."

She nodded. "Three million."

He rammed the pistol under her chin. "Five."

She grunted *no* and shook her head. Was that what this was

about? He thought if he threatened her personally, she could get more money?

"I saw you land. Private jet. You and some FBI dweeb."

"I wanted to get here as soon as I could." Her words were a muffled mess, but he seemed to understand her.

"Private jet. Must have cost thousands. Ten thousand maybe."

She shrugged. "FBI."

"FBI?" His gaze bore into her. "You're not trying to cheat me? You have my money. Right?"

She grunted *yes* and tried to nod, pushing against his gun as her head bobbed up and down.

He grabbed her hair and jammed the gun hard into the flesh of her neck. "You. Have. My. Money?"

She widened her eyes and whimpered. Maybe he'd lay off if he thought he was hurting her. "Yes, yes."

His malevolent gaze roamed over her face. She angled her head to relieve the pressure from the muzzle against her jaw.

He grunted and pushed her head back by her hair. "I'm settling for three. You should be grateful."

She nodded as best she could.

He removed the gun's barrel from her jaw. "Three million. Not a penny less. Used bills. No trackers or tracers. No funky powder that glows under a black light. Just you and my money."

She coughed and rolled her head down, compressing her chin against her neck. She panted. "I can do that."

He nodded. "Good. Because if you don't, your boy dies."

She lifted her head up, still breathing hard. "Do you have him?"

Gotting frowned. "You trying to be funny?"

She shook her head. Her heart pounded.

Gotting snarled, "Of course I have him. And in case you're thinking of doing something clever right now, if I don't get back to him, he dies."

She closed her eyes a moment longer than a blink and nodded.

He grinned. "He won't die quick. Cold, dehydration, or the fumes. All can kill him. None work fast."

Jess grunted. "Okay."

He jammed the gun to her forehead and pushed her head back. "*You*. You will do it."

She nodded rapidly. "Me. Just me."

Meeting him face to face had revived her memory. Thirteen years ago, he'd been a sullen man in her apartment building who stared and never spoke. He'd been creepy then, and he was creepier now. She hadn't thought him dangerous then, but now she knew better.

He eased the gun away. "Good. You do one thing I've told you not to do, or one thing I don't like, and poof. I'm gone. And if I'm gone, so is your baby. Understand?"

She nodded. "Yes."

He must have been satisfied because he reached up and ripped off the duct tape. She felt the sting as it pulled her skin.

Jess took a deep breath. "You won't get a cent if Peter isn't alive and well treated."

Gotting rubbed the gun against her cheek. "You just get me my money."

She looked down then back up, and straight into his eyes. "If Peter is hurt in any way—"

"You'll what?" He looked her up and down. "Write an article about me? A stern telling off? Damn me in print? You haven't got the balls to do anything to stop me. Not thirteen years ago and not now."

The last thing Jess wanted was for Gotting to worry that his money was in jeopardy. Just the opposite. She needed him to be overly confident. To make mistakes.

She bit her lip. "How do we do the exchange?"

Gotting sneered. "You think I'm going to tell you that so you can set up some trap? You really do think I'm stupid."

Jess shook her head. "You're not stupid. We both know that the handover is the tricky part. I want to make sure it goes off smoothly. You've told me Peter's life depends on it. I don't want to screw anything up."

"Well, that's good. You be ready tomorrow with a car and my money in a suitcase, just like I told you."

"And after that?"

"You wait here. At the hotel. You'll get your instructions."

Gotting checked Jess's bonds before he stood to leave. "I know you think your FBI friends will help you. Maybe you believe they'll catch me. But think on this. I know the drill. I have the right to remain silent. And I will. And if I do, your precious boy will die."

CHAPTER SIXTY-FIVE

Thursday, November 30
5:30 a.m.
Gunnison, Colorado

GOTTING CHOSE TO SLEEP in the derelict cabin. It was a fifty-fifty decision compared to the Yukon. He'd kept all his clothes on, layering his own coat over the stolen ski jacket. He'd pulled down the fleece hat as far as it would go. His joints ached when the alarm on his watch rang at 5:30 a.m.

His breath condensed in the air. He levered himself up onto his feet and walked circles to stretch out his muscles. His limp was more pronounced in the cold.

He walked one more circle, then hammered on the metal door. There was no response. He hammered again but heard nothing.

He could still get his money, even if the boy had died, but he might be more useful alive. It would give him more bargaining options if anything went south.

Gotting dragged an old table across the floor. It was warped and moldy but made of thick chunks of wood. He leaned it against the door, an inch under the big metal handle. He slid back the lock bolt. It rasped as rusty metal scraped against rusty metal, and the door inched open.

Peter slammed his body into the door. The door shook. The hardware jolted back a fraction. The boy grunted and screamed. His shoes were scrabbling for grip and he put all his weight into his effort.

Gotting held the table under the door handle. The boy's force was grinding the handle into the wood, binding the two together harder. He waited a full thirty seconds for the boy to adjust his body position. He was preparing for a second attempt. Gotting leaned on the door, closing the gap, and clicked the bolt back in place.

Peter shouted, his voice rough and gravelly, but little more than a mumble through the metal.

Gotting adjusted the table, shoring it up under the handle. He scraped up sand and dust with his hands, and poured it into the giant lock, seizing the mechanism.

Whether Peter was dead or alive wouldn't affect getting his money. But it would be game over if he escaped.

He checked he had his gloves and goggles and stepped outside. Light snow was falling. The Yukon was completely covered, making its bulk even larger in the faint dawn light.

His snowboard boots gripped the soft snow firmly. One advantage snowboarders had over skiers was the ability to walk almost normally.

He found some broken branches and used them to brush the snow from the Yukon. Normally, he would only have bothered with the windows, but he cleared the whole vehicle. The last thing he wanted was some chunk of snow blinding him at the wrong moment.

He checked the snowboard was in the rear before starting the Yukon. The engine churned into life. He let it idle a few moments before putting it in gear. Fortunately, the owner had kept the gas tank well filled.

The big SUV slithered down the trail to the main road. Despite the four-wheel drive, it wasn't great descending hills. The main road was a mixture of snow and slush. It wasn't a busy route, but enough traffic had been by to keep the snow from hardening.

He had sixty miles to go. He kept the heater blowing on the windshield and the wipers going to stop the glass from misting up.

The route slowly climbed. He passed through a few sleeping towns, their lights filtering through the snowflakes. He kept rigidly to their posted speed limits.

Cars drove by in the opposite direction. When a car approached him from behind, he pulled over. He wasn't being a good citizen, he didn't want anyone following him.

He knew his route by heart. He reached his final turn. The road weaved as it climbed. The slope grew steeper. The road led out of one valley and into the next. The valleys ran parallel to each other, and the road he was on was the only link for a good ten miles in each direction.

The snow grew heavier. They were the same thin flakes, but there were more of them. The temperature dropped. The snow stuck to the road. The passage of cars wasn't enough to turn it to slush, their wheels merely tamped it down into hard pack.

He passed over the top of the ridge. The wind whistled around the Yukon.

He looked behind him. There was no sign of his tracks. A good thing as long as it didn't prevent Kimball getting up to the top of the ridge.

360 | DIANE CAPRI

On the right, he could make out the Zuma Loda ski area through the snow. The lights of the town were on. Yellow pools of warmth inviting skiers for the day.

The ski lifts were stationary, their wires trailing in haphazard routes down the mountain. A few hundred yards to his right, a group of workers was clearing the overnight snow from a chairlift.

He made a three-point turn, headed back up the road, and stopped a couple hundred feet short of the peak. He reversed the Yukon through a rough gap in the trees on the opposite side of the road to the Zuma Loda ski area. He guessed that under the blanket of snow there was a footpath, but it suited his purpose.

His tire tracks were almost invisible. A few more minutes of snow and no one would know he was there. He turned off the engine and headlights. He flipped the interior light to the off position and tested it by opening the door. There was no light. All was good.

He exited the Yukon, and walked along the road, toward the mountain's peak. The snow grew thin. The wind blew it into swirls around the trees. He zipped up the hood of the ski jacket. It was thin material and barely windproof. The jacket was a fashionable make. He cursed the person who'd put style before substance.

The wind picked up as he crested the peak. The snow was traveling almost horizontally. Visibility was down to perhaps a mile or two.

He looked back the way he'd come. It was downhill, but when Kimball arrived, a mile would barely give him a minute or two. He found a spot on the edge of some trees. It afforded shelter and gave him the best view of the road down the mountain and valley. It would form a good sighting spot to watch for Kimball's approach.

He strained to see through the falling flakes. He could hear a delivery truck lumbering up the hill. As soon as he caught sight of the vehicle, he checked the time on his watch and ran. He dodged his way out of the trees to the main road then followed the edge toward the Yukon. The gravel on the side of the road gave better grip than the smooth tarmac.

He ran hard. His arms swinging and his heart pumping. His lungs strained in the thin air. He was almost to the Yukon when he stumbled to a stop. He folded double, supporting his upper body weight with his elbows on his knees, and panted. Stars swam across his vision. He staggered back and leaned against a tree.

Damn.

The truck drove by. The noise of its laboring engine replaced by the squeal of its brakes as it rolled downhill.

He checked his watch. It had been a minute and forty-five seconds since he first saw the truck. That meant he couldn't run when he saw Kimball's Jeep. Even if he made it to the Yukon, he'd be in no state to take her on and escape.

The path he'd parked on led through the trees up to the peak. It was a straighter route, but it'd be more difficult to run.

He took the floor mat from the passenger side of the Yukon. It was a two-foot square, nylon carpet on one side and hardened plastic on the other.

He walked the path back to the peak, sat on the floor mat, and waited to get his breath back. He angled himself down the path and pushed off. He had to work with his feet to keep himself going straight, but he arrived at the Yukon in just over forty seconds.

He breathed a sigh of relief. He would have almost a minute to get himself ready, and he would be in good shape to take her on.

Satisfied with the first half of his scheme, he climbed into the rear of the Yukon and tested the snowboard's bindings. They zipped up snug with just one strap. He practiced putting his feet in and out of the binding. If his plan was going to work, he was going to have to be fast and unobtrusive. Nothing attracted attention more than fumbling and fighting with your gear on the slopes.

He carried the snowboard across the road, and through the trees to the opposite side. There was a walking trail, rough underfoot and about fifty yards long. The trail ended with a danger sign and the Zuma Loda ski resort emblem. He laughed. There was no danger, they just wanted to frighten people away from skiing without buying a lift pass.

Down the mountain, a chairlift started to move. Minutely at first. Groaning and clanking until it got up to speed.

The town was lighting up. The workers were in full swing. A few determined skiers and snowboarders were eating an early breakfast, waiting to jump on the first lift to the top of the groomed area. Some would go farther. Hiking another five-hundred feet up through a narrow passage to the mountain's peak.

There was the real terrain. Backcountry stuff. Off-piste as the French like to call it. Gnarly. It was the stuff he'd sought out when he'd lived in Colorado. The high he'd had blasting down the mountain through the biting cold air was its own drug.

He'd do it again. But not today.

He chose a tree on the edge of the woods and leaned the snowboard against it.

He practiced reaching for the board and clipping his boots into the bindings. The tree was ideally located on the flat ground and at the edge of a run. He could step into the board's bindings and use the tree to push himself onto the run. It was only a green, the easiest slope, but it would be enough for him to leave behind anyone on foot.

He trudged back to the Yukon. It had gained a few flakes in the time he'd gone. He brushed the windows. He could hear the clanking of a chairlift in the distance. The cold air carried noises clearly.

He went over his plan again. This was it. He had to get the money. The police, the FBI, and the Kimball woman all knew him. There was no way back. But with three million cash he could leave the country on his own terms. He'd get a boat and head south.

He switched on his phone and pulled out the receipt for the express delivery envelope. A search engine gave him an expected delivery time of 9:50 a.m. He had three hours.

He didn't mind. The handover had a lot of things in common with kidnapping. Of course, kidnapping babies and young kids was a lot easier than giving the feds the slip, but it all came down to the same thing. Timing. They wouldn't have any idea where he was, and when they finally got a clue, it would be too late because he would be long gone.

He set an alarm on his phone. At exactly 9:50 a.m. he'd go back to his sighting spot in the trees. At 10:10 he'd call Kimball. Minutes later, she'd fall into the trap, and he'd be three million richer.

He ran the engine a few minutes for warmth and settled down to wait for his alarm.

CHAPTER SIXTY-SIX

Thursday, November 30
9:30 a.m.
Vista Hermosa, Colorado

GOTTING HAD SAID THE instructions would arrive at the hotel, so Jess rose early after a fitful sleep. She ate a light breakfast and drank two espressos. She was ready to go at a moment's notice.

Lynette Tierney had arrived early. After a few moments of conversation, she sat in a chair, hands clutched together and rocking back and forth.

Fernandez was outside with two other officers, keeping watch up and down the road, scrutinizing each approaching vehicle. They'd been doing it for two hours, but they'd seen no one suspicious.

The FBI had alerted the Post Office and national delivery companies. None of them reported having an envelope or package to be delivered to Jess or to the hotel. The hotel had given permission to trace calls, and an agent from the FBI office was at the telecom company's switching exchange.

Jess paced the length of the hotel lobby and rubbed her wrists. She'd raised the alarm soon after Gotting had left, but the exertion required to get the duct tape off had left her skin raw.

His visit had been all about power. He wanted to prove she should take his threats about surveillance seriously. And he had done it through threatening the one thing she loved the most.

Peter.

His message wasn't wasted on her. He was heartless. Ruthless. Soulless. Anyone in his crosshairs was in mortal danger. He thought his visit would frighten her into submission, make her force the FBI to stay out of the way.

He couldn't have been more wrong. He'd grossly underestimated her in more ways than one.

She was the last mother he'd ever do this to. Never again.

Her phone alerted her to an email from Stephenson. He wished her good luck and hoped that she didn't need it. She sent him a quick thank you as she walked back across the lobby.

A black Lincoln Town Car pulled into the parking lot. Jess stood by the window, watching. The car stopped under the awning outside the main door. Henry Morris stepped out.

Jess ran outside. Morris grinned.

She hugged him. "How on earth—"

"I checked out. Doctors weren't happy, but neither was I. We reached an agreement. I have to go in for a checkup tomorrow."

She stepped back. "Are you okay?"

"I'm going to have to take it easy." He shifted his weight. "I wanted to be here to help."

Fernandez put his hand on Morris's shoulder. "He's going to be a passenger in my Jeep, and nothing else. Director's orders."

Jess took Morris inside the hotel and introduced Lynette Tierney.

A woman wearing jeans and a bright yellow parka crossed the road from the small garage opposite. Jess stiffened when she handed a padded envelope to Fernandez. They talked for a moment before she returned to the garage and Fernandez came into the hotel.

"Is that what I think it is?" Jess said.

Fernandez ran his hand across the envelope. "Seems like just paper." He held out the letter. "Addressed to you care of the garage across the street."

"He's full of surprises."

Fernandez donned nitrile gloves. "Let's hope this is the last surprise."

The envelope contained a single sheet of paper with directions. The list was handwritten in block capitals. He held the paper by the corners.

An FBI technician shone a black light over the page and shook his head. "Nothing obvious."

Fernandez laid the page on a larger sheet of paper and photographed the text.

The technician dusted both sides of the page for prints and shook his head. "Nothing."

Jess took a picture of the page, and the technician made photocopies.

Fernandez laid out a map and traced the directions with a pen.

"That's a long way," Jess said.

Fernandez nodded. "Highway 285 south then 216 west through Pineland Valley."

Morris pointed at the list. "He's making you pick up a burner phone on the way, so give us the number as soon as you get it."

Next to the location of the phone was a note that the phone was under observation, and if anyone picked it up before Jess, Peter was dead. "You think he has a partner?"

"We'll have to assume he does. But unless he's got a large team, he can't be watching everything. We won't risk picking up the phone early. Once we have the number, we can trace calls right away."

Jess nodded. "The directions don't end with the word *handover*."

Fernandez sucked air in through his teeth. "No."

"He's going to be watching me on the way, and if you're there at the next set of instructions..."

Fernandez consulted the map. "I can put some men in the area pretty quickly. Drive slowly. Give us time."

Jess nodded. "Just bear in mind, I can handle myself. I won't be suing you for keeping farther back until we've exchanged."

"We'll be out of sight, Jess."

The technician handed Jess a copy of the map mounted on cardboard. It was small enough to hold with one hand. The route was highlighted in yellow marker. "We've programmed it into the Jeep as well," he said.

Fernandez's phone rang. He listened for a few moments and hung up. "The money is on its way." He took a deep breath. "Time to put you in a bulletproof vest."

She nodded. "Let's get going."

CHAPTER SIXTY-SEVEN

Thursday, November 30
10:00 a.m.
Vista Hermosa, Colorado

THE BULLETPROOF VEST WAS bulky. Despite its claims of comfort and the reassurance it gave her, it did little to slow her racing heart. She adjusted her seat to compensate for being an inch closer to the Jeep's pedals.

Morris put a red, hard-sided suitcase in the passenger seat footwell. He patted the handle. "Stock suitcase. No trackers. Nothing. Once you hand this over, it's his. Unless we have eyeballs on him, we'll never see it again."

"I'm not letting go until I have Peter."

He nodded. "And no hero stuff. Once you have Peter, you head in the other direction as fast as you can."

She nodded.

"Agreed?" he prompted.

"Yeah."

"I'm serious, Jess."

370 | DIANE CAPRI

"How many others did Gotting kidnap?"

Morris sighed. "Fernandez and I pulled every string imaginable to even get you near this handover. It's all about you and Peter. Gotting gets away, and no problem. He'll turn up again. Three million dollars in his pocket, and he'll stand out like a sore thumb."

"You think he's that stupid?"

"That's for time to tell. But we're not that stupid either. We have a large team. Slim chance he's going to go anywhere other than back to prison."

She pursed her lips. "Yeah. You make damn sure of that."

He winked. "You got it." He closed the passenger door. "Ready?"

She gripped the steering wheel, checked the gun under her seat, and started the V8. "Ready."

Fernandez started another Jeep Wrangler. Morris jumped into the passenger seat. He was already talking into a radio mic as Jess pulled away. They didn't immediately follow, and she left town unable to spot anyone behind her.

The directions were simple. South on 285 to 216. She edged the Jeep over the speed limit, taking to the outside lane to overtake slower moving traffic and eighteen-wheelers.

"Ease off, Jess." Morris's voice came through the Jeep's speakers with a clarity that made her feel he was in the vehicle. It was reassuring to know he was there.

"Sorry," she said and slowed to join the flow in the inside lane.

"Better," he said.

The navigation system kept her updated on the distance to US-216.

Twelve miles after turning onto 216, she slowed to search for the small roadside picnic area listed on the directions. US-216 was quieter than 285. The falling snow was sticking to the road more than on the busier highway.

She found the picnic site. It was occupied by two cars. She stopped behind them, squeezing into what little space was left, the rear of the Jeep sticking out into the road.

She crushed herself down to be able to look into the cars. One had an older couple, the other held a man eating a sandwich.

She checked the directions for the location of the phone. The list gave a number for a telegraph pole. From the Jeep, she could see the pole in the picnic site was two short of the number she needed. She gambled the numbers rose in the uphill direction and set off.

As she passed the cars, she made a point of standing in front of each and taking a picture of the occupants. The old couple frowned. The single guy flipped his middle finger and left in a cloud of diesel smoke. She checked she had the registration plates and mailed the pictures to Fernandez.

The next telegraph pole was surrounded by thick undergrowth, but fortunately the next was clear. She found a plastic supermarket bag taped to the rear. It contained a cheap burner phone.

She jogged back to the Jeep. The snow was getting thicker. She sat in the Wrangler with the heater running and switched on the phone. "There was a phone. Burner. No surprise." She worked her way through the menu, found the phone's number, and read it out. Fernandez confirmed the number.

The next step in the instructions was to continue for five miles. There was no phone number in the instructions. "I guess he'll call me," she said to the empty Jeep.

"Guess so. Just remember, take it easy. Gives us more time if he pulls something," Morris said through the vehicle's speakers. The reception was getting weaker in the mountains. His voice didn't have the presence it had earlier.

Jess pulled around the older couple's car, and back onto the road. Every fiber of her being wanted to go faster, but the tarmac was slippery even with the Jeep's off-road tires and four-wheel drive.

She ran the heater on the windscreen and the wipers front and rear. After a mile, she caught up with a low-slung sports car struggling with the conditions. To her relief, it pulled off onto the side road by a sign that read Timberline Creek. The road appeared to lead to expensive mountain homes.

The burner phone rang. Jess jolted at the distorted bell sounding from its small speaker. There was no hard shoulder to the road. She slowed to a crawl and the Jeep's giant tires bounced up onto low rocks, leaving her half off the road for traffic to pass.

She grabbed the phone on its third ring. "Yes?"

"Where are you?" Gotting's voice was unmistakable. He peppered his words with expletives.

"US-216."

"What?"

"US-216." She uttered the numbers slowly.

Gotting swore. "What are you doing on 216?"

"It's in your directions."

"You're trying to mess with me. You're trying to—"

"I'm not trying to do anything. Your instructions said 216."

"No, they did not."

"I have them here. It says—"

"I've had it. You're trying to play games. Don't say I didn't warn you."

"No, no. Listen. Your instructions say US-216. They did. I have them here."

Gotting breathed hard. "You're supposed to be on US-261, not 216."

"Okay, okay. I can turn around. I can find 261. I can be there."

There was a long silence.

"Where are you?" Gotting said, his voice angry.

"216. I'm..." she twisted in her seat and looked at the home sign. "I'm by some big houses. Timberline Creek. I can look up 261 now. I can—"

"Two miles ahead. Take the left. Plateau Creek Road. It goes over the mountain to 261. Then turn left. Call me when you reach 261 or Peter here is going to meet a sad end."

"No, wait. I need—"

The line clicked. Gotting had gone.

CHAPTER SIXTY-EIGHT

Thursday, November 30
10:15 a.m.
Pineland Valley, Colorado

JESS TOSSED THE BURNER phone into a cup holder and stomped on the gas. The Wrangler shimmied, its wheels scrabbling for grip as it bounced off the rocks and back onto the tarmac. She fought the steering for a moment to keep the vehicle going straight down the road.

Two miles. She punched a button to reset the trip meter and watched it count up.

Morris's voice rasped from the Jeep's speakers. "Jess. Slow down. We've got a problem."

"Could you hear him?"

"Just about."

"He almost lost it."

"The directions definitely say 216, Jess."

"So? He made a mistake. He's an idiot. He was probably drugged up when he wrote the instructions. Either way, I'm not risking Peter. He wants me on 261, that's where I'm going to be."

"Jess. We're all in Pineland Valley."

"So?"

"The only way into Lakeland is back to US-285 or over Plateau Creek Road. Which means it's either thirty minutes going around the mountain, or we risk being seen on Plateau Creek."

Jess eased off the gas. "Where are you?"

"According to our tracker, three miles behind you. But with this weather, that's four minutes."

She pushed back down on the accelerator, and the Jeep forged ahead. "Okay. Four minutes. That gives me plenty of time to get through the road. He can't be watching us everywhere. Just don't drive in a convoy, and we'll be all right."

"Jess—"

"He was on the verge of losing it, Henry. I've got to show him I'm trying. I've got to show him I can be trusted."

"Jess we had people ahead and behind you. Now, we'll all be behind. It's not good. Makes us weaker. We won't be able to support you as well."

The trip meter closed in on two miles. There was a road on the left. She slowed. The sign was partly covered in snow, only the word "Plate" was visible, but it was enough. She turned hard, the rear of the Jeep fishtailing in the snow and slush. "Morris, I'm going over Plateau Creek. You copy?"

There was no reply as she barreled up the mountain road.

CHAPTER SIXTY-NINE

Thursday, November 30
10:16 a.m.
Plateau Creek, Colorado

GOTTING COULDN'T BELIEVE HIS luck. Not only had Kimball fallen for the idea she was on the wrong road, but by identifying her position accurately, she'd given him a few extra minutes notification of her arrival.

He jumped onto the floor mat and bounced down the path to the Yukon.

His adrenaline was getting to him. He sat in the driver's seat a few moments. He had his old coat over the light blue ski jacket. He had his hat and gloves on. He pulled on his ski goggles and tightened his seat belt. What would fight off the extreme cold would also help prevent serious injury in what he was about to do.

He rolled down the Yukon's windows. Less glass meant less chance of injury. The metal on metal sounds from the chairlift a few hundred feet away wafted through the openings.

He started the engine. The noise would prevent him from hearing Kimball's approach. He'd have to depend on visual identification. Not that it should be that hard. The feds would have chosen a dark color to stand out in the snow.

Kimball's Jeep appeared over the crest of the road.

He selected first gear, revving the engine while holding the big SUV on the brakes.

With luck, the impact would render Kimball immobile, if not dead.

CHAPTER SEVENTY

Thursday, November 30
10:30 a.m.
Plateau Creek, Colorado

JESS EASED OFF THE accelerator. The road was leveling out.
If it weren't for the snow, the view would have been stunning in
all directions. She was at the peak between Pineland Valley and
Lakeland Pass. The road was white with snow. The only
indication that she was actually on the road was because the
snow was flatter than on the sides.

The road angled down. She backed off the accelerator even
further. The Wrangler had four-wheel drive, which was great for
going faster, but under braking, it was no better than a two-wheel
drive car.

Trees loomed on either side of the road. Their presence had
kept some of the snow from the road, but it was still well
covered. The slope ahead looked ominous. Beyond the trees, it
dropped out of sight.

"Morris? Fernandez? Can you hear me?"

Static rasped from the speakers. She thought she heard a voice but couldn't make out any words.

"Morris—"

A blur flashed through her peripheral vision. She twisted her head to the left. A brown SUV burst from the trees. It covered the road in a second. She wrenched the wheel right, but it made no difference.

The SUV smashed into the rear of the Jeep. Metal crumpled and glass shattered. The Jeep twisted, the rear of the vehicle slewing around. She stomped on the brakes and gripped the wheel as the Wrangler hurtled into the undergrowth.

The Jeep came to a halt, rocking on its suspension. Her fingers held a crushing grip on the steering wheel. She took a deep breath. The impact couldn't have been that bad, the airbags hadn't gone off. The Jeep should still be drivable.

She whipped open the door. How could the SUV driver have been so stupid?

She slid out of the Jeep's seat and turned toward the SUV.

A black-gloved fist flashed. A swinging blow. It caught the right side of her face, pounding into her cheekbone and grinding across her nose. Her balance swam. She collapsed sideways into the Jeep's rear door, her hands slapping against the metalwork. She glimpsed Earle Gotting's face as her knees gave way and she tumbled to the ground.

He'd tricked her. He'd forced her over the mountains and into his ambush.

Gotting swung his leg to kick her. She grabbed his ankle. He swept down a blow from above. His gloved fist smashing a glancing blow to her ear. Lights flashed in her vision. Pain bloomed in her head. If she stood any chance of fighting back, she had to get off the ground.

She rolled onto her knees and launched herself upright. Gotting kicked toward the side of her knee and she collapsed away from the full force of his blow.

He grabbed her hair, holding her head still as he rammed his gun in front of her face. "Where's my money?"

Jess grabbed his sleeve. "We had a deal!"

He jerked her head sideways, breaking her grip on his sleeve. Her head bounced against the Jeep.

"The deal is you give me my money!" He shoved the gun into the soft flesh under her chin. "Now!"

"Where's Peter?"

He wrenched her up by her hair, dragging her to the open driver's door. "Where's my money!"

"I need Peter!"

Gotting saw the suitcase in the passenger footwell. He still had the gun shoved under her chin. She grabbed his sleeve. "No. You don't get it until I get Peter."

He snarled, kept his grip on her hair, and dragged her around the rear of the vehicle to the passenger door.

He kicked the door. "Open it."

"Not until I get—"

He shook her head. "Open it!"

He yanked her hair hard. The pain burned like a storm of a thousand needles. She grabbed his wrist. "I can't—"

He threw her backward, grunting with the effort. She stumbled and rolled onto the ground.

He whipped open the Jeep's door and leaned in for the suitcase.

Jess scrambled toward the rear of the Jeep.

Gotting hoisted the suitcase onto the passenger seat. He glanced at Jess, still on the ground, and turned back to the case. The luggage locks thunked open.

Jess reached for the rear wheel arch. It was packed with snow and slush. She drove her fingers into the cold and yanked out the slippery bag.

The suitcase locks thumped shut.

She was holding the barrel of the Glock.

Gotting leaned back out of the Jeep, the case in one hand, his gun in the other.

She snatched the Glocks' grip with her other hand, pushed her finger onto the trigger through the plastic bag and fired without aiming. She didn't want to kill him. He was her only link to Peter.

The gun boomed. The noise bounced off the hard side of the Jeep and echoed down the valley.

Gotting's eyes went wide. He jerked backward, raised his gun and fired.

The bullet went over Jess's head. She scrambled toward the back of the Jeep, firing as she moved, aiming wide.

Gotting screamed.

She reached the back of the Jeep.

Gotting fired. The Jeep's rear window shattered. He continued firing, the bullets making metallic ticking sounds as they pierced the Jeep's metalwork.

Gotting grunted in pain. One of her bullets must have hit him.

She dropped flat, her arms under the Jeep, cradling the Glock and aiming twelve inches away from his feet. She fired once. A cloud of snow erupted beside his foot.

Gotting dodged away from the Jeep, swearing as he went.

Jess rolled onto her feet, the gun in front of her as she peered around the side of the Jeep.

He was scrabbling away, disappearing into the woods.

She raced for the Yukon, her boots slipping on the thickening snow. The driver's door was open, and the engine was still running. She jumped up into the driver's seat and craned to see into the rear seats.

No sign of Peter.

She ran back to the Jeep and stabbed the starter button. The V8 growled into life. "Fernandez," she shouted. "If you can hear me, Gotting attacked me on the top of Plateau Creek. He has the money. No sign of Peter. I'm going after him."

Jess rammed the Jeep into gear. Chasing Gotting through the trees was likely to get her shot. He could be waiting for her. But the trees were only a band that started at the road's peak and ran along its side.

She slung the Jeep through a one-eighty. The tail end slew round farther than she expected and snapped back hard as she straightened the wheel. The impact must have bent the rear of the vehicle.

She headed a couple of hundred feet back up the hill to where the trees started, checked the Jeep was in four-wheel drive and bounced off-road.

The snow was soft, the smooth surface hid lumps and potholes. The Jeep crashed and banged over the terrain, the engine revved, dipping when more torque was required, but the Wrangler never slowed.

Two Jeeps were climbing Plateau Creek Road. She angled hers toward them and flashed the headlights. "Morris! Fernandez! I'm here. Can you see me?"

"Jess," came the distorted response. "We're on our way. Stay back."

She flashed her lights again. "Can you see my lights?"

"Yes. We're trying to close off the roads. We heard shots."

"He didn't hit me. He's on foot. He abandoned a Yukon. I'm going after him."

"Wait for us."

"He took the money, and he didn't have Peter. He's getting away."

"Wait, Jess."

"I'll keep him in sight."

She turned back down the slope. To her right, a chairlift station was busy with skiers. Some stared at her. The ski runs from the chairlift angled away from the road. A wide swath of unprepared snow separated the trees from the trail.

She drove closer to the woods than the ski runs. The thicker snow slowed the Jeep, and as the slope increased, its resistance was a blessing. A display by the rev counter told her the Jeep's pitch and roll. She was at twenty degrees of each, and already it felt uncomfortable.

She scanned the trees and saw no sign of movement. The jeep bucked over a pothole, wrenching the wheel from her hands. She grabbed hard and yanked it back as she stomped on the brakes. The Jeep rocked for a moment.

Ahead of her was a line through the snow. A snowboard's track. It started where she estimated Gotting had attacked her. A black object lay stretched out on the snow by the trees. Straining in her seat until her head touched the roof, she could make out that the black object was his jacket.

She followed the snowboard's track. It wasn't traveling straight down in a headlong rush. A hundred yards away, Gotting struggled to cross the trail on a snowboard. The red suitcase was unwieldy and slowing his progress toward a clump of trees on the far side.

"Fernandez. He's on a snowboard. Red suitcase and light

blue jacket. Heading about ninety degrees away from the road."

Fernandez's reply was a mixture of buzz and crackle.

She put the Jeep in its lowest gear and headed for the trail. Skiers and boarders were flying by, shouting and waving their fists. She switched on the hazard flashers and kept up a rhythm of honking the horn.

The lines of skiers scurried to the far side of the slope. She edged onto the trail. In theory, it would be easier to drive on the manicured surface, but she'd skied plenty and knew there'd be little texture for the Jeep's knobby tires to grip.

She was right. She was crossing the slope with twenty-five degrees of roll. The Jeep see-sawed down the slope, first the front losing grip, then the rear. She swung the wheel aiming to keep up her progress across the trail, honking the horn as she went.

Skiers came to a stop and lined the hill above her. A man in a red ski patrol uniform raced down the slope on a snowmobile. The skiers opened a gap for him to travel through.

Gotting disappeared into the trees. She pressed a fraction harder on the accelerator. The Jeep lost traction against the pull of gravity, sliding sideways down the slope and turning as it went.

She fought back her instinct to stomp the brakes and spun the wheel to steer into the slide. The Wrangler responded and the wheels aligned with the direction of travel.

She regained momentary control of the vehicle. The Jeep picked up speed. The trees loomed close. She had no choice, she stomped on the brakes. The Jeep went into a full-on skid, rotating ninety degrees before it hit the trees.

The passenger side absorbed the brunt of the impact. The airbags exploded, throwing Jess back in her seat. Her ears rang

386 | D I A N E C A P R I

as acrid smoke filled the vehicle. The engine quit. The lifeless Jeep bumped over the rough ground, turning as it went, until the rear of the vehicle came to rest against a trunk.

Wind rushed through the missing windows and cleared the smoke. She was facing uphill. The snowmobile was barreling toward her. The first few skiers set off to pass on the far side of the run.

She opened her door. Her head swam. She breathed deep. The snowmobile slowed as it approached. She reached under the seat and pulled the second Glock free.

She stood on the driver's seat and held onto the roof rails to gain height. Between the thin trees was indistinct movement. Gotting wasn't that far ahead.

"What are you doing?" shouted the ski patrol.

She jumped from the Jeep and worked her way toward him, digging the toes of her boots into the snow.

"I need your ride," she said.

He leaned forward, a frown visible behind his goggles. "What?"

She reached him and grabbed the handlebars. "I need this."

The man's eyes fell on the gun. "Er…"

"I'm with the FBI. Chasing a kidnapper. Get off." In the circumstances, she didn't feel she was stretching the truth, and she didn't care.

He shook his head. "No. I…are you serious."

She hefted the gun. "Do I look like I'm joking?"

He held his hands up. "Okay, okay."

"Get off."

He dismounted the snowmobile, his gazed fixed on the Glock.

She sat on the sled. "Call the police."

She twisted the throttle, and the machine snapped forward,

almost throwing her off the back. She plunged down the slope, leaning back in the seat. She circled around the end of the trees.

Gotting was crossing a rough section to the next run. He had a backpack in place of the suitcase. He'd switched the contents.

She leaned into the hill and crossed the trail.

Gotting was leaping and pushing, fighting against the lack of slope.

She opened the throttle. The snowmobile bounced and wobbled as it crested tiny dips and swells in the trail. She steered up and down a fraction to avoid a group of skiers hurling a barrage of angry shouts.

She reached the rough area as Gotting made it onto the next trail. She held the throttle open. The engine's roar deepened as it worked hard to propel the snowmobile through the softer, deeper snow.

Gotting turned and fired. Jess ducked down. She couldn't return fire with so many people around and she wouldn't stop. The distance between them reduced rapidly. Gotting ran out of ammo, threw his gun toward her, and set off down the slope.

She kept her hand on the throttle, sweeping round above him. He headed straight down the fall line, accelerating rapidly. She leaned back in the snowmobile's seat because the weight of the machine threatened to pull her over, head first.

Gotting slowed a fraction before turning toward another bank of trees.

Jess hurtled past him with her leg out. She caught his hip with the sole of her boot. A good solid impact. Gotting was thrown flat. The force rotated her body, twisting the handlebars and inducing a heart-stopping rocking motion. She eased off the throttle and leaned into the hill. The rocking stopped, and she raced around in an arc.

Gotting was sliding down the slope, trying to rotate his body and get back on the snowboard.

She matched his speed with the snowmobile, staying above him.

His slide stopped. Jess did the same, ten feet away, with the Glock trained on him. "Don't even think about moving."

He stood up. One boot had come free of the snowboard. He struggled to kick the second boot free. Finally, the board separated and skittered down the hill.

He stepped toward her. "You think I'm scared of you?"

"You should be. I'm an excellent shot. I could have hit you a dozen times." She held the gun pointed steadily at his groin. "Where's Peter?"

He laughed. "You're going to shoot me?" He held his arms out. "Here? Where there's a ton of people."

A trio of snowmobiles started up the hill, two riders apiece.

"Where's my son?"

He laughed. "I told you what would happen."

"Where. Is. My. Son!"

"Ain't nothing you can do to find your little boy. He's a gonna die!" He went for the Glock in her hands.

Jess whipped the gun out of his reach, but he caught her jacket, yanking her from the snowmobile. The Glock spun out of her hand and vanished down the slope.

She lashed out with her boot, catching him in the groin with a solid kick. He grunted and threw her to the ground.

She rolled onto her knees and sprang to her feet. He was still folded in two. He looked up at her. She pounded her fist into his face. The cartilage in his nose bucked and twisted. He yowled. She grabbed his stringy thin hair, wrenched his head forward, and hammered her fist into his face a second time.

Blood poured from his nose and lip.

"Where's my son?" she shouted.

Gotting sank onto the snow.

She raised her fist.

Gotting looked at her, blood running down his face, and sneered. "He's never been yours, and you ain't gonna have him now."

She swung her fist for the center of his face.

He jerked backward, breaking free of her grip, and slid down the snowy slope.

Jess fell onto the side of the snowmobile, fighting to avoid the hot and still running engine.

She used the handlebars to pull herself up to her knees.

Gotting was thirty yards down the slope, on his stomach and scrabbling across the frictionless surface, going for her Glock.

She looked around. The trees were twenty yards away on either side.

Gotting grabbed the gun. He was still on his back. He leveled the gun toward Jess and fired. The gun boomed in the wide-open space and the shot went wide. A cloud of snow erupted to her right.

Offense was her only defense.

She levered herself up and lay flat on the snowmobile's saddle, her hands on the handle bars.

The Glock boomed again. Three shots. All three hit much too close. The metal of the snowmobile rang with each bullet's impact.

She twisted the throttle wide open, gripping the handlebars as tight as she could. The vehicle bounded forward, almost throwing her off behind.

She stayed flat while steering directly toward Gotting.

He rolled up onto his feet and fired again and again, emptying the clip.

The snowmobile covered the gap in seconds. At the last moment, he threw himself backward, but the snowmobile ran over the top of him.

The vehicle bucked and threw Jess off before it came to a stop, its tracks digging into the snow while she continued to slide down the slope.

Gotting lay still, buried in the snow.

She finally slowed to a stop. Her hands and knees stung from the impact, but she kept her eyes locked on Gotting.

The trio of snowmobiles arrived. The first stopped beside Jess, the other two continued onto Gotting.

Fernandez dismounted and held his hand out to help her up. "You okay?"

She didn't speak. Her fists were tight, and her teeth were clamped hard shut. Given the chance, she'd beat the answers out of Gotting. Where was Peter? That's all she wanted to know. She panted like a bull before a charge.

One of the agents checked Gotting for a pulse. He looked at Fernandez and shook his head.

Jess breathed out like she'd been punched in the gut. "Peter's not in Gotting's Yukon. He wouldn't tell me where to find my boy," she said, her teeth still clenched tight.

"We'll find him, Jess."

"How?"

Fernandez said, "Forensics. We'll go over the Yukon, and his Audi in the parking lot. Soil samples and all sorts of things can help."

She shook her head. "That'll take days. Gotting was taunting me. He said Peter won't last long."

"We've got CSI coming from Denver and Colorado Springs. We're doing everything we can."

She looked back up the slope. "He was parked in the trees. Ready. He intended to ambush me on that road all along. He planned his getaway on the snowboard."

"He was heading for his Audi."

"Is Peter in the car?"

Fernandez shook his head. "And we have men combing the woods around the Yukon. If Peter's there we'll find him."

She looked around at the mountains. "He could be anywhere."

Fernandez nodded, with a sympathetic smile. "We're not giving up, Jess."

CHAPTER SEVENTY-ONE

Thursday, November 30
11:00 a.m.
Zuma Loda Ski Area, Colorado

JESS SAT IN MORRIS'S Jeep, the heater blowing hard. He'd insisted she get some warmth.

Her knuckles burned from punching Gotting, but she was sorry she hadn't punched him several more times.

Morris was on the phone, calling every police department for miles around and questioning every record of suspicious activity. Gotting must have holed up somewhere, but Morris had found nothing helpful so far.

The Jeep's windows were misting up. The snow had intensified. Visibility was down to less than a quarter mile. She cracked open a window.

Jess clenched her fists. "He knew what he was doing. He planned…" She took a deep breath. "He planned to let Peter die. He was always going to let Peter die."

Morris put his hand on Jess's shoulder. "We've got leads Jess. We're following up everything. CSI is working on the Yukon. CBI is reviewing every traffic camera they can."

Her phone rang. She answered immediately. "Jess Kimball."

"Ross Tierney. Get moving. Out of the parking lot and turn left."

Jess spun around. "You're here?"

"I'll explain when you're on the move."

She covered the mouthpiece. "Tierney has something. Drive."

Morris shoved the Jeep into gear and raced out of the parking lot. Fernandez saw them leaving and followed in a second Jeep.

Jess put her phone on speaker. "Okay, we're on the way."

Ross Tierney's voice rasped from the car's stereo. "Take Plateau Creek Road back to 216. Four miles then turn left on 149. It's a winding road, but it'll be quickest."

"What have you found?" Jess said.

"You realize I can't just use Air Force assets as if they were my own?"

"Yes, but…"

"I want my son back just as badly as you do. We're training a lot of drone pilots. We have seven Night Crows in your vicinity."

Jess leaned forward. "Seven?"

"Should have been eight. One of them is a hangar queen. We've been doing a wide-area moving track sweep since dawn. We record everything. Once something happens, we can rewind the recording to find the target's origin."

Morris ran the wipers on full speed and the heat blasting on the windshield. The Jeep rocked in the wind as they reached the peak and Gotting's Yukon. The CSI team stared as the convoy of Jeeps barreled past.

"So, you know Peter's location?" Jess said.

"Not yet. Gotting started outside the area we were sweeping. But we know he can't have driven more than a few miles because his Yukon had a low heat signature when it entered the search area."

Morris slowed on the downslope. The Wrangler's transmission whined as it took some of the load, controlling their rate of descent.

"Where do we go after we turn onto 149?" Jess said.

"Our best guess is the Yukon started on that road, somewhere between five and ten miles from Gunnison."

Jess brought up a map on the Jeep's dashboard. "It's going to be seventy-five minutes before we can get there. Can you cover that area with your drones?"

"We're trying. The snow is thinning quickly, and we have a few possible buildings, but nothing certain yet. There's a lot of holiday cabins in the area. I'll let you know as soon as I have something."

Tierney hung up.

Morris used the Wrangler's speakerphone to call Gunnison PD and the Colorado Bureau of Investigation. Within a minute, five more cars were converging on 149, south of Gunnison.

He rallied his way along 216 and onto 149. The road narrowed. It was almost all turns. The agents in the Jeep behind kept pace.

Jess studied CO-149 on her phone as she held onto a grab handle.

The land looked hilly on either side of the road. The map image showed nothing but trees. There were numerous turnings off the road, presumably leading to houses under the tree canopy. "There's a lot of pines obscuring the buildings. And there's a lot of buildings."

"Gunnison PD will be there well before us. They'll know the area and the residents. That should cut down the number of places to search."

Morris kept his foot down. The Jeep made light work of the snow and slush, but 149 was a twisting road that prevented rapid progress. The snow changed from the large fluffy clumps on the top of Plateau Creek to a needle-fine dust.

Jess jolted when her phone buzzed. Tierney spoke immediately after she answered the call.

"I'm sending a text with GPS coordinates now. Two possibilities. One's a weekend place that looks like it's been broken into, the other is a derelict structure built against the side of an escarpment. The derelict place has tire tracks, now covered by snow, so they must have been earlier this morning. It's consistent with our back-track of his Yukon."

Jess typed the coordinates into the Jeep's navigation system. "We'll be there in fourteen minutes."

"Good. We're still looking for other high probability targets."

Tierney hung up.

Morris pushed his foot down on the gas.

CHAPTER SEVENTY-TWO

Thursday, November 30
Noon
Gunnison, Colorado

MORRIS SLOWED AS THEY closed in on the GPS coordinates. A police cruiser was parked by a lane on the side of the road, lights flashing.

He displayed his badge to get them by an officer at the bottom of the lane.

The path sloped upward. Tracks showed several vehicles had traveled the lane already. They passed a derelict shelter and came to a stop. The lane ran out at a line of three police Ford Explorers. Morris parked the Jeep, careful not to block any of the police vehicles.

Jess jumped out. Foot traffic had made a line through the undergrowth. She raced to follow the path. Morris was a few steps behind her, grunting to control his pain.

They emerged into an open area. In front of them was a forty-foot, vertical rock face. A large dilapidated wooden building appeared to be leaning against the rock. An officer stood by one corner of the building. Jess ran to him. "Is there a boy inside?"

Morris held out his badge.

The officer nodded. "There's someone inside. He—"

Jess pushed past and ducked into the building through a large hatch.

The building was basically one open space. Moss grew in corners. The air was damp and fetid. A large rusted wood-burning stove lay on its side. Rotting furniture was strewn about.

The rear wall was bare rock.

In the middle of the wall, four officers were leaning on crowbars, trying to pry open a giant metal door. The ground around them was littered with tools.

"Is he alive?" Jess called.

One of the officers nodded. "He's making noises."

The officers adjusted their crowbars and heaved their weight into the door again. It creaked but didn't open.

Jess pointed to the stove. "We need to use the weight of the door. Lever it down from the top by standing on this."

One of the officers stared at her. She patted the stove. "Stand on it. Lever the door from the top."

The officers dragged the stove to the door. It was big enough for three of them to stand on. They dug crowbars into the gap at the top of the door.

They leaned in. The door creaked and bulged.

The fourth officer dug a crowbar into the gap by the lock.

The metal screeched like an angry bird before it bent. Paint and rust crumbled off, but the door and its frame flexed back into position.

Jess grabbed an ax from tools on the ground. "Again!"

The officers leveraged their weight into the top of the door. The metal creaked. The last officer wedged his crowbar into the gap on the side.

Jess pounded the ax into the gap by the door handle.

The officer inched his crowbar farther into the gap.

She wrestled the ax from the door and slammed it into the widening gap.

The officer repositioned his crowbar.

She swung the ax again. There was a bang like a gunshot. A cloud of rust burst into the air. The door jolted. The frame cracked around the ax. Bolts and chunks of metal rattled from the lock.

The officers jumped from the stove.

She wrenched the door open. Inside the space so dark she could see nothing. She stepped into the blackness. "Steven?"

Someone groaned to her left.

Morris pushed through and shone a flashlight into the space.

Jess stood in a rough-hewn tunnel.

Ten feet from the door, a figure was curled in a ball on what looked like the remains of a table. "Peter!"

Jess dropped to her knees. He was wrapped in a thick parka, the hood pulled tight over his head, his hands rammed in his pockets. His eyes were closed.

She held her hand in front of his face. "He's breathing."

His whole body shook. "C…c, c, c…,"

She stepped back as the officers lifted Peter onto a stretcher.

They threw a thick blanket over him as they carried him out of the building.

Jess followed. The officers lifted the stretcher as they plowed through the undergrowth without stopping.

The rear of one of the Explorers was open. They slid the stretcher straight in and closed the rear door.

Jess dived into the rear seat. The Ford's heaters were running full blast. An officer was setting up an IV.

Peter's eyes were still closed.

The officer taped the tube into Peter's hand and held up the bag of fluids. "Go!"

The Explorer took off, bumping and sliding its way down the trail. They turned for Gunnison, lights flashing and the driver pushing hard through the snow.

Morris followed in the Jeep.

Jess leaned over the seat and rested her hand on her son's still trembling arm.

A group of doctors and nurses stood waiting at the emergency room. Peter was on a gurney within a minute. They cut off his wet clothes, wrapped him in dry, warm blankets, and worked on feeding him thin warm soup.

Jess stood back, letting the medical team work.

Morris arrived. He put his arm around Jess's shoulder. They waited silently, watching the doctor and listening to the bleeps from the machines monitoring Peter's vital signs.

Fernandez arrived, followed minutes later by Lynette Tierney.

Lynette sat by Peter. His eyes were open but staring blankly. He seemed to recognize her. They held hands.

Jess sat on a chair in the corner. Doctors and nurses came and went. Machines were adjusted, and the bag of fluids was changed.

Sometime later, Lynette approached Jess. "Let me introduce you."

Jess looked at Peter. Wires and tubes snaked around him. He still lay on his side, but he was uncurling from the position he must have been in for a long time in the tunnel.

Jess shook her head. "There hasn't been a day when I haven't thought about finding him." She pursed her lips. "But it was never about me." She swallowed. "Right now, he needs his normal world for reassurance. He needs you." It pained her to say it after thirteen years of hoping for that moment, but she knew she was right.

Lynette nodded. "He knows he's adopted. So as soon as he's better…"

Jess watched Peter pull the blankets closer around himself. "When he's ready," she said.

Ross arrived. He was torn between thanking Jess and checking on his son, so Jess and Morris left the Tierneys in the emergency room.

Fernandez was in the foyer, finishing up paperwork at the reception desk.

"Gotting planned to leave Peter to die," she whispered.

Fernandez nodded. "I suspect so. He was very lucky."

Jess nodded. "We all were."

"There's a ton of things still to do." He glanced at Morris. "I could go get things sorted out if the Denver branch authorizes it."

Morris held out his hand. "Consider it authorized."

They shook hands. Fernandez signed the last piece of paper, wished Jess well, and left.

She sent an email to Stephenson that said, "Peter found, recovering." He replied immediately saying he was thrilled and that he wanted to hear about it when she had a chance to take it all in. It left her wondering just how long that would be.

An hour later, Ross Tierney came out to find her. "He's doing pretty well, Jess. Conscious, body temperature rising well, and he wants pizza, so he must be getting back to normal."

She walked into Peter's room with Ross. When he stood aside, she moved closer to the bed. Peter reached for her hand and looked into her eyes. Through her own glassy tears she heard the words she had spent her life waiting for.

"Hello, Mom."

CHAPTER SEVENTY-THREE

Christmas Day
Colorado Springs, Colorado

THE DRIVE FROM DENVER to Colorado Springs took a little over an hour in Jess's Dodge Charger. The roads were clear, but a thick layer of snow blanketed the fields. Henry talked work all the way. She had the feeling it was going to take a few days of peace and quiet for him to completely switch off.

The Tierney house was decked out with lights. In the garden, an oversized Santa ornament looked very festive covered in white snow about a foot deep.

Jess parked in front of the garage. When they climbed out, Henry massaged his side where the bullet had hit. He was almost totally recovered, but the ride from Denver had his muscles kinked, he said. Carter Pierce had offered a private jet for the trip, but Jess said the pilot should be home with his family today, too.

The trunk was full of presents, all festively wrapped for the gift exchange. A couple of the labels had loosened during the drive. She worked to reattach them as Peter came down the walk from the front door in a T-shirt and no coat, despite the subzero cold. His eyes sparkled, and his blond curls bounced in the breeze, just as Henry said hers did.

Steven. Think of him as Peter if you must, but call him Steven now. She'd reminded herself many times in the past few weeks, but she hadn't quite managed to make the switch.

Her son would always be Peter to her. But he'd never known himself by any other name. She didn't want to upset or confuse him any more than the whole situation already had.

He looked fit and strong again, she was pleased to see. The doctors had kept him off football for a week but released him because he'd made a complete physical recovery. He'd been a minor celebrity at school when he returned, but he was quickly putting the whole affair behind him.

Jess had visited Colorado Springs every weekend. She tried not to monopolize his time, but she knew he looked forward to her visits because he could talk her into spending Sundays skiing. In all the years she had searched for him, she never considered what a pushover she'd become.

He gave her a big grin and an equally big hug.

Ross and Henry each carried a load of presents into the house. There were a few remaining.

"Shall I take those?" Peter said.

"Please do," Jess smiled. He was still very formal around her, but he was softening.

He scooped up the presents. "I'll put them under the tree," he said with a huge grin that lit his face with delight. He carried the packages into the house, reading the labels along the way.

Lynette stood at the open front door. "Come on in where it's warm. We're all ready."

Jess gave her a hug and walked inside. The house smelled like gingerbread and pine. Instrumental holiday music wafted from speakers in another room.

Behind Lynette was a red-haired girl with a fresh face and a touch of lipstick on her welcoming smile.

Jess held her arms out. "You must be Michelle."

"And you're Jess, of course." Michelle's voice was sweet and sincere as they hugged. "I'm just home for the week, then back to college. Everyone's told me all about you."

Lynette took the coats and gestured, "Have a seat in the living room."

The room was filled with enough decorations to fill a retail store display. Lights and Christmas cards filled every flat surface. Peter knelt at the edge of a huge heavily decorated tree, arranging the presents.

"Here's a little something to warm you up." Ross brought two coffees with piles of whipped cream from the kitchen. He handed one to Morris and one to Jess.

Lynette offered a knowing smile. "He got one of those milk frothing things for Christmas. I suspect everything will have foam on top from now on."

Morris took a sip and toasted Ross with his cup. "Beats office coffee any day."

"Thanks, Ross." Jess took the cup and looked at Peter. "What gifts did you get?"

He shrugged. "Bunch of things. Just...you know..."

"Show her the headset," Michelle said.

Peter picked up what looked like a giant pair of sunglasses, but the front was solid black. "Xhead. It's a virtual reality headset. Tracks where you look. Makes you feel like you're in a car or a plane or a—"

406 | DIANE CAPRI

"Made me fall over," Lynette grinned.

Jess picked out a small present from the pile she had brought. "Better open this then."

He peeled back the tape and unfolded the wrapping without tearing the paper. "Cool. A racing simulator."

"Maybe you'll be as good at driving as Jess one of these days," Ross said kindly.

Peter turned it over and read the details on the back. "Oh, wait. It's for an Xhead." He frowned at Jess. "You knew?"

She winked. "Can't keep much secret between parents."

Michelle laughed. "Oh, yes you can." She pointed her brother to the presents by the tree. "Give Jess hers."

He picked up a small box.

Michelle rolled her eyes. "Not the pen."

"Oh, way to go on the surprise front."

"You got me a pen?" Jess grinned. Everything about Peter was endearing to her. Even spats with his sister.

Michelle pointed to the presents again. "Give her the other one."

Peter picked up a present that looked suspiciously like a board game. His cheeks reddened as he sheepishly handed it to Jess.

Lynette sat on the couch beside Jess. She directed Peter to sit on Jess's other side.

Michelle perched on the arm of the couch.

Jess peeled back the wrapping paper. Inside was a blue photo album with the words "For Mom, with love, Peter" written in neat cursive that she recognized by now.

Her boy had never given her a present before. Jess sniffled and her eyes filled. She took a deep breath and turned to the first page.

A happy, healthy toddler dressed in a one-piece pajama with a tiny rocket applique looked up. He was strapped snuggly into a new car seat. Wispy blond hair curled beguilingly around big eyes and a mischievous smile.

"That was the day we picked him up," Lynette said proudly. "Wasn't he gorgeous?"

"The most beautiful little boy ever," Jess said softly as she ran her finger over the picture, tracing around the edge of Peter's face.

Emotion welled up and thickened her tongue. She blinked hard, fighting back tears. But her eyes only grew wetter, making it harder to see his bubbly smile. "Exactly as I remembered him."

Morris leaned over and pushed a box of tissues into her lap. She took one and wiped her eyes. "I bought that outfit. It was what he was wearing…"

"Oh no," Lynette said, wrapping her arm around Jess as tears welled up in her eyes, too.

Jess lost herself to her emotions. For a moment, the room was silent while the two women regained composure.

Morris put his hand on Jess's shoulder.

"We thought you'd like it." Peter's face crunched into dismay. "We didn't mean to upset you."

Jess squeezed his hand. "You didn't. Not at all. I love it. This might be the best Christmas gift I've ever received."

"We searched through all the pictures we could find," Michelle said.

Jess flipped on through the book. Lynette pointed out pictures, providing a running commentary on the events surrounding each one. Peter holding Lynette's hand outside a brick building on his first day of kindergarten. Peter in a ski suit and helmet on tiny skis. Peter with a lunch box, standing by another brick school building.

"The first day of real school," Lynette smiled. "Didn't want to hold my hand that day."

"Mooooooom," he protested.

Jess laughed.

"Show her the video," Michelle said.

Lynette flipped to the back of the book and took a memory stick from a little pocket. Peter plugged it into the TV.

Jess didn't trust herself to speak. She took a deep breath and braced herself.

Excited baby sounds filled the room as Peter walked on the screen holding onto Michelle's fingers in his tiny fists. The pair playing in the snow. A birthday party with a big number six on the cake in front of Peter. A group of boys playing soccer in a backyard. Scenes from school, including one where Peter played a set of tympani drums in an orchestra on stage at a concert. It was a great piece of music, with lots of applause from the audience afterward.

"You're really good," Jess said.

"Dad says I could get to be as good as Stewart Copeland. You know, the drummer from his favorite band, The Police?" Peter glanced at Ross, who smiled. "We're hoping to go to state finals next year."

The video ended with a freeze frame of Peter gazing into the camera. Jess turned to look at him. He wore the same expression now. Head slightly tilted and that big, joyful smile.

After a moment, the screen went blank, and Peter put the memory stick back in the book. He closed the book, patted the cover, and handed it back to her.

Her heart almost burst. She wanted to tell him that she had

thought about him every day, that she had worried every night when she went to sleep, and that she'd hoped more than anything that he was happy. But she didn't say any of that.

Because Peter was happy. He'd grown up a normal boy in a loving family. None of what had happened was his fault, and she would never be the one to cause him pain.

She turned to Morris. "You want to tell them?"

He shook his head.

"What?" Lynette's eyebrows raised.

Jess said, "Fernandez called yesterday. They reunited the last family. Fifty-six children."

The sheer number was hard to comprehend. That Gotting, Norell, and Belk had managed to keep their scheme hidden for so long was equally difficult to believe.

Lynette clapped her hands together. "That's marvelous."

Ross nodded. "Amazing. And the Norells?"

"The trial starts next month."

"So much heartache they caused. They should never get out of prison," Ross said.

"They won't," Morris replied. "We have a ton of evidence. After we figured out the logistics of the whole scheme, we were able to trace all of the families. Fifty-six cases of kidnapping and extortion will keep them locked up forever."

"How did they deal with the birth certificates? That's the part that's still puzzling me," Ross said.

"They forged all of the necessary documents, including the birth certificates and all the consent forms. Then they legally amended the forged birth certificates to show the new names of the adoptive parents and children," Henry explained. "Which means all of the adoptions are illegal."

Lynette's eyes widened, and she glanced nervously at her

children. "That doesn't mean the adoptions can be undone, does it?"

"It could in some cases, I guess," Henry said. "Only lawyers with a solid understanding of the law would have been able to pull this off. It's going to take a while to get it all figured out."

Jess remained quiet. She'd consulted with lawyers in Denver. They'd told her that Peter's adoption was illegal. Since she'd never consented to the adoption, her parental rights remained in place. She'd spent many sleepless nights during the past few weeks over this issue. Should she take Peter back? Remove him from the only life he'd ever known? The questions gnawed the lining of her stomach raw.

After a moment, Ross noticed his wife's anxiety and changed the subject. "What's going on with Anna? Are we all set for next weekend?"

Jess cleared her throat and replied, "We are. She'll fly in from Florida on Thursday. She's really excited to meet you all in person."

Peter nodded enthusiastically. "I can't wait to meet her. It's been amazing for me to find out about you. But a half-sister, too? How cool is that?!"

"You sure you can cope with all of us?" Lynette asked. "We booked a hotel room, but still. This is a big crowd for your apartment."

"It'll be a squeeze, but we'll manage for couple days," Jess said.

"And we're all going skiing, right?" Peter said.

Jess nodded. "We'll fly out to Vail on Saturday and stay overnight. It's all arranged. Carter Pierce insisted on picking up the tab."

"That's not necessary, Jess," Ross said, a little stiffly. "We can pay our own way."

Henry squeezed Jess's shoulder and replied quietly, "He wants to do it, Ross. Sometimes the best thing we can do is accept gifts given freely from the heart."

Ross frowned, but he nodded and said no more.

A buzzer sounded. Lynette rushed off to the kitchen to finish making dinner. Jess followed, glad for the distraction. They cut and peeled vegetables while Peter and Michelle set the table with Christmas china and festive napkins.

Jess overheard Ross and Henry talking in the living room about justice for kidnappers and how the reunited families were coping before they switched to football.

Another hour later the meal was ready. Henry said grace. They passed dishes as they talked. Ross poured glasses of hearty red wine for the adults and sparkling water for Peter and Michelle.

After dinner and cleanup, Ross made more coffee with whipped foam. Everyone filtered into the living room. Jess and Lynette sat on the couch, sipping coffee and flipping through the picture album one more time. Henry fell asleep in front of the television. Michelle took selfies with every new piece of clothing she'd unwrapped. Peter raced his way through the afternoon with his virtual reality headset.

Jess sighed. This was the most normal Christmas Day she'd spent in a very long time. She remembered holidays like this when she was a child. But while Peter was missing, she'd avoided Christmas and every other family gathering.

Now, she saw he'd thrived here. He'd lived a good and happy life, surrounded by parents and an older sister who loved him. The Tierneys had provided Peter with a better life than she could have done on her own back then.

She'd spent thirteen years looking for him, and nothing would give them that time back, but now the years faded away. The Tierneys had welcomed her with open arms, even as they must have feared she'd take Peter. They'd behaved gracefully, demonstrating they were good people who loved her son as much as she did.

How could she possibly take Peter away from all of this? But how could she possibly give him up again? Either choice was unthinkable.

Henry went into the kitchen for more coffee, and Jess followed. He asked, "Are you okay?"

She nodded. "More than okay. All those years. I hoped Peter had found a family like this to love him. But I was afraid he hadn't. I worried about him every minute. In some ways, this feels like a miracle to me."

Henry wrapped his arms around her. "What about Anna? She's Richard's daughter. Which makes her Peter's half-sister. I know how you felt about him and you haven't spent much time with her. You don't know what kind of kid she's become. Are you sure you want to get involved with her and all of this?"

"Richard's been gone a long time, and Anna's only a child. She deserves to know her brother. He's fifteen already, Henry. He'll be going to college soon. We need to take advantage of the time we have now. And that includes Anna, doesn't it?" Jess shook her head and leaned into Henry's embrace. "We'll all be fine. We have to be. For Peter's sake."

Henry kissed her. When she pulled back, he said, "You know, all those years your days were consumed with only one goal. Finding Peter. What are you going to do with yourself now that you've found him? Have you thought about that?"

"I have. There are still way too many victims in this country who need justice, Henry. I'm a reporter with a platform while *Taboo* is still in business, at least." She grinned. "I'll keep on keeping on. Since I still haven't won the lotto, I'm going back to work. What else would I do?"

THE END

ABOUT THE AUTHOR

DIANE CAPRI is the *New York Times*, *USA Today*, and worldwide bestselling author. She's a recovering lawyer and snowbird who divides her time between Florida and Michigan. An active member of Mystery Writers of America, Authors Guild, International Thriller Writers, Alliance of Independent Authors, and Sisters in Crime, she loves to hear from readers and is hard at work on her next novel.

Please connect with Diane online:
http://www.DianeCapri.com
Twitter: http://twitter.com/@DianeCapri
Facebook: http://www.facebook.com/Diane.Capri1
http://www.facebook.com/DianeCapriBooks

Printed in Great Britain
by Amazon